THE DEVIL'S ONLY FRIEND

TOR BOOKS BY DAN WELLS

I Am Not a Serial Killer
Mr. Monster
I Don't Want to Kill You
The Hollow City
The Devil's Only Friend

THE DEVIL'S ONLY FRIEND

DAN WELLS

TOR®

A TOM DOHERTY ASSOCIATES BOOK

NEW YORK

This is a work of fiction. All of the characters, organizations, and events portrayed in this novel are either products of the author's imagination or are used fictitiously.

THE DEVIL'S ONLY FRIEND

A Tor Book
Published by Tom Doherty Associates, LLC
175 Fifth Avenue
New York, NY 10010

www.tor-forge.com

The Library of Congress Cataloging-in-Publication Data is available upon request.

ISBN 978-0-7653-8066-1 (hardcover)
ISBN 978-0-7653-8067-8 (trade paperback)
ISBN 978-1-4668-7497-8 (e-book)

First Edition: June 2015

Printed in the United States of America

0 9 8 7 6 5 4 3 2 1

This, this the doom must be
Of all who've loved, and lived to see
The few bright things they thought would stay
For ever near them, die away.

—THOMAS MOORE, "ALONE IN CROWDS TO WANDER ON"

THE DEVIL'S ONLY FRIEND

1

I'm good now. I promise.

My name is John Wayne Cleaver and I was born in a little town in the middle of nowhere called Clayton. You know those little towns on the side of the road, the ones where you drive through and you don't notice them, or maybe you stop for gas and think, "what a dump, who would ever live here?" Well, I did, for sixteen years. And I wish I could say that it was boring, and that nothing ever happened, and that we lived in a sleepy haze of naive innocence far from the troubles of the modern world, but I can't. I killed people. Not as many as other people, I'll grant you, but that's not much consolation, is it? If someone sat next to you on a bus, held out his hand and said, "Hi, I'm John, I've only killed a couple of people," that wouldn't exactly put your mind at ease. But yes, I've killed, and some of them were demons, true, but some of them were people. That I didn't kill the people personally is beside the point; they are dead because of me. That changes you. You start to look at things differently, at lives and their fragility. It's like we're all Humpty Dumpty, held together by tiny, cracking shells, perched up on a wall like it's no big deal. We think we're invincible, and then one little crack and boom, out comes more blood and guts and screams than you'd ever thought could be inside a single body. And when that blood goes, everything else goes with it—breath, thought, movement. Existence. One minute you're alive and then suddenly you're not.

I used to wonder if it went somewhere. If the thing that used to be your "life" actually left your body and physically went somewhere else. Conservation of matter and energy and all that. But I've seen death, and life doesn't go anywhere, and I think that's because life doesn't exist, not really. Life isn't a thing, it's a condition; we switch it on and we switch it off. For all we talk about taking a life, there's nothing there to take.

But I'm good now. I promise. I've killed, and whatever bloodlust I used to have is sated. I wake up in the morning and I go to my tutor and I go to my counseling and I go to my job with the FBI, helping to track down other killers, and I say the right things and I do the right things and nobody's afraid of me and everything is good. I watch travel shows. I cook. I do logic puzzles to keep myself occupied. And then sometimes at night I go to the butcher shop and I buy the biggest roast they have and I bring it home and I cover the room in plastic and I hack the meat to pieces with a kitchen knife, slashing and ripping and chopping and grunting until there's nothing left but scraps. Then I roll up the plastic, meat and blood and all, and I throw it away and everything is clean and calm again.

Because I'm good now.

I promise.

"I love you, John."

I used to think I would have loved to hear Brooke Watson say those words. Now they broke my heart every time. I never thought I had a heart until it was broken. It's hard to see the point of something that only ever causes pain.

"You don't love me," I said, shifting my weight in the uncomfortable hospital chair. We were sitting in the dementia wing of a rest home in a dirty little Midwestern city called Fort Bruce. It was bigger than Clayton, the town where Brooke and I grew up, but that's not saying much. We'd left Clayton almost a year ago, when Brooke was just starting to lose her mind. She'd been getting worse and worse ever since. "Your name is Brooke Watson," I told her, "and you're my friend."

She shook her head. "My name is Nobody."

"Nobody was a demon," I said. "You called her a 'Withered.'"

Her expression grew dark. "The Withered are evil."

I looked out the barred window, seeing the slate-gray sky over the week-old January snow that covered the city like a layer of ash. New snow is clean; old snow is black and coarse and full of dirt and garbage.

I looked back at Brooke. "That's right," I said. "The Withered are evil, and you're not one of them. 'Nobody' was a monster and she possessed you, but she's gone now. She's dead, and you have her memories, but you're not her. You're Brooke." I looked at her, wondering again—for the thousandth time—how to help her. Her mind seemed to come and go like a breeze, ethereal and impossible to predict.

"Possessed" wasn't really the right word for what had happened, but it was close; possession implies a spirit or a ghost, but Brooke was taken over by a physical entity—a monster made of ash and grease, a black sludge that, in her more lucid moments, Brooke called "soulstuff." The demon known as Nobody was made of it and crawled inside her bloodstream and moved her like a puppet. I suppose the best word would be to say that Brooke was "invaded," but honestly, when you're talking about a bodily invasion and using words like "best," things are pretty screwed up and you might as well just not talk about them at all. But that's life in the demon-hunting business, I guess.

Yay.

Brooke looked over my shoulder, her eyes locked on some distant memory rather than the hospital wall barely ten feet away. Kelly Ishida, the cop on our little team of hunters, had covered the wall with posters of flowers and landscapes, but that seemed almost insulting. Brooke's mind was buried under thousands of years of nightmare memory, from when her mind had merged with that of a demon who'd spent millennia invading body after body, girl after girl, only to inevitably grow disillusioned and kill itself—and the host bodies—over and over. Were some pictures of flowers supposed to make that go away?

"My name is Lucinda," said Brooke, stating it almost slyly, like she was telling me a secret. "I used to sell flowers in the market, but now I'm stuck in here." She paused a moment and then her eyes fixed on me. "I don't like it in here." A small tear welled up in the corner of her eye, growing bigger and bigger until it spilled over her eyelid and trickled down the side of her face. I watched it roll down her skin, leaving a thin, wet trail. I focused on the tear because it helped me to ignore all the horrible things that surrounded it. Her voice seemed far away and quiet. "Can you get me out of here?"

Here, as I said, was the lockdown wing of the Whiteflower Assisted Living Center. We traveled a lot, following Brooke's patchy memories of various Withered; we'd spent about four months in St. Louis, hunting a demon named Ithho who stole people's fingers, and then nearly seven months in Callister, hunting a demon who could only hear people in pain. "Demon" wasn't really the right word any more than "possessed" was, now that we knew more about what they were—which still wasn't much, frankly, but at least we knew they weren't the typical boogeymen from Catholicism or Judaism or any other big religion. We'd come to Fort Bruce because of an unprecedented two Withered in the same city, and we'd been here about three months, gathering information. And because Fort Bruce didn't have a real mental institution, Brooke was in Whiteflower with a bunch of dementia patients. She was the youngest patient by several decades, but aside from that it was a pretty good fit: her room and the floor were locked, she was under constant surveillance, and the staff was experienced with both memory problems and suicide risks. One of the few things Brooke remembered consistently was killing herself and surviving it tens of thousands of times. Her perception of things was a little screwed up.

"You need to stay here for now," I said. I said it almost every day, no matter how much I hated it. A year ago I wouldn't have said anything—I probably would have just left, if we're being perfectly honest. Being a heartless wallflower had been so much easier than feeling guilty all the time. "You're sick, and they can help you here."

"I'm not sick, I'm Lucinda."

Lucinda was one of the people Nobody had killed over the centuries, and her memories were mingled in with all the others jumbled up in Brooke's head. Dr. Trujillo, our team's psychologist, had counted more than thirty different personalities so far, but he said few of them surfaced more than once. Lucinda had popped up three or four times so far, and I wondered what it was about Brooke's situation here that called that specific girl to mind. Had she been in an institution or a hospital? Few of Nobody's victims were that modern, if we understood her correctly; most were hundreds, if not thousands, of years old. How had Nobody found Lucinda, and where? What had attracted her to the girl's life, and what had eventually caused her to end it?

How did Brooke remember dying?

"Your name is Brooke Watson," I said again. "My name is John Wayne Cleaver." I hesitated, knowing what I wanted to say and not daring to speak it out loud. I sat with my mouth open, struggling with the words, and finally just said them, softly in case Dr. Trujillo was listening. "I'm going to get you out of here—I don't know when, but I promise. Out of this hospital, out of the team, out of everything. We're going to run away."

"Are we going to get married?"

Her words were like an ice pick in my chest, and I shook my head. "No, Brooke, you don't love me."

"I love you more than anything," she said fiercely. "I've loved you for a thousand years—I've loved you since the sun was born and the stars sang songs to wake it up. I love you more than life and breath and body and soul. Do you want me to show—"

"No," I said, trying to calm her. "Just stop. I'll get you out of here, but you have to stop saying that."

"It'll be our secret, then."

"No," I repeated. "It'll be our nothing. You don't love me."

She paused for a moment, studying me with eyes that looked far too old for a seventeen-year-old girl. "I know all about nothing," she said softly. "I'm Nobody."

I sighed. "You and me both, Brooke. You and me both."

Nathan Gentry tapped his fingers on the conference-room table. "This chick is crazy."

Of all the people on our team, Nathan would be the easiest to kill. Not that I wanted to kill any of them, necessarily, but I had a plan for it in case I needed to. It never hurts to be prepared. Nathan was soft without being fat, an ideal mix of "out of shape" and "uninsulated" that left his vital organs right at the surface, without any muscle or fat to get in the way. For the others I needed a plan, but for Nathan all I'd need was a knife: slash the gut or the legs to slow him down, get in close, and cut his throat. He'd fight, but I'd win. If he was distracted at the time, buried in a book with his earbuds in the way he spent most of his time, it'd be even easier.

I kind of hoped, if the time ever came, that he didn't make it easy.

I wasn't supposed to think about that, obviously. I had rules to keep myself from hurting anybody, rules I'd been following since I was barely seven years old—ever since I'd discovered, with a dead gopher's blood trickling down my hands, that I was different from other people. That I was a sociopath, cut off from the rest of the world, surrounded by normal people but forever and relentlessly alone. I had rules to help keep my most dangerous impulses safely locked away. But I also had a job, and my job was to plan killings. All day, every day, I studied our targets, discovered their weaknesses, and figured out exactly how to kill them. It's a skill set I'm particularly gifted at, but not one that's easy to turn off.

I looked away from Nathan and back at our surveillance photos, forcing myself to focus on the task at hand. The "chick" Nathan thought was crazy was Mary Gardner, and he kind of had a point, though that didn't make me hate him any less. I deflected my hatred into what I hoped was playful teasing.

"Sensitivity training," I reminded him. As government employees we had a lot of sensitivity training, and it had become one of our go-to punchlines for any kind of joke, insult, or banter. I liked having running gags like this because they made it easier for me to know what the others would find funny and what they'd find off-putting. I couldn't always tell on my own.

"Sorry," said Nathan, "this 'woman' is crazy." The cadence of his voice was off, in a pattern I'd come to recognize as frustrated sarcasm. I suppressed a smile, knowing I'd gotten to him.

"That's not what he meant," said Kelly, and her voice had a fair bit of frustration in it as well. "He means that you shouldn't use 'crazy' as an epithet, since John has a mental-health issue too."

Kelly Ishida would be much harder to kill. She'd trained as a cop and worked homicide for six years, according to her file, so she knew how to handle herself. Her file also said that she was twenty-nine years old, but if I'd seen her on the street I would have sworn she was twenty-two. Twenty-three at the oldest. She was about my height, Japanese-American, with long black hair and dark eyes. I also knew that she slept very lightly and kept a gun on her nightstand, neither of which is a sign of a particularly healthy psyche; I assumed it had something to do with the incident that caused her to leave the police force and join our team, but I didn't know for sure yet. The exact details were redacted from her file, but whatever it was had left her with a lot of trust issues. Not as many as she thought, though; she still had me pick up her coffee almost every day. When the time came—if the time came—I could poison her virtually at will.

"Us crazy people have to stick together," I said, still studying the surveillance photos. I had seen something in one of them, and after another moment of thought I slid it across the table to Kelly; trust issues or not, she was an excellent detective. The photo was mostly identical to all our other photos of Mary Gardner—a nurse's uniform, a sweater, and a blue hospital face mask—but this one had a key difference. I tapped an odd shadow in the center. "Look at this bulge by her waist."

Kelly took the photo, examining it closely. "Sweaters do this sometimes, so it's hard to be sure what's under there. You think it's a gun?"

"It's not a hip," I said, "unless she has very weird hips."

"Sensitivity training," said Diana, and I suppressed another smile. Diana Lucas was the only other person on the team who ever joined in my jokes. Not only would killing her be physically hard—she was former military and as tough as a brick—but I'd regret it afterward. We weren't friends, per se, but we got along, united in our shared annoyance with Nathan, if nothing else. Nathan always told her they had to stick together, as the only black people on the team, and I think that annoyed her more than anything else. She'd even punched him once. I sincerely hoped I never had to kill Diana.

I looked back at Kelly. "Compare that photo to this one," I said, sliding another image across the table. "This is an older shot, from a few weeks ago, so she's wearing different clothes and we're seeing it from a different angle. The bulge is still there. It's too consistent to be a random fold in a sweater."

"Maybe," said Kelly. She pulled out magnifying glass—a real live magnifying glass, like an old-timey detective. It was one of Kelly's quirks. I kept waiting for her to pull out a pipe and a Sherlock Holmes hat. "Could be a gun," she said, studying the photo intently. "Do we have any other shots of that side?"

"What's the big deal about a gun?" asked Nathan, watching as I sifted through the photos. "She's some kind of supernatural monster anyway, right? Seems like a gun should be the least of our problems."

"Sensitivity training," I said.

"Oh, come on, what now?" asked Nathan, his voice even more frustrated than before. "We're not allowed to call the monsters monsters anymore? Are we worried about offending them?"

"I was actually warning myself that time," I said, finding another photo and passing it over to Kelly. "I'm about to call you an idiot, and I was saving everyone else the trouble of pointing it out."

"Hey—" said Nathan, but I cut him off.

"You're an idiot," I said. "But to be fair you're also new, so maybe you haven't done all the reading yet."

"I've done more reading than anyone in this building," said Nathan. "Or did you forget that I'm literally a doctor of library science?"

Diana rolled her eyes—we couldn't forget Nathan's credentials because he shoved them in our faces every chance he got.

"I'll let you know if any science libraries start bleeding," I said. "Between now and then, apply your research with a little common sense. I assume you read the report on my second contact with a Withered?"

"Of course I did," said Nathan. "That's exactly what I'm talking about. If this woman can turn her hands into claws or whatever, a gun seems like the least of our worries."

I nodded. "So if she has supernatural weapons that make a gun redundant, why does she carry a gun?"

"Not every Withered has claws," said Diana, explaining the line of reasoning more patiently than I was. "Some of them—like the second one John ran into, named Clark Forman—have no apparent means of defense at all, and no superhuman powers beyond whatever basic . . . whatever . . . that makes them a Withered in the first place. Forman carried a gun specifically because he *didn't* have any claws. If our information is correct, Mary Gardner drains the health of others to keep herself healthy, which is why she works as a nurse. Nothing about that profile suggests that she has a form of supernatural defense, and if she carries a gun, that only serves to support this analysis."

"Okay, that makes sense," said Nathan. "I'd never thought of it that way."

I nodded. "That's because you're an idiot."

"Seriously," said Nathan, slapping the table, "why do we even put up with this kid? What are you, sixteen?"

"Seventeen."

"Seventeen years old and mouthy as hell, and we just have to sit here and take it because you're some kind of superpsycho?"

He looked at Diana. "Is this out of respect for his abilities as a sociopathic murderer, or because we're all afraid he's going to snap and kill us?"

Nathan was older than I was by a good ten years; much younger than his credentials would suggest, though, because he, like most of the rest of the team, was a bit of a prodigy in his area of expertise. According to his file he had two masters and two doctoral degrees, most of them related to one form of research or another. He knew more about Mediterranean history than anybody I knew, which was especially impressive since one of the people I knew was Brooke/Nobody, who'd lived there for literally centuries. I knew this about Nathan because of his file, but also because he told us constantly, just like he always told us how he'd climbed his way out of the ghetto in Philadelphia, paying his own way through school and earning his first Ph.D. from Harvard before the age of twenty. He had accomplished a lot, and I respected that; what bugged me is that he knew so much about everything, and all he seemed to talk about was himself. How could I not antagonize him for that?

"He's just staring at me," said Nathan.

"He does that," said Diana. "You don't get used to it." As much as I admired Diana, I was always secretly proud that I could unnerve her like that. She'd trained in the USAF Security Forces, one of the only armed services in America that trained women as snipers, and she had been their rising star. She'd been on the team since before I joined, so I wasn't sure of the circumstances; the exact details were redacted from her file, just like Kelly's. To be fair, so were mine—the team knew I'd killed three Withered, and they knew my mom had died in the final attack, but they didn't know how. And they didn't know anything about Marci.

I realized I was gripping the table edge so tightly my fingertips were turning white from the pressure. I couldn't let myself think about Marci anymore. I counted my number pattern, a mental exercise that helped me calm down: one, one, two, three, five, eight, thirteen, twenty-one, thirty-four. *Deep breath, in and out.*

"This is definitely a gun," said Kelly, still hunched over the photos. "That's a good catch, John. I'll call the others."

"What does that tell us for sure, though?" asked Nathan. "She works late hours in a bad part of town; maybe she wants to be able to defend herself without morphing into a monster every time."

"That's entirely possible," said Kelly. "On the other hand, our records say nothing about a concealed weapons permit, and yet she's wearing one in a hospital. That's two laws she's breaking, which seems a little unnecessary for standard self-defense. We've had her under surveillance for weeks and we didn't know anything about this gun until now. That means she really, really wants one, and she really, really doesn't want anyone to know she has it, and those two together seem like a pretty good sign that something weird is going on."

"That's a lot of reallys," I said.

"Sensitivity training," said Nathan. I raised my eyebrow and he scowled. "Everyone else got to say it."

The door to the conference room opened without a knock, and Linda Ostler stepped in: the woman who'd organized our team and the de facto leader of the US government's secret war against the supernatural. Her file listed her as fifty-three, which made her older than even Trujillo, and she had the force of will to back that age up with an aura of hard-won experience and authority. Kelly stood up immediately; some remnant of her training as a cop, I assumed.

"Agent Ostler," said Kelly, "I was just about to call you—we've found something new in the Gardner case—"

"Thank you, Ms. Ishida, but I'm afraid it will have to wait. Agent Potash called, and we're moving on Cody French."

"Now?" asked Diana.

"Immediately," said Ostler. "Potash is observing him, and we have reason to believe that our window of opportunity is about to open. If John's analysis is correct, we have about three hours to kill him before that window closes again, possibly for weeks."

"Everybody suit up, then," said Diana, already walking to the door. "I'll meet you at the car in ten." She brushed past Ostler and disappeared down the hall.

Kelly looked at me. "Are you ready for this?"

"I'm jumping for joy."

"Do you need me for anything?" asked Nathan. "I'm not a field agent, but I've been training in firearms and I—"

"Guns won't help on this one," said Kelly. "Diana won't even be much use, unless it goes wrong, at which point having extra people there will only makes things harder." She looked at me. "This one's all John and Potash."

"Then why are you going?" asked Nathan.

She turned back to him, her gaze icy. "I'm going because, unlike you, I *am* a field agent, and I've actually *finished* my firearms training, and I know exactly how the plan is supposed to go down. We may need you in the future, Mr. Gentry, but until then we need you to stay here." He fell silent, and I followed Kelly and Ostler into the hall.

"He's actually 'Dr.' Gentry," I said, "and it's very rude of you to forget his title. Do you know how hard he had to work for that? He pulled himself out of the ghetto in Philadelphia—"

"Dr. Gentry is a good model of where you could be in a few years, John," said Agent Ostler. "Put your natural intelligence to good use and get a real degree or two."

"And annoy everyone around me."

"You already annoy everyone around you," said Ostler. "At least Nathan doesn't do it on purpose."

I had a plan to kill Ostler, too. I looked forward to it with relish.

I lived in a small apartment two doors down from a demon named Cody French. Becoming his neighbor had been my idea: we'd come to Fort Bruce to study him, after all, trying to find a way to kill him, and what better way than by interacting with him directly? That was what I'd brought to the team, more than anything else: not so much my expertise as my approach. The US government had been peripherally aware of the demons for decades, just as many other nations over the years had been. But knowing about them and hunting them were two different things. Whatever the Withered were, they were supernatural, and that made them hard to predict, hard to track, and hard to kill. How could you plan for something that had the power to do or even be something completely unexpected? Ostler had inherited an investigation team with a long history of fleeting glimpses and near misses, and meanwhile I'd killed three of the things, all on my own. There wasn't any real trick to it—I planned their deaths the same way I planned my teammates'. Spend time with them, figure out their weak spots, and then push on those weak spots until they die. I make friends with them, and then I kill them.

Being my friend is not, statistically speaking, very safe.

We knew about Cody French the same way we knew about all the other Withered: Brooke told us. Brooke was a childhood friend of mine, the girl next door, and I'd had something of a crush on her for years. I say "something" because sociopaths don't have crushes the way normal people do. Looking back, through the lens of counseling, I can say more accurately that I had an obsessive fixation on the *idea* of Brooke, an idea that had very little to do with Brooke herself. I'd wanted what Brooke represented—some Platonic ideal of innocence and beauty—not because I wanted to share it but because I wanted to possess it. Not exactly the basis for a stable relationship. She, as it turns out, had a much more normal attraction to me—I almost said "healthy" in that sentence, but that's kind of laughable, isn't it? She'd thought I was nice and asked me out a couple of times, and ended up chained to a chair in a madman's kitchen. She was eventually possessed by a suicidal demon named Nobody. With any hope of a normal life destroyed, she'd joined Ostler's team the same time I did. I don't know what her parents thought she was doing, but I bet they imagined it as a lot more glamorous and heroic than it was.

But even a statement like "she joined the team" wasn't really accurate. *I* joined the team; Brooke was more of a tool that the team used. She wanted to be more when she was lucid, but honestly, she had several thousand years of suicidal, homicidal, everything-o-cidal monster memories trapped inside of her head. Most days she could barely dress herself.

I told you it's not safe to be my friend.

So Brooke's job was to comb through Nobody's memory for every scrap of Withered-related information she could find, and once we put together enough of the pieces we'd move to their city, trying to be as quiet and unobtrusive as we could, and set up a temporary office. We interfaced with the police, using Kelly as a liaison, but mostly we kept to ourselves—the mind-wrecking secret that the world was infested with supernatural monsters was not the kind of thing people took to easily, and we'd found it was simpler to work in the shadows than to try to train a different police force in Withered-hunting tactics every few months. We'd settle in, start our surveillance, and then it was my turn: Brooke found the Withered, but I was the one who figured out how to kill them. Albert Potash did most of the actual killing, with Diana as backup, and Kelly, Nathan, and Dr. Trujillo helped out with whatever else we needed.

I probably need to explain how the Withered work. We still didn't know exactly where they came from—Brooke's memory was selective, to say the least—but somehow each of them gave something up in return for greater power. The first one I'd ever met, my neighbor Bill Crowley, had no identity of his own—no face, no body—but he could steal the bodies of others. He'd lived for centuries, for millennia really, hopping from body to body, sometimes as a king, sometimes worshipped as a god, but eventually just hanging out in Clayton, trying to get by. I think they got tired after so long, after seeing so much and being so constantly on the fringes of the world. They never really belonged anywhere, and I can tell you that gets old fast, and I'm only seventeen. To spend thousands of years not belonging . . . it's no wonder Cody French ended up in a one-bedroom hole with a ragged old dog and a dead-end job. Whatever zeal he'd once had, whatever ambition, had run out ages ago.

Cody couldn't sleep. It's not that he didn't need to, he literally couldn't do it, not with sleeping pills or even pummeling himself unconscious, and I was fairly certain he'd taken both to a dangerous extreme at various points in his life. Think about that for a minute: all the other Withered were falling apart at the mental seams after so much relentless existence, but they'd only been awake for, on an average human sleep schedule, two thirds of it. Cody had experienced every minute of every hour of every day, day after day after year after century. What do you do with all that time? How do you not go insane? Cody had chosen books, and he was one of the most well-read people I'd ever known, but that can get you only so far. He'd filled the rest of his time with drinking, using alcohol to create a mindless stupor that wasn't exactly sleep, but filled a similar role. It helped him to forget, to relax, to turn off his brain for just a few precious minutes here and there.

And sometimes he took it a little farther.

"He's knocking on your door, Cleaver," said a voice on the radio. Albert Potash—I'd guess you'd call him our team's muscle—was not a patient man. I enjoyed pushing Nathan's buttons, but Potash I just tried to avoid altogether. I had no idea how to kill him.

"We're coming as fast as we can," said Kelly, keeping her hands firmly on the wheel. "The roads are icy. Keep your shirt on."

Cody French was a hard man to hurt: he had the reflexes of

a wild animal, a mind that never relaxed, and the combat training of a man who'd spent thousands of years trying to find something to do with his time. On top of that he had a shocking level of regeneration, having passed our "speed-bump test" with flying colors. That test was more or less what it sounded like: the second step of every hunt we went on, after we'd picked up some basic information about who the target was and how they worked, was to hit them with a car. If that took care of them, easy peasy; if not, we dug in for the long haul and tried to find a way around their supernatural healing. Our second week in Fort Bruce, Potash had run a red light in a diesel trailer and broadsided Cody French's car while the Withered was on his way to work. The car was totaled and the inside was covered with blood, but Cody had been essentially unharmed when they pulled him from the wreck—he'd healed before the bystanders had even been able to reach him. So we needed something more personalized, and we spent a long time studying him from afar, looking for a weakness. And then Cody asked his neighbor, the quiet, unassuming John Cleaver, to watch his dog for a few hours.

Just hours? That dog spent all day alone sometimes, so what could a few hours possibly matter? Sure, he had a girl there, but he had girls all the time. Why was this time different? Turned out that girl landed in county lockup a few days later, raving and delusional, though with no signs of outward abuse. That's the kind of thing that sets off all our alarm bells. Animals made me nervous in general, and under any other circumstance I would never have even touched his dog—I'd hurt some animals very badly as a child and I had rules to keep myself away from any similar temptations—but this was my in, so I'd smiled and nodded and said yes, and Cody had introduced me to his basset hound, named Boy Dog—and no, I have no idea why anyone would choose such a stupid name. Cody only laughed when I asked him. I petted Boy Dog as calmly as I could, played the friendly neighbor, and stepped into the life of a damaged monster. Over the course of the next month or so I'd figured it out: When Cody French's life got too bad, when he just couldn't stand being awake anymore and all he wanted was a rest, he'd pick up a girl—usually a hooker, someone desperate and already a little shady—and take them back to his apartment and pour everything he had into them. Not his memories, but his awareness. The part of his brain that could never turn off, that could never stop or slow down for even a second, he dumped into someone else. Then he slept, and she went mad.

"The dog's with another neighbor," said Potash. "How close are you?"

"Five minutes at the most," said Kelly, "unless you want us to die in a car accident on our way there."

"The dog's not part of the plan anyway," I said. "Better to have it somewhere else, so I'm free to move around."

Potash's voice crackled on the radio. "This girl looks younger than you are."

"Probably a runaway," said Kelly. "Someone who won't go to the cops, and who doesn't have anyone taking care of her. Twenty bucks says she's already got a drug problem, so her hallucinations won't look out of place if anyone looks too deep at her case."

Diana spoke up from the back seat. "If we take him out fast, can we save her?"

The car was silent.

"I don't know," I said at last. "I don't know exactly how he works. Killing him might end the transfer early, or it might make it permanent."

"So then we're damning her with the same curse he has?" asked Diana. "What good does that do?"

"She can't transfer it to anyone else," I said, "and she can't live forever."

"Better to just kill her in the same hit," said Potash.

"Absolutely not," said Kelly. "Better to take her into custody and observe her—maybe she'll be fine."

"She won't be," I said.

"And you don't care about her?" asked Diana.

I stared out the windows, the world flying by as Kelly sped through the city, and clenched my hands in a fist while I recited my number sequence: one, one, two, three, five, eight, thirteen. Dr. Trujillo would be so proud. I took a deep breath and thought about Diana's question again, more calmly this time. I turned her words back on her: "What good would caring do?"

"This entire thing is your plan," said Diana. "You couldn't find any way of hurting him without also destroying an innocent girl?"

"It's not like I'm happy about it—"

"But you're not sad about it either," said Diana. "We're about to straight up ruin someone's life, all in the interest of killing someone else, and you don't care the least, tiny bit about either one of them."

"What good would that do?" I asked again. This was my plan, like she said, and I'd thought it through from every possible angle. Caring about the target could get us all killed, and going in soft to avoid collateral damage could be just as dangerous. "He can recover from damage faster than we can deal it," I said, "which means we have to deal a hard, precise blow that he can't recover from. That means cutting his head off, and *that* means we have to get him while he's incapacitated, and *that* means we have to wait until after he starts the transfer. It's the only time he can't defend himself. We have to do this, and we have to do it *this way*, and I could spend my energy being sad about that or I could spend it making sure it works, and that we get him, and that after this one last girl he never hurts anyone else again."

Diana growled. "Normal people don't just turn off their human nature every time it gets inconvenient—"

"Sucks to be them, then," I said.

"We don't need to argue about this right now," said Kelly. "Sometimes you have to turn off your empathy to get the job done—I learned it in the force, you learned it in the military, John learned it . . . I shudder to think where John learned it. Let's just get the job done."

A limp body in a bathtub full of blood. A broken mirror. A burning car and a twisting scream.

Twenty-one. Thirty-four. Fifty-five. Eighty-nine. One hundred forty-four.

Turn it all off and don't feel anything.

"It's about time," said Potash, spotting us from his window as Kelly pulled into the apartment parking lot. There were two rows of buildings and a parking lot between them, with crumbling, open-air walkways, and stairs leading up to the apartments. It was winter, and the curbs were crusted with dirty, jagged ice. Kelly pulled to a stop behind the high, cinder block wall around the Dumpster, concealing us from anyone who might be looking out of Cody French's window. Diana got out without a word, carrying the duffel with her disassembled rifle.

"Give Diana five minutes to get in place," said Potash, on the radio, "and meet me at the door."

"Three minutes," said Diana, her whisper barely audible on the shared frequency. "How incompetent do you think I am?"

"Radio silence," said Kelly. "Go."

We all had our jobs and we'd gone over them a dozen times at the rented office space, getting ready for this exact situation whenever the opportunity appeared. Kelly would stay in the parking lot, her badge in hand, ready to deal with any questions or nosy neighbors. Ideally we wouldn't need her at all. Diana would be perched in the other apartment we'd rented, directly across from Cody's, with her rifle aimed and ready to shoot anyone who chased us out his door. Ideally we wouldn't need her either. I had a stolen key to Cody's door, and as the one who'd planned the hit, it was my job to observe the situation and make the call to proceed or pull out. I'd go in, make sure he was as helpless as we needed, and then . . .

. . . and then I wouldn't kill him. Potash, with a stainless-steel machete, would wait for my signal and take off Cody's head in one clean stroke.

I could feel that machete in my hand, feel the grip and the heft and the sudden, perfect resistance as it severed the spine. This was my plan. I'd practiced it a hundred times in my head. A thousand times. Sometimes in my head I had to kill the girl, too. You never knew what complications might arise.

But I never got to do it for real.

I got out of the car and walked to the stairs, pulling the key from my back pocket. Albert Potash timed it perfectly, arriving at the door from the other direction exactly as I got there. He was an older man, lean and fit, his graying hair still trimmed to the short, military cut his kind never seemed to let go. I didn't know exactly where he'd gotten his training, but he was some kind of ex-special forces supersoldier, the kind of man a government creates, uses, and then denies all knowledge of forever. I wasn't surprised, when I'd looked in his file, to find it completely empty. I'd spent my short life dreaming of death, of ending one life after another, stabbing and choking and poisoning and more. He'd spent his life actually doing it. I hated him passionately.

I raised my key to the lock, but he stopped me with a sudden gesture, listening to something I couldn't hear. After a moment he looked back at me again, rolling his hand to signal me to hurry. I unlocked the door in a rush, pushing it open as soon as the bolt scraped free of the frame, and stepped inside. Potash moved in behind me, silent as a ghost, pulling the machete from its black vinyl sheath so quickly I didn't even see him do it—it was covered one second and gleaming faintly in the dim light the next.

The front room was dark, the windows covered with blankets, and I could hear the noise now: a muffled grunting, like someone was struggling to speak. The layout of the apartment was essentially the same as mine: a small living room with an attached kitchen, which is where we stood now; a short hallway that led to two closed doors, with a bathroom on the left and bedroom on the right. I pointed to the bedroom door, and Potash stepped forward silently. He rested his hand on the doorknob, paused a moment, then quietly pushed it open.

The room beyond wasn't a den of horrors. No bodies hung from the ceiling, no eyes peered out from cracks in the wall. There was a simple wooden bed with a thin mattress, and Cody asleep facedown in the middle. Nearby, on the floor, bound and gagged and tied to the bedpost, was a teenage girl. I estimated her to be about fifteen years old, fully clothed, eyes haggard, but wide awake and terrified.

"Listen to me," said Potash firmly, crouching down beside her. "I can't untie you yet, but I need to know what's happened here. Did this man bring you in?"

The girl squeezed her eyes shut, shaking her head violently.

Potash glanced at me. "Is she saying no or is she already crazy?"

"He gave her his supernatural awareness," I whispered. "She could hear us outside before we even unlocked the door; it probably sounds like you're screaming in her ear." I lowered my voice to the barest breath. "We're here to help you. Did this man bring you here?"

She calmed and, after a moment, she nodded.

"Did he drug you?"

She stared at me, probably trying to decide how much trouble she'd get into for answering. She apparently decided it was worth it, and nodded.

"We good to go?" asked Potash.

"She's moved the bed almost eight inches," I said, pointing at the depressions the bed legs had left in the carpet. "If her struggling hasn't woken him up, nothing we do is going to."

"This feels too easy," he said, but I didn't answer. If you do it right, it's always easy. This was the great and dreadful end of everything I did, the paradox that made my life one long, successful hell. Months to find a weakness, more months to exploit it, endless nights of planning and practice, building up and building up until that one, perfectly executed strike that I don't even get to make. Potash walked to the bed, aimed his machete, and cut off Cody's head. The demon's eyes snapped open, his mouth gaping in a caricature of speech, but it was too late. The bright red blood pumping from his neck turned to black, greasy ash, and his body crumbled to nothing. The girl screamed, but it wasn't enough. It was never enough. There was no danger, no thrill, no visceral *thunk* as the machete vibrated in my hands.

Months of built-up tension and nothing to release it.

"It's done," said Potash in his radio, breaking the silence now that the job was done. He wiped his blade on the blanket and looked at the girl, passed out by his feet. "The runaway fainted, so I guess she isn't stuck with Withered senses forever."

"Get her out here," said Kelly. "I'll take her to a hospital while you and John go through the house."

Standard procedure: we go through the house, looking for anything we can find that might give us a hint about other Withered. Finish one hunt and get started on the next one, building more anticipation. I held my hands in tight fists, pushing out the blood until my knuckles were white as bone.

No rest for the wicked.

2

Here's a logic puzzle for you: there are four people, named Grant, Bill, Marci, and April. Each one has a different eye color: blue, brown, green, and hazel. Each one has a different role: girlfriend, neighbor, therapist, and mother. Each one died in a different way: a stabbing, a slit throat, slit wrists, and fire. One of the women died alone. The other woman died without a blade. One of the men killed the other one and then he, in turn, was killed by a child. All of them loved the child, but the child didn't save any of them. Can you solve the puzzle and find the answer?

Do you even know what answer you're looking for?

"Good morning, John." Dr. Trujillo was an older man, short and squat, his white hair making a stark contrast with his bronze skin. Him I'd probably poison, though there were other options depending on the circumstance. His shirt was wrinkled enough that I assumed he must have spent the night on the cot in the room next to Brooke's—we'd paid Whiteflower extra to get a second room, and Trujillo slept there more often than not. He stood when I walked toward him. "I heard about the project yesterday; I'm glad it went well."

We always called them "projects" in public. "Job" felt too crass, "mission" attracted too much attention, and "government authorized murder of a supernatural monster" just didn't have that sassy ring to it.

"It pays the bills," I said. He tilted his head analytically, and I rolled my eyes. "Is she awake?"

"Let me ask you a question first," he said, as if my permission had anything to do with it. "When you say that our work 'pays the bills,' what do you mean? Obviously it's true, but it's not a way you've ever characterized our work before."

"Do we have to do this right now?"

"I'm your psychologist, John, assigned to this unit specifically to help keep you and Brooke on an even keel. The reasons why you do the work you do are every bit as important as the work itself, and if you've begun to think—"

"Is she awake yet?"

"If you've begun to think of yourself less as a protector of human life and more as a contract killer, that's exactly the kind of thing I need to be watching out for."

Trujillo was the most zealous therapist I'd ever had, but on the plus side, having a lot of therapists meant I'd gotten really good at pissing them off. "Actually I prefer to swing as far as I can in the opposite direction," I said. "I have a full-on messiah complex now. I don't just protect people, I'm the outright savior of mankind." I spread my arms beatifically.

"Now you're just being belligerent," said Trujillo. "That's a deflection tactic, and we've talked about this before."

"I don't need to deflect anything," I said, "I'm impervious to harm. Try it—you packing? I'm sure there's a zip gun or a shiv somewhere in this place, it's a psych ward. Of course, if you try to harm me you'll be damned for eternity and live forever without My grace."

Trujillo put his fingers on the bridge of his nose, sighing or pressing down on a headache. "Why do you do this, John?"

"If I tell you, it's cheating. You're supposed to figure it out on your own."

"I'm here to help you."

"I'm here to see Brooke," I said. "Is she awake yet?"

He stared at me a moment, exasperated. I got to see his exasperated face a lot. "If not now, can we at least talk about this later?"

"Does it matter if I say no?"

"You can always say no," he said, "but you know what will happen if you do. I can't sign off on your psychiatric readiness to perform your job unless you open up to me."

"In your defense," I said, "the illusion of freedom is one of my favorite illusions. Also that one where you can pull a quarter out of someone's ear; I love that one."

"This does not have to be a confrontational relationship, John."

"Then why do I have to ask you four times if my friend is awake yet?"

He blew out a rough sigh, throwing one hand in the air and then pointing it at Brooke's door. "Yes, she's awake." He turned and walked back toward the side room, talking over his shoulder. "You're not likely to get much out of her today, but you're welcome to try. And we *will* talk about this later."

"Bless you, my son."

He grunted and disappeared into the second room. I walked to Brooke's door and peeked in the window. She was sitting up on the bed, cross-legged, her long blond hair hanging like a tangled curtain around her shoulders. Her face was turned up, her eyes staring blankly at the ceiling, and her left hand was tracing intricate patterns in the bedspread. I opened the door—it was only locked from the inside—and she turned toward me.

"*Bunâ ziua.*" Her left hand, unattended, was still drawing on the blanket.

"What language is that?"

"I don't know," she said, "what language is this?"

"English," I told her.

She didn't say anything, but simply stared.

Brooke had always been thin, but a year of mental incapacitation had left her gaunt, her blue eyes sunken deep in her pale, white face. Trujillo said some of that was the drugs they had her on—they made food taste bad, so she never ate unless they forced her. Protein shakes when she was in a good mood, restraints and IV drips when she wasn't. Her entire room had been cleared of anything dangerous, partly for our safety but mostly for hers: there were no cords, no glass, no sharp edges. Even the power outlets were nailed into the wall, because screws were too easy to extract and misuse.

"Do you remember me?" I asked.

"Of course I remember you," said Brooke, and her eyes focused on me suddenly. "I love you."

I sighed. "No you don't," I said. "You're Brooke Watson, remember? You're not Nobody."

"My name is Hulla."

We'd known the Withered as Nobody back when I was hunting it, but in her more lucid moments Brooke could remember the thing's real name. Hulla was, according to Nathan, an old Sumerian name, but that didn't tell us much; we already knew the Withered were ancient. Did Hulla come from Sumer, or just borrow a name when she got there?

"Do you love me back, Ghita?"

"I'm John," I said. "You're Brooke and I'm John."

Her hand was still drawing, all by itself, like it wasn't even a part of her at all.

"I saw Meshara last night."

"These are not real people," I said. "Not anymore. You live in Whiteflower Assisted Living Center in a town called Fort Bruce. My name is John Wayne Cleaver. Do you remember any of this?" I couldn't tell how much of her was Brooke and how much was Hulla; how much was crazy and how much was drugs designed to control the crazy. I could only imagine how much worse it was for her.

"Of course I remember you," she said again. "You lived on my street. We were friends. I married you and I died the next day."

"I'm not Ghita," I said, "I don't even know who that is. My name is John, and this is—"

"This is the Whiteflower Assisted Living Center," said Brooke. "My name is Nobody and I was born ten thousand years ago in a shepherd's hut on the slopes of the great mountain. And Meshara was there and now he's here."

I sat up straighter; this was different than her usual ranting. She called me by old names occasionally, thinking I was someone from her past, but she'd never referred to anyone else that way except for the actual Withered: the two we'd known in Clayton were named Mkhai and Kanta, just like Nobody was named Hulla. These were their old names, the names they used for each other; to hear her use such a name for someone she'd seen last night, and to connect it with something so deep in the past, was troubling, to say the least. Who was this Meshara? "You saw somebody here?" I asked. "You recognized him?"

"In the lobby downstairs," she said. "The doctor took me for a walk. I almost didn't recognize him, it's been so long. Maybe a hundred years."

We thought there were only two Withered in Fort Bruce. If there were three . . . "Did you tell Trujillo who you saw?"

"I don't like Dr. Trujillo." Brooke scowled. "He never lets me cut my own food."

"Can you describe Meshara to me?"

"He's sad."

"What does he look like?"

"He looks sad."

I stood up and walked to the door; I needed to talk to Trujillo. "Could you point him out to me if you saw him again?"

Her voice changed suddenly, losing the odd, disconnected tone she always seemed to use when she was remembering things and becoming suddenly sharp and pained. "Please don't leave me."

"I'm coming back, I just need to—"

"No one ever comes back."

"I promise," I said, and knocked on the door. "Just try to remember everything you can about Meshara, okay? Can you do that?"

"He's here," said Brooke.

"I know, and I need you to remember everything you can about him—"

"Not Meshara," said Brooke. "The doctor."

Half a second later Trujillo stepped into view through the window and did a visual check of the room before opening the door. "Is everything okay?"

I shot one last look at Brooke; she had tears on her cheeks and look of abject despair in her pale, haunted eyes. I turned away, stepped into the hall, and closed the door firmly behind me.

"Did you take her on a walk last night?"

"Yes, down to the lobby and back. We bought some candy from the vending machine."

"She's found another Withered, here in Whiteflower."

His brow furrowed in worry. "There were only supposed to be two in the city."

"Exactly," I said. "And if there's an extra one, and if he's here, right under our noses, it only means one thing: the Withered are hunting *us* now."

"Ghita is a Romanian name," said Nathan. "Her greeting was also Romanian: '*bună ziua*' means 'good morning.' That's all in line with the kind of flashbacks we tend to see from Brooke: she woke up with the wrong memories on the surface of her consciousness, and so she thought she was a Romanian villager. Not exactly the worst-case scenario for her, all things considered."

"And Meshara?" asked Agent Ostler. The entire team was gathered around a table in our office, a rented space across the street from Whiteflower. I could tell by the way they were fidgeting—drumming their fingers on the table, glancing at the windows, shifting their weight from foot to foot without bothering to sit down—that they were just as tense as I was.

"That one's not Romanian," said Nathan. "I haven't had time to look into it too deeply, but my preliminary research suggests that Meshara is Sumerian, like Hulla, which suggests in turn that this is another Withered. Kudos to John for spotting it."

I ignored the compliment, taking as it a bald attempt to get back on my good side after yesterday's argument. The joke was on him for thinking I had a good side. "How do we track him down?" I asked.

"I was able to pull last night's security footage from the lobby cameras," said Kelly, laying a stack of low-res photos on the table, hastily printed on plain white office paper. She pointed at the top photo and tapped her finger on an average-looking man in a loose jacket. "I took these to Brooke and she identified this man as Meshara."

Potash pulled the photo toward his side of the table, rotating it for a better look at the image. "Is this our best shot of him?"

Kelly nodded. "This isn't a convenience store, where the cameras are positioned to get clear face shots of the customers at the counter. Whiteflower's main security risk is patients leaving unaccompanied, so their lobby camera is a wide-angle pointed at the front door. The image you're looking at comes from a hallway camera and offers a slightly better look at his face than the one in the lobby."

I dug through the pile of photos, looking for the lobby image. It was just a few photos down, marked with a red circle from Kelly's meeting with Brooke. The jacket looked the same as the hallway image, but the face was hard to discern—dark hair, no beard or mustache, paunchy. An incredibly average-looking man.

"Do we have a name yet?" asked Ostler.

"I've sent it back to headquarters for facial recognition," said Kelly, "but without a better image the computer's not likely to find anything. This is one we're probably going to end up doing by hand, so I hope you're all excited to sit down with old case binders and start flipping."

"There's got to be a better way," said Nathan. "Are there traffic cameras outside? I haven't noticed."

"In Fort Bruce?" asked Diana. "Come back in five years."

"There's a camera in the parking lot," said Kelly, "but it's out of order. I can try going to the other businesses in the area and hope we get lucky, but unless he stopped at a gas station immediately before or after his visit that's almost guaranteed to be a dead end."

"Brooke said nothing to me," said Trujillo, "so if I had no idea she saw anything, this Withered might not know either. Our best hope for now is that he still thinks we don't know about him."

"He?" asked Potash. "Or they? This could be a sign of a much larger counterattack than we're imagining." The group started grumbling, but I ignored them and studied the photo. There was something about it . . .

"Don't jump to conclusions," said Ostler, trying to regain control. "The last thing we need is a panic."

"The last thing we need is to get murdered," said Nathan. "It could be weeks before we figure out who this guy is, and by then we could all be—"

"Did you ask at the front desk?" I asked. Kelly looked at me, and I turned the photo to face her. "Look at his position there—he's either just changed directions for no reason in the middle of the room, or he's walking away from the receptionist."

The room went quiet, and Kelly studied the image a moment before closing her eyes. "I'm trying to remember the layout of the lobby. Leaving the front desk at that angle would take him toward . . ."

"The dining room," I said, and looked at Trujillo. "Did you walk through there?"

"We never do," said Trujillo. "Too many knives."

I looked at Ostler. "The dining room is for residents and their guests only; unless he's accompanying somebody, he wouldn't even be allowed in."

"Why does this matter?" asked Nathan.

"Because it means Meshara has a cover story," said Ostler, picking up my line of thought. "If he was just walking around watching people the nurses would get suspicious, so he's made friends with a resident. That's his excuse for being there. And that means he's been there more than once, which means the people at the front desk might recognize him."

"It'll be an Alzheimer's patient," I said. "Someone who doesn't remember anyone, so no one will think it's weird that he doesn't remember this guy."

"How do you know that?" asked Diana.

"I don't know for sure," I said. "But that's the way I'd do it."

Ostler looked at Kelly. "Ms. Ishida?"

Kelly stood up, taking the better of the two photos with her. "I'll check it out. Potash, come with me—nobody should be alone now that we know we're being followed." The two of them left, and the rest of us looked at each other.

"What does this mean?" asked Trujillo. "Practically, I mean? I've worked on serial-killer cases, but never one where the investigators were being hunted. Has this ever happened before?"

"Nobody was hunting John," said Nathan. "I mean, the Withered named Nobody was hunting John."

"That's a weird name for a Withered," I said. "Is 'Nobody was hunting John' also Sumerian?"

"This is serious," said Diana. "Can you please stop making jokes for five damn minutes?"

"Let me fill in some gaps for you," said Ostler. "In the process of hunting John, the Withered named Nobody killed four girls John knew, including his girlfriend, then tried to kill Brooke, then burned John's mother alive. So maybe humor is a defense mechanism, and you need to cut him a little slack."

So now they knew my history. Judging by their silence, it kind of freaked them out.

Trujillo was the first to speak. "So I take it the answer to my question is 'yes, we're in incredible danger.' "

"All I knew about Nobody was her name," I said. "We know Meshara's name, face, and location, and we have a good lead on finding more, plus anything else we can get out of Brooke. We can do this."

"And how many of us die in the process?" asked Nathan.

"Better us than civilians," said Diana.

"I am a civilian!" Nathan shouted.

"We knew the risks when we got into this," said Ostler. "Even you, civilian or not. If they want to make this a war, we have the tools, the experience, and the weapons to fight it."

"Our first step needs to be Mary Gardner," said Trujillo. "If there's more than one Withered working together, we have to assume she's a part of it. If we take her out as fast as we can, we remove one enemy soldier before they have a chance to hit us. That could throw their whole plan into disarray and buy us the time we need to track down this Meshara."

"We're not ready to move on Mary," I said. "I haven't figured out her weakness yet."

"She passed the speed-bump test," said Nathan, "so we know it's going to be tricky."

"Maybe the speed-bump test is part of our problem," said Diana. "If the Withered talk to each other at all, and this suggests that they do, then the fact that each one of them's been in a major, unexplained car accident recently can't help but look like a clue."

"So we don't speed bump Meshara," I said. "Make them think we don't know about him yet."

"All that does is deny us information," said Nathan. "Even if it denies them information, too, it's still a wash at best, and a needless precaution if Brooke has communicated with him in any way. Dammit!" He smacked the table with his hands, like he'd just remembered something terrible. "She's thinks she's one of them! For all we know she's been talking to him all along!"

"She wouldn't do that," I said, though I knew it was a hollow assurance. We could never be sure what Brooke would do. I shook my head. "All we have to do is the same thing we always do: get to know them, make a plan, and strike. And we've already made good progress, despite barely knowing about this guy for three hours. We know he's hunting us, we know he's using a patient as a cover, and we know he can't shape shift the way some of the others can."

"How do we know that?" asked Ostler.

"Because Brooke recognized him," I said, "after what she claimed to be a hundred years. If he could shape shift in that time, he would have. So unless the receptionist throws Kelly some insane curveball down there, we've got a good head start on figuring out what he does, and how, and how to stop him." Ostler's phone rang. "Speak of the devil."

Ostler set her phone in the middle of the table. "Ms. Ishida, you're on speaker."

"His name is Elijah Sexton," said Kelly. "The receptionist knew him immediately. He visits a man named Merrill Evans—an Alzheimer's patient, just like John guessed."

"Nice one!" Nathan held up his hand for a high five, but I ignored him.

"Now get ready for the weird part," said Kelly. "He's been visiting here ever since Merrill Evans checked in. That was almost twenty years ago." She sighed. "Either that's a really deep cover story, or we don't have any idea what's really going on here."

3

"I don't want you in my house," I said.

"That's not your call," said Potash.

We were going back to my apartment; Potash was driving. That was a frustration of its own: I was seventeen and I could drive just fine, but they never let me. I had my own car, but whenever I was with the rest of the team—which was always—I had to let one of them drive. I was a child to them. Worse, though, Potash had a duffel bag in the back seat, full of what he claimed to be the sum of his material possessions. I felt my throat starting to constrict, imagining the invasion of my living space. I couldn't do it.

"It's my house," I said, "of course it's my call. Why do you think I live by myself—because I love people so much? It's part of my deal with Ostler: Kelly and Diana share a place; you and Nathan and Trujillo share a place; I live alone. This isn't up for discussion."

"You're right," said Potash, still looking at the road.

"It isn't." Now that Meshara and who knew how many others were hunting for us, no one on the team was allowed to be alone, even at home.

"Have you considered that I'm a dangerous psychopath?" I asked. "Sleeping in the same apartment as me could be severely hazardous to your health and well-being."

Potash glanced at me, a silent, emotionless look that expressed precisely how little danger a scrawny teenager posed to a special forces soldier. "Have you considered that that's exactly why they chose me to be the one to join you?"

"Even if I'm not a danger to you," I said, "what about other people? How many guns do you have in that duffel bag? Is it a 50 percent ratio of clothes to weapons, or somehow more than that? I have a very strict no-weapons policy in my house—"

"All the more reason you shouldn't be alone."

"—and I do that to avoid temptations. I'm trying very hard not to become a serial murderer and the last thing I need is a bunch of guns and knives all over my house."

"There are no weapons in my duffel bag," said Potash. "I have a concealed gun on my person, which you will never see or touch. Everything else is stored off site."

"It's a one-bedroom apartment," I said. "I have nowhere for you to sleep."

"I sleep on the floor."

"I don't even—" I stopped suddenly, surprised by what he'd said. "I was expecting you to ask for the couch."

"I prefer floors. I don't actually own a bed, even at home."

I sighed, running out of feasible plans to dissuade him. "You're insane."

"Then we should get along fine."

"Sensitivity training," I snarled. I closed my eyes, trying to think of the problems this would cause and searching for preemptive solutions. "I'm a vegetarian," I said, "and rather militant about it. No meat of any kind in the house. You so much as order a pepperoni pizza, you eat it outside."

"Does fish count?"

"Of course fish counts."

"Some vegetarians don't count fish."

"I do," I said. "I'm not protesting the American meat industry, I'm trying to not kill anything. Have you ever thought about your meat as an animal? Your teeth biting through the flesh of a living thing that somebody killed and put on a fire? No animals of any kind."

Potash nodded. "Eggs?"

"Eggs are fine," I said. I stared out the window, clenching my fist inside my coat pocket. "You can eat all the f—" I stopped and closed my eyes. My apartment was my haven; it was the one place I could go to be away from everyone. In Clayton we'd lived over my mother's mortuary, so I'd had my own room and the embalming room as my private, silent sanctuaries. Now I had neither. We moved around the country, killing as we went, and all I had to keep myself stable was the knowledge that wherever we went I would always have a place to myself. I needed one.

Now I'd lost even that.

When we reached my apartment I showed Potash the living room: a single chair pointed at a TV.

"I thought you said you had a couch," said Potash.

"I said I was expecting you to ask for a couch," I answered. "I was kind of looking forward to telling you I didn't have one.

It's not as weird as not owning a bed, though, so don't point any fingers." I left him to set up his own sleeping area and retreated to the kitchen, where I started making a salad. I wasn't kidding about my vegetarianism—while I would gladly have made that my diet just to piss him off, I really did avoid meat and had for a few years. I'd come to embrace cooking as a "safe" hobby that helped me keep my mind off of other things. Now, raging at this home invasion, I chopped yellow peppers with my teeth clenched in fury, slicing tomatoes and shredding carrots and ripping chunks of lettuce with my bare hands. I covered the mass of vegetables with sunflower seeds and olive oil and sat down at the kitchen table with my mind still roiling. There was no wall between the meager kitchen and the tiny front room, so I watched Potash in angry silence as he finished his spartan preparations. Maybe if I burned the apartment down they'd let me be alone again. I was only halfway finished with my dinner when he stowed his bag in the corner and sat down across from me at the table.

"I eat alone," I said.

"You used to do everything alone," he responded. "Eating is one of many things that will have to change under this arrangement."

"Or you could just go, and I can keep my routine the way I like it."

Nathan or Ostler or Trujillo would have sighed, or shaken their heads, or given some outward expression of frustration. Potash only looked at me. "I have trouble believing that while our entire team is being hunted by monsters, putting your life in direct and immediate danger, you care more about your routine than your safety."

"My routine is my safety," I said. "I have a specific way of doing things. I have rules."

"And what happens if you don't follow them?"

I held myself as still as I could, focusing on the wall so no other images could enter my mind. "I'd rather not be forced into a demonstration."

"I can buy my own food," he said simply, "but you'll have to go with me to the store, or this whole living arrangement is meaningless. We're always together. It's late now, so we can go tomorrow."

"I can be out late," I said, "I'm not a child."

"No one ever says that but children."

I pushed my salad away, suddenly sickened by the idea of food. The kitchen table was mostly covered in papers, and I gestured to them as calmly as I could. "This is where I study—another thing I do alone. I need to figure out how to kill Mary Gardner, so just . . . back off for a while, okay? Disappear."

"You only have three rooms," said Potash. "I either invade your bedroom, which I doubt you want, or I sit in the bathroom all night, or you see me out here."

"I choose bathroom."

"I wasn't offering you a choice," said Potash, "I was pointing out that full avoidance is impossible." His voice was maddeningly calm, and I had to exert every ounce of my self-control to maintain a similar expression. I felt like a tornado turned inside out: the windless eye of the storm was on the outside, placid and emotionless, but trapped in the middle was a raging vortex of movement and fury and violence. I took a deep breath, staring at my half-eaten salad and my piles of carefully ordered papers and my living room without a couch. I should move to the bedroom, I knew—it was the only way to work in privacy—but that would mean giving in, and I felt a hot, irrational aversion to even considering it. Better to sit here getting nothing done and making him uncomfortable than to retreat to the back room and let him rule the front uncontested. I tried to think of how to do it rudely, knowing there was no way to just "not move" dramatically, when someone knocked on the door.

Potash and I looked at each other.

"Probably a neighbor," said Potash softly. "Someone on the team would have called first."

"The only neighbor I know is dead," I whispered, standing. "I'll answer it, but if it's a Withered I'd better see that concealed weapon you keep bragging about."

Potash said nothing, only standing to follow me and then stopping just where the opened door would hide him from the visitor. I heard a foot shuffle outside,and a low canine yelp. I frowned and opened the door.

"Oh good, you're home." It was Christina Tucker from apartment 201; I'd seen her collecting her mail now and then, and walking to and from her car. She had a white Honda Civic with one missing hubcap and she worked part-time at a bank where she earned just barely enough to pay the rent. She hated her mother and broke up with her boyfriend three weeks ago. At night she slept with a face mask and a white-noise machine, and you probably don't want to know how I know all of that. "I'm Christina," she said, brushing hair from her eyes. "I live in 201."

"I think I've seen you around."

She was bent nearly in half, holding Boy Dog by the collar. "Do you know where Mr. French is?" she asked. "The guy in

202? Nobody really knows him, but I've seen you talking to him and I know you take care of his dog sometimes."

Withered bodies collapse into ash when they die, so there was no decaying body for anyone to smell and get suspicious. We hadn't reported his death, so unless his boss called the landlord, it was unlikely anyone here would realize he was gone until the rent came due at the end of the month. I looked at the big basset hound, then back at Christina. "I haven't seen him."

She tugged on the basset hound's leash, dragging the heavy dog forward a few inches. "He left his dog with me yesterday and hasn't come back. I can't keep him anymore and I don't want him just running around the complex pooping on everything." She tugged the leash again, pulling the dog closer to my doorway. "I suppose we could call the pound, but I don't really know how that works—I don't know if he could get the dog back when he shows up again, or if they'd sell him to somebody, or God forbid they put him to sleep." She tugged again. "Can you watch him?"

"The dog?"

"Yes." Tug. "I've seen you take care of him before, maybe he'll be better for you. It will only be a day or two, I'm sure."

I have rules about animals: I don't own them, I don't touch them, I don't even talk to them. I'd watched Boy Dog for an hour or two, twice, so that I could get closer to Cody French and kill him. Now that he was dead I needed to stay as far away as I could. Especially now that I had Potash in the house—adding a dog to the equation would be idiotic. Worst of all, despite Christina's uninformed promise, I knew that French wasn't coming back. If I took this dog, it would be forever. It would be stupid and irresponsible.

I started to form a protest, stepping slightly to the side to give Christina a better view of how little space I had, but she seemed to interpret the move as an invitation to let go of the leash. Boy Dog wandered in, walked straight to Potash's makeshift bedroll, and peed on the blankets. Potash muttered a low curse, and I turned back to Christina.

"I'll take him."

I gathered my papers and retreated to my bedroom, shutting the door to study and letting Potash deal with Boy Dog. He wasn't exactly a difficult dog—he was a basset hound, which is barely one step up from a furry statue. Give him a warm place to lie down and he'd lie there for hours without moving. The fact that he had claimed Potash's bed gave me a petty sense of satisfaction, and I turned my attention to Mary Gardner.

I pored through my own notes, assembled over weeks of part-time volunteer work on Mary's floor of the hospital. She lived under the human guise of a nurse, forty-six years old, competent and caring and boundlessly sympathetic to the parents of those children who died in her care. She was very careful about her kills—we had to give her that. If not for Brooke's assurance, we would never have suspected that the children under Mary's care had died from anything other than the diseases they were already being treated for. Many of her victims, we suspected, weren't under her direct care at all, though we'd been observing the hospital long enough to tie her, at least superficially, to the approximate time and place of most of the deaths on three floors of the building. If she were human, we'd have enough evidence to at least get her fired, but we couldn't afford that with a Withered. Drive her away and she'd just start killing somewhere else, and we didn't have the time or the resources to follow her all over the world. We had to kill her here, once and for all, and the sooner we could manage it, the fewer children she'd take with her on the way out. Our own danger from Meshara was a secondary concern for now, though as Trujillo had pointed out, every dead Withered made us that much safer.

The one thing we hadn't figured out was the actual mechanism of Mary's kills; she seemed to gain some kind of healing boost from the process, as her cycles of health and illness seemed to follow the deaths fairly clearly, but she was never around when the victims died. My best guess at this point was a delayed reaction: she'd slip into a sick child's room, "take" something from them—hell if I knew what it was, energy or something—and then her health would improve, and then the child would die, sometimes hours later, sometimes a day or more.

Ostler and the others insisted that Mary's killing of children made her more evil than the others, more heinous and irredeemable. I figured a victim was a victim; she didn't target children out of generic evilness, but because something about her process required it. Finding out what that something was could be the key to the whole mystery.

I needed someone to talk to, to bounce ideas off of. Kelly was good for this, and sometimes Trujillo, though he talked back too much to be of any real use as a sounding board. Either way, they were both working on their own branches of the project tonight, and I had to make do without them. In the old days I'd had Max, and then I'd used Marci, but I supposed I'd be paying for that mistake for the rest of my life. I couldn't use just anyone . . . and I guessed, at the moment, I couldn't use anyone at all.

I haven't told you about Marci yet, though I've mentioned her a couple of times. She's not exactly easy to talk about. Sociopathy is a tricky disease to describe—it's not an absence of emotion, but an absence of empathy. You look at another human being, or even an animal, and feel no connection whatsoever: you don't feel good when they're happy, you don't feel bad when they get hurt, you're completely cut off. Maybe you feel jealous when they get something you want, but that's not a connection to them—that's all focused on yourself. What you want and what you're willing to do to get it. And if that means hurting someone, well, you don't care. Your needs are more important than anyone else's, because you're more important than anyone else. Nobody else counts.

Marci was different.

And now Marci was dead.

I looked around at my room, almost as if I expected to see her there, pale and half formed, like a shadow in reverse. I don't know what a ghost looks like, or if ghosts are even real—the Withered are, so who knows what else is possible?

"Are you here?" I whispered. Instantly I felt the tears in the corners of my eyes, hot and cold at the same time, my face burning with anger and embarrassment. I shouldn't try to talk to her. I know she's not there. But if anyone could be, if there really was something after this—maybe another life, or even just a dead reflection of this one—I wanted her to be there. I wanted her to be here.

I dried my eyes, rubbing them harshly with the palms of my hands. Marci was gone, and I couldn't change that. Worse, she was gone because I hadn't stopped her killer fast enough. I wasn't going to make that mistake again. I'd follow this new demon straight into hell before I let it kill anyone I knew.

I couldn't turn to Potash for help—if he didn't take me seriously, how seriously would he take the discussion? I'd have to work on my own.

The central question of criminal profiling is this: what does the killer do that he doesn't have to do? Find that, and you find everything. As much as the average person wouldn't believe it, serial killers have very clear, often very simple reasons for what they do—reasons you probably disagree with if you're not a killer, but a bad reason is still a reason, and the reasons we do things affect the way that we do them. Imagine you're closing a door: why are you closing it? If you're leaving your house to go to school or to work, you probably close the door firmly behind you and make sure it's locked before you go. If you're sneaking out at night, you probably close it softly and slowly, doing everything as quietly as you can so nobody hears. If you're leaving because you just had an argument, you might slam the door behind you and walk away without looking to see if it stayed closed. All you really have to do is close the door, but the way you close it says everything. Killing is the same. The way you choose your victim, isolate it, kill it, even the way you leave the body—whether you arrange it like killers in the movies, or just run away and hope nobody sees you. These choices, even if they're subconscious, can tell investigators even more about you than your fingerprints.

The Withered, though they kill for different reasons, still have reasons. Crowley stole body parts from his victims, and while a normal serial killer might do that as a way of remembering the kill, Crowley did it because he was rebuilding his body. It was supernatural, and impossible to decipher in the beginning, but it still helped me to figure him out. It still helped me to kill him.

Mary killed children, exclusively. She killed remotely, or on a delay. I got out a clean sheet of paper, hoping that the process of taking notes could substitute for a human sounding board, and wrote down everything I knew about her methods. She got to know some of her victims before she killed them, but not all. Was that a crucial part of the process? Did it affect the outcome? Maybe that was why she worked as a nurse: because she needed prolonged contact to make it happen. Whatever "it" was. If all she needed was the occasional sick child, she could get the same access as a janitor or even a volunteer who visited once a week. And yet she was a nurse. Why?

I looked through my stack of papers for her timeline. Ostler had bought me a laptop to work on and sent all of these documents through e-mail, but I hated that machine. Living on my own, with no one breathing down my neck or checking my Internet history, I'd spent nearly a week binge-watching every horrible thing I could find—entire message boards and websites about death, displaying the most graphic images and even videos of head wounds, shark bites, gunshots, and more. I'd nearly lost control then, and I'd even fallen back on my old habits and started a Dumpster fire or two, on the far side of town where no one would link it to me. Nothing serious, just a little safety valve to release the pressure that was building up inside of me, pouring it out in a burst of flame and heat and dancing red—

No. Stay focused. Push it away.

I have a job to do.

I looked at the printout of our reconstructed timeline. Mary didn't seem to kill on any predictable schedule: sometimes one a month, sometimes more, sometimes less. Two of her kills were less than a week apart. Kelly was convinced this meant there were more we didn't know about, but I doubted it. If two per week was Mary's standard schedule, and we just didn't know about the others, where were they? How could she kill that many people and keep them hidden? Fort Bruce simply wasn't big enough. The hospital was the most advanced in the region, and people came in from all over hoping to get the best care they could. That created a large enough population for Mary to hide her activities. Obviously it was possible that some of the kills we attributed to her were not, and some of the kills we thought were unrelated were actually hers, but even if we gave her credit for every dead child in the hospital, it didn't add up to the frequency Kelly suggested.

But that left us with the original problem: why the erratic schedule? She seemed to kill for health reasons, like Crowley had—rejuvenating themselves every time their bodies got too degraded to function properly—but Crowley had followed a predictable pattern. When his kills got closer together, it was because his degeneration was accelerating. Mary's pace seemed to speed up and slow down almost at random. There had to be an explanation, and if Kelly's was wrong, what was right?

The bedroom door opened abruptly, and Potash dragged Boy Dog in from the hall with a grunt. "He's staying in your room."

"I can't have him in here," I said, practically jumping up. "I have rules—"

Potash growled. "You said yes to him, you deal with him."

"I have rules," I said again, though I knew it would mean

nothing to Potash. I stared at Boy Dog, panting placidly on the floor, then looked up at Potash. "We'll give him back."

"She won't take him back."

"Then we'll . . ." I hesitated, knowing that anything I said would put the dog in danger. Put him out on the street? Leave him tied to someone else's door? Send him to a pound? My rule said to avoid animals, but the purpose behind it was to protect them. I couldn't let myself hurt an animal, even through inaction. I'd hurt too many people that way already.

"I'll call the animal shelter," said Potash, "but you keep him in here until they come."

"Wait," I said. "We have to give him to someone who wants him."

For the first time, his facade cracked and he stared at me in a grimace of complete confusion. "Why?"

"Because I won't let him get hurt."

"The shelter won't hurt him."

"But they won't help him either," I said. "I have rules."

He stared at the dog a minute. "So what do you want to do?"

I want to hit this dog with the sharp edge of a shovel until I can't recognize it anymore. I closed my eyes and breathed. "I want to put an ad in the . . . I don't know. No one reads the paper, and I don't use the Internet. Craigslist? Is that a thing?"

"Yes, that's a thing. You don't have your laptop?"

"I leave it at work."

"That's not the point of a laptop."

"Do you have one?" I asked. "Or a phone?"

"Not a smartphone." He stepped backward into the hall. "We'll post an ad tomorrow. I'm closing this so he can't get back out."

"Okay—" I started, but he shut the door, and I heard his footsteps walk away. I looked at the dog. "Hey."

It didn't respond.

"I don't want to hurt you, okay?" I'd had him here before, and he'd been fine. It was only a few hours, though, and this would be all night. I sat back down, watching Boy Dog like I expected him to attack, or turn into a bowl of flowers. He looked back, mouth open, panting softly. "How'd you get your name?" I asked. "Why Boy Dog, instead of . . . anything else in the entire world? Everybody has a reason."

What did Mary Gardner do that she didn't have to do?

4

I caught Agent Ostler in the lobby of the building where we rented an office. "Children are weak."

She looked at me a moment. "Is this something you need to talk to Dr. Trujillo about?"

"No," I said, "it's about Mary Gardner. She targets children because they're weak. She needs somebody weak."

"She kills the terminally ill; they're all weak."

"But children are weaker," I said. "Not just physically, but their immune systems. They haven't been exposed to as many diseases as adults, so they haven't built up the antibodies to fight them off. Children recover from disease more quickly because they're resilient, but they're also far more likely to get sick in the first place. That's how she does it."

Ostler started walking again, forcing me to hurry to catch up. "Are you suggesting that she's the one putting these children in the hospital in the first place?

That would mean contacting them months or even years before they die; we have no evidence for that kind of behavior."

"That's not what I'm saying at all," I said, following her into the elevator. "I'm saying we have it backwards. We thought she was taking something from the children, whether it was their health or their healing power or whatever, which is why she gets healthy and they die. But why does it have to be so complicated? How do you take 'healing power' from someone? It doesn't make sense."

"None of it makes sense," said Ostler. "They're supernatural creatures who don't follow any rules."

"But they do," I said. "They always do, whether we understand those rules or not. And the simpler answer is always the best. Mary Gardner isn't stealing some kind of healing power, she's targeting already-sick children and giving them her own illnesses."

Ostler turned to me, paying real attention for the first time that morning. "That would mean . . ."

"It explains everything," I said. The elevator stopped on our floor, and we stepped into the hall. Potash was already there, telling the same thing to Kelly, but they stopped to listen to me. "It explains why she targets kids," I continued, "because it's easier to give them her sickness. It explains why the deaths all appear to be natural causes—because they are natural causes, just like any other disease. It explains why they die on such a weird schedule—because she's not the one killing them. She's just giving them a disease and then *that* kills them."

"But the timing is too close—the correlation between her health and their deaths is too close to be random," said Ostler. "There might be a variance of a few days, but that doesn't account for some of the seven-week gaps we've seen in the timeline."

"This theory explains that, too," I said. "The Withered are defined by what they lack, and we know from Brooke that Mary Gardner lacks health. We thought she had to steal it from other people, but then why steal health from sick children? That's like . . . eating gum off the bottom of a table: it might help a little, but it's the most inefficient way of getting the job done. Our problem is we didn't think it through: if she doesn't have any health, what is she going to do? Think about it. What's going to happen to her *all the time*?"

Ostler closed her eyes, in an expression that said she felt as stupid as I did when I finally figured it out. "She's going to get sick."

"Exactly," I said. "We were so worried about the gun in those photos, we didn't pay attention to the real clue: she's wearing a paper face mask in almost all of them, even at home. If she has no health of her own she's going to get sick all the time. She wears a face mask and slathers herself in hand sanitizer and does every other precaution she can think of, but sooner or later she's going to catch something and it's going to hit her hard. A cold could kill her. Those seven-week gaps are just the times she caught an innocuous disease that wasn't lethal to anyone else when she gave it away."

"Then why does she work in a hospital?" asked Ostler. "She'd be exposed to all kinds of pathogens in there."

I nodded. "But she'd be able to dump them off immediately, without arousing any suspicion. A hospital is dangerous to her, but it's also the only place she can live without showing up on every epidemic tracking program there is. She's trapped in a feedback loop, always getting sick and always getting better. She couldn't leave the hospital if she wanted to."

"Immortal," said Ostler, "but only because she gives her death away, over and over and over."

"What does this mean?" asked Kelly. "Now that we know how she works, can we move on her?"

"We move immediately," said Potash. "She works afternoon shifts this week; surveillance suggests she'll be at home right now, sealed off from the rest of the world, which we now know to be a defensive tactic against germs. She'll be at her weakest, and she'll be isolated. We leave in fifteen minutes."

"I want heavy protocols on this," said Ostler, though everyone was already moving, collecting the others and gathering equipment for the attack. "Cleaver on the street out front, Lucas positioned behind the house with her rifle, Potash and Ishida at the front door." She looked at me. "We don't need you to verify a trance, like with Cody French, and Ishida has more combat experience. You're sure Mary Gardner won't hulk out or grow claws or . . . anything like that?"

"She'll have a gun," I said, "but that's it. Worst-case scenario she gives us pneumonia or something, but none of us are children with compromised immune systems, so we should be fine. We ought to hit the hospital after, though, and chug vitamins like a sewer worker, but we should be fine."

"Pray that you are," said Ostler. "No matter how much you think you know, never forget that these are demons."

"I thought you didn't like that word."

"I don't like killing, either," said Ostler, "but we do what we have to do."

Kelly drove again, and I sat in the back seat, breathing deeply, counting out my number pattern: one, one, two, three, five, eight, thirteen, twenty-one. We were on our way to kill again—we were on our way for Potash to kill again. They made me plan it and they made me watch, but they never let me have that moment.

Kelly Ishida had her hair up in a ponytail, showing the back of her neck through the gap between her seat and her headrest. I could see the bumps of her spine pressing up under the skin, see the tiny wisps of black hair too small to get tied up in the ponytail. The subtle imperfections in her skin, the pores and follicles and one pale chicken-pox scar at the base of her hairline. I would stab her right there, just beneath the scar, between the two tendons connecting the skull to the collarbone. Sever the spinal column with a single strike. If I did it right now, while her eyes were on the road, she wouldn't even know what I was doing until it was too late.

Thirty-four, fifty-five, eighty-nine, one hundred forty-four, two hundred thirty-three.

"What else have we figured out about Meshara?" asked Potash. "If they're working together, he might be at her house. We still don't know what he can do."

"He 'remembers,'" said Diana. "Trujillo spent all night with Brooke, but that's all he got. I didn't know you could remember someone to death, but that's what I love about this job."

"Wait," I said, "was Nathan alone last night? Why does Nathan get to be alone and I have to live with Potash?"

"Our surveillance has never placed Mary Gardner and Meshara together," said Kelly, ignoring me. "I went through as many of our old photos and videos as I could last night, and he's not in any of them."

"Maybe they know we're watching Mary," said Diana, "so they're staying out of the way to hide themselves."

"That could mean this is an ambush," said Potash.

"We need backup," said Kelly.

"We don't have backup," said Diana. "Even if we called the local police, we couldn't brief them in time to be helpful, and once they knew everything we wouldn't be able operate freely in the city."

"Then we make do with what we have," said Potash, turning from the front seat to hand me something. "Take this."

It was a gun.

I stared at it, not moving an inch.

Potash jiggled the gun, prompting me again to take it. "Have you ever used a gun before?"

"Once," I said, but it wasn't what they were thinking. The only shot I'd ever fired was a hole in the top of my car, to pour a can of gas on Brooke's head and burn her. I didn't touch his gun, considering this other idea instead. "We could light her house on fire."

"Don't be ridiculous," said Kelly.

"Is it?" asked Diana. "If it gets the job done . . ."

"We can't just light a criminal's house on fire," said Kelly, "that's against every—"

"She's not a criminal," I said quickly. "She's a monster. Our job is to kill her by any means necessary, and if that means burning her house down then we burn it down, and it's not against any laws or regulations because our entire team is operating beyond the law. We do whatever it takes to get the job done."

"This isn't the only job we have to get done," said Potash. "We have at least one more Withered to take care of in this city, and an attack as visible as a house fire will make it almost impossible to act. Diana's right about the police—if they know what we're doing, if they know we're here at all—"

"Drop me off here and I'll walk the rest of the way," I said, feeling more desperate than I expected at the prospect of lighting a major fire. I lit small ones now and then, when I could get away from the rest of the team, but a whole house . . . I felt short of breath. "I can get into the yard without anyone seeing me, and no will ever know we're the ones who set it—"

"Even if you can," said Kelly, "we can't guarantee she won't get out before it burns. She's not incapacitated like Cody French was, she's just taking the morning off from work. We'd have to station Diana outside to pick her off when she runs, and at that point we're just doing the same thing we always do, just way more publicly."

"It was a good idea," said Diana, patting my leg. "Maybe on another project." I wanted to shove her hand away, but I knew it was overemotional. Three minutes ago I hadn't even thought about a fire, and now I wanted it so bad I could already smell the smoke. Three hundred seventy-seven, six hundred ten, nine hundred eight-seven, fifteen hundred ninety-seven.

Potash offered the gun again. "You said you've used one once. Are you comfortable using one again?"

"Not really," I said. My breath was only slowly returning to normal. "I don't want to shoot you by accident." *Though if you don't get out of my house soon I might want to shoot you on purpose.* I paused again, collecting myself. "Do you have a knife?"

He shared a quick glance with Kelly and holstered his gun. "Can you use a knife?"

"I've been cutting open corpses since I was ten," I said, exaggerating only slightly.

"But in combat?" he asked. "With a Withered?"

"Do your job and I won't have to," I said. "If the plan goes to hell, better a knife than nothing."

He pulled a combat knife from some hidden fold of his jacket; it was about ten inches long and wrapped in a nylon sheath. I opened the snaps that held it in place and pulled the blade about halfway out; it was five, maybe six inches of the total length, stainless steel with a nonreflective coating. I ran my finger along the groove in the side of the metal: a blood gutter, so the knife wouldn't get caught by the suction of a deep wound. I slid it back in, snapped the sheath closed, and tucked the whole thing into the pocket of my heavy winter coat.

"It's right up here," said Kelly. "We've staked this place out before, so you all know the layout, and we've practiced so you all know the drill. Radio silence. Diana, this is your stop. We'll give you five minutes." She pulled over in front of a plain beige house behind Mary Gardner's, and Diana got out with her unmarked duffel bag. The neighbors were gone during the day, but we'd already duplicated their key, and Diana was inside before we'd even turned the corner at the end of the block. She would wait at the top bedroom window with her rifle, to stop Gardner from escaping out the back.

Potash screwed a suppressor onto the end of his gun—not the one he'd offered me, I noticed, which meant he had at least two. Who knew how many he was carrying? I wondered if he really did have more than one at my house and where he hid them.

Mind on the job. Kelly would follow him in and wait by the front door, cutting off the other exit. My role was to stay in the car and hope nothing went wrong. I touched the hilt of the combat knife and tried to convince myself that "nothing" was what I really wanted.

The street was quiet, with most people gone for the day to school or work. There'd be a few homemakers around, but they wouldn't see anything. Kelly parked across the street from Mary's house and left me the car keys as we traded seats. I put my hands on the wheel, gripping it tightly to help stabilize my shaking. Kelly and Potash did a final check of their weapons, hid them in their coats, and got out of the car. I watched them walk to the front door, pull out a duplicated key, and let themselves in. It was 10:26 in the morning. They closed the door behind them.

I waited.

Ostler insisted on a communications blackout during every project. Maybe she was worried about people overhearing us? If Meshara and whoever else was with him had radios of their own, they could listen in and warn Mary we were coming, so the rule made sense, but that didn't make it any easier to sit in the car and wonder what was happening. I listened for the sound of Potash's gun—even with a suppressor it would make a loud thump, like a pneumatic staple gun. Any people sitting in one of these houses might not notice it at all, but I was waiting for it and I—

The sound that came was a full gunshot, unsuppressed. That meant it wasn't Potash, and that meant something had gone very wrong. Was it Kelly or Mary? I sat up straighter, staring across the street at the now-silent house. There was a small circle in the bedroom window, up on the second floor; I peered at it closer, almost certain that it was a bullet hole. I couldn't tell for sure at that distance. I looked at the other windows, at the front door, at anything and everything hoping desperately to see some sign of what was going on. Our radio silence ended when the Withered was dead; they could call me then, like we'd called Kelly when we'd killed Cody French. I clutched my radio in my hand, my knuckles white, but it didn't make a sound.

A curtain moved in the bedroom window—a sudden bulge, like it was being pressed against the glass from the inside. It moved to the side, then fell back to hang normally again. Was someone struggling, or was it just a current of air? I clutched my knife, wondering what to do.

I got out of the car and walked across the street.

The front yard was covered in snow, and a narrow path was shoveled along the walk. The steps to the porch were painted concrete, crusted with a scattered layer of rock salt. I put a hand to the door, wary, wondering if I should pull my knife out now, to be ready, or if it was better to wait until I was out of view of the street. Someone had to have heard the shot; surely the neighbors were watching me now. I pretended to knock, making no noise but trying to give the visual impression that I wasn't a part of this, that I was just an innocent bystander. I waited, listening, and heard a low crash, like someone had broken a vase or a window somewhere deep in the house. I put my hand on the doorknob, turned it, and went inside.

The front door led into a narrow hallway papered in a floral pink. A hat rack and umbrella stand stood nearby, and beyond them I glimpsed a small living room that seemed almost Victorian: ornate wooden furniture upholstered with thick, embroidered cushions. The lamp on a small corner table was hung with fringe. The effect was classy but threadbare, the kind of furniture you might see in the home of a ninety-year-old woman. Mary, of course, was much older. I supposed she'd had this furniture since it was first made, over a century ago.

I heard another crash, maybe upstairs, and pulled the combat knife from my pocket. I stayed as silent as I could, not wanting to alert Mary to a third enemy in her house. I was not a trained fighter, so if I was going to have any meaningful effect on this situation, surprise would be a far more effective weapon than the knife ever could. I unsnapped the sheath and revealed the black blade, holding it in front of me in an upside-down grip, point toward the floor. Another crash, and a grunt. Definitely upstairs, and somehow recognizably feminine. Kelly, or Mary? Where was Potash? I tried the first step, found that it didn't squeak, and slowly shifted my weight to the second, then the third. The ceiling thumped, somewhere to my right, like something heavy had fallen—heavy but soft; not a piece of furniture, but a body. I moved to the fourth step and, hearing the faintest trace of a creak as I started to place my weight on it, quickly picked up my foot to stop the sound. I tried the other side of the step, slowly and carefully, and when it stayed silent I moved to the next. The thump upstairs was followed by a scrape, then a pause, then a sudden flurry of footsteps. I moved to the sixth stair. The seventh. I was halfway up.

A window shattered above and behind me, loud and bright, and after a moment of shock I raced back down and threw open the front door, cursing myself for leaving an exit unguarded—if Mary had jumped out a front window she could run for safety, on the wrong side of the building for Diana to stop her. I saw a foot, sprawled in the snow, and stepped out for a better look. Kelly was facedown on the white lawn, her left side covered with blood, her head bent at an impossible angle. Her spine must have been snapped nearly in half, though whether it was from the fall or the fight itself I didn't know. She hadn't screamed, during or even before the fall.

Mary Gardner was more deadly than we'd ever imagined, and now the whole neighborhood knew we were here—and yet I froze, staring at Kelly's twisted body like I was in a trance. Her broken shape in the snow was curled beautifully, like a flower, her arms splayed out like the tendrils of a dark black fern. Black and gray, with drops of bright red blood melting deep pink pockets in the snow. Her hair billowed around her head like she was a mermaid in a pale white sea, frozen in a moment of single, perfect beauty. I took a step toward it, then a few more. I was halfway down the stairs from the porch before the sound of another crash echoed down from upstairs. Potash was still up there, and the fight was still going. I took another step forward. How many times had I imagined Kelly dead, and now here she was, right in front of me. The Withered disintegrated when they died; I hadn't touched a body in months. I reached out to it—and saw the knife in my hand.

A knife. Mary Gardner was still upstairs. I looked up at the window, then back at the door.

Then back at the body, still as a photograph.

Another crash. Mary was killing Potash—I didn't know how, but the process sounded brutal. My only advantage was that she didn't know I was there. This was what I needed—to work alone, without anyone knowing where or who I was. Even if the neighbors knew about Kelly, Mary didn't know about me; someone might call the police, but I had a few minutes to salvage this kill. To do it myself. I gripped my knife tighter and slipped back inside, quietly locking the door behind me. I took the stairs faster this time, knowing which spots to avoid. The walls of the second floor hallway were covered in the same pink wallpaper as the first, though it was brighter here, where the sun hadn't reached it to fade out the color. The crash had come from . . . there. That was almost certainly the room Kelly had fallen out of. The door was open, though I couldn't see anything from my vantage point, and whatever was inside the room couldn't see me. I listened and heard heavy, labored breathing.

"You've ruined everything," said a woman's voice. She had the hushed, clipped tones of a person barely controlling her fury. "Do you think I can stay here now? What am I supposed to say when the police come? That the man who attacked me had pneumonia so bad he couldn't even walk? Who's going to believe that?"

More labored breathing, and a loud crash, like someone had smashed a vase or a lamp. I crept closer to the door.

"People are going to ask questions," said the woman, and I heard another crash. The gasping breather grunted, only to succumb to a fit of coughing so bad he might have been vomiting. I wondered how her sickness-shunting power worked—if she had some way of increasing the intensity. An ancient goddess of plagues, amping up a common cold until it destroyed a grown man's lungs in minutes. "Some of the parents are already suspicious, they have been for years, and now you come in and add more fuel to the fire. 'Nurse Gardner killed my daughter! She's a vector of disease; she's Typhoid Mary!' " Another crash. I stood by the edge of the door, my back pressed against the wall, the knife raised to my chest so I could strike out in a split second if I had to. Maybe I already had to; I couldn't think clearly. I wanted to attack her, to stab her and twist the knife and feel her hot blood pumping out on my hand—but for that very reason I knew that I shouldn't. There was a threshold here, and I didn't dare to cross it. Potash grunted again, like he was trying to speak, but his voice was nothing but a broken wheeze, so painful it made me cringe just to hear it.

"I wanted to leave you for Rack," said Mary. I heard a click of what could only be a gun, and I knew I couldn't wait any longer. I gripped the knife tighter, screaming silently at myself to stay and go at the same time. "You deserve a death so much worse than I can—"

I swung around the doorjamb, saw Mary Gardner's back as she stood over Potash's body, and plunged my knife in with a strangled shout. It was exactly like I'd dreamed it: a sudden slowing as the blade met flesh, the metal sinking into the meat, glancing off a bone, jarring my hand like a thrill of pleasure. She stiffened and screamed, hanging for a moment in midair before her strength disappeared and she started to collapse. The weight of her body fought against my grip on the knife, but I grit my teeth and held my hand firm, and the body slid off with a slow, bloody slurp.

I'd killed her.

She landed in a lifeless heap, and I felt a sickening rush, like water flowing into a void. All that work, all that waiting, all that planning and dreaming and imagining what it would be like, and . . . that was it? My peripheral vision seemed to disappear, tunneling in on this one single body. I dropped to my knees, reaching out my left hand to touch her back, but shying away at the last moment. Her pale blue nurse's shirt was slowly turning red as her blood spread across it. Should I roll her over? Should I see her face? Should I say something or do something or punch her or bite her or—

My breath became shallow, my heart hammered in my chest. How many times had I dreamed about stabbing someone? I used to dream about stabbing Brooke, or Marci, or even my mother; shameful, terrifying fantasies I'd tried for years to get free of, killing everyone who was close to me. I'd dreamed about killing my father so many times I'd lost count. And now I'd finally done it, knife and all, to this . . . nobody. And it meant nothing.

I felt a greater rage than I'd ever felt before.

My knife was in her back again, before I even knew how it got there, then I saw my arm raise and the blood drip from the knife and I screamed and drove it in a third time, piercing flesh and snapping bone, and again and again, up and down, my teeth clenched in a frenzy of stabbing and hacking until the body dissolved around my knife, the flesh turning black, the air filling with the acrid stench of burning grease, the body discorporating into ash and sludge and slime. It sunk into the carpet, a smoldering, shapeless blob—and still I stabbed it, until the knife stuck deep in the floor and the jolt knocked my hand away. I gasped for breath. Mary's gun, lost under her body when she fell, became visible again as the sizzling ash sizzled away around it.

A grunt. I looked up at Potash, who was too weak to breathe, propped against the wall like a broken doll.

He'd seen everything.

5

I volunteered to embalm Kelly, but I don't think they took the offer seriously. Instead we holed up in our office, waiting for the world to calm down.

"They got a photo of me," I said, looking at my laptop.

"We're lucky that's all they got," said Diana. She'd managed to slip out of her sniper's nest unseen, since all the commotion was one street over. I hadn't been so lucky, though she was right that I had been, all things considered, as lucky as we could have hoped for. Three different neighbors had seen Kelly's body and called the police, who had arrived, guns drawn, almost fifteen minutes before Ostler managed to flash her FBI badge and smooth things over. Fifteen minutes wasn't much—they hadn't gotten me back to the station for fingerprints, they hadn't had time to interrogate me, they hadn't even found my name because we didn't carry ID. But the neighbors had been watching. One of them had a cell phone, and a picture of the mysterious teenager sitting in the back of a cop car had been on Twitter within minutes.

That was last night. We'd barely dared to move since.

"Potash is stable," said Nathan, setting down his phone. "Trujillo says they have him in protective custody at the hospital, no press allowed."

Diana looked at me, than back at Nathan. "Is he breathing?"

"Not on his own; he's on a machine. They think it's some kind of pulmonary embolism, because of how fast it came on."

"It's pneumonia," I said, remembering Mary's words.

"We know what you think it is," said Nathan, though his tone suggested more impatience than recognition. "Let's let the doctors do the diagnosing for now, okay? She's been killing people with this . . . whatever it is . . . for thousands of years. We're lucky he's still alive at all—and if he wasn't, you'd be the one responsible."

"Nathan," snapped Diana, but he bulldozed past her warning with a snarl.

"You told us it was safe," he continued. I laid my hands flat against the table, trying to stay calm, keeping my eyes fixed on the laptop screen without seeing anything on it. "You told us all she could do was make sick kids sicker, not kill a grown man's lungs with a flick of her wrist! And she threw Kelly through the damn window, which you also conveniently forgot to mention she could do! And meanwhile you had the gall to sit outside in the car and let them face this thing alone—"

"Nathan!" said Diana again, in a voice that left no room for argument.

Thirteen, twenty-one, thirty-four, fifty-five, eighty-nine. The counting wasn't working.

They didn't know I'd stabbed her.

"We have bigger problems to worry about," said Diana. "Ostler's bosses are going to be pissed, and who knows what fallout will come from that? We're practically a joke as it is, and now we've lost an agent and caused a public scene. Ostler's at the police station right now trying to convince them there are monsters under the bed, but we can't afford to bring the cops in. Rumors are going to start, word is going to spread, and our entire operation is going to be raked by headquarters. I'll be amazed if we don't get recalled and fired."

"That's the best possible thing that could happen to us," said Nathan. "Not only are the Withered fighting back now, but even the ones who don't know we're coming can still kill us with impunity. We need to get out of here yesterday."

"Don't worry about the FBI," I said. "Worry about whoever else out there is watching."

"The police are the only ones who know anything," said Nathan. "They kept the press out of it completely."

"The police found two people and one dead body," I said, "sitting in the middle of an obvious fight scene, yet we all claim to be on the same team. If you don't know what the sludge is, the person we claim to have killed doesn't even exist. People are going to talk, even if it's just the cops, and rumors are going to spread. Best-case scenario, they'll think it's a government cover-up, but worst case, someone puts it all together and figures out we killed a demon."

"That's ridiculous," said Nathan. "Nobody else even believes these things are real."

"Somebody does," I said. "Somewhere out there, somebody suspects, and this is only going to confirm it. There've been too many news stories, too many unanswered questions, and those pile up—they'll wonder about the sludge, they'll wonder about me, maybe they'll put the two together and get even more curious. I've been publicly involved with missing bodies and mysterious sludge three times before, you know." I pointed at the computer screen. "And now my picture's on the Internet."

With Kelly dead and Ostler running ragged trying to keep our story quiet—and with Potash too sick to speak—nobody remembered the stipulation that I should never be alone. That night after work I found an old jacket and a ball cap in the building's lost and found, and waited inside the rear service door for the most blue-collar person I could find. A custodian left around six, bundled up tight against the cold, and I fell in step beside him, chatting idly about the weather, feigning friendliness so that anyone who happened to be watching would miss the mysterious boy from an unexplained murder and see only a pair of working-class Joes. I didn't know who might be watching—Meshara or the other demons, or maybe someone completely unexpected—but that gave me all the more reason to hide. I rode the bus home, sitting in the back on a hard plastic seat, staring out the window at the dirty black snow lining the sides of the roads. I didn't *like* being alone, any more than I really *liked* anything. But I preferred it. It was simpler.

Boy Dog was waiting for me when I got home, wagging his tail in the biggest display of energy I'd ever seen from him. Potash and I had gone shopping that morning before work—had it really only been one day?—and left a large plate of dry food and a bowl of water on the floor of the kitchen. Both dishes were overturned now, mixed and scattered across the floor, and I could smell the powerful scent of hound-dog urine in every corner of the room. But he was only marking his territory: there were no major puddles, and no droppings, so I told him he was a good boy and took him outside to do his business. Cody French, monster or not, had trained his dog well.

I took Boy Dog back inside and cleaned up the mess on the kitchen floor, sopping up the soggy chunks of kibble with an old towel. I poured him another dish of water and another pile of food, then sat in the lone chair in the living room, staring at the blank TV. I didn't turn it on.

I'd stabbed a woman to death.

Obviously she wasn't a woman, not really, but she had been when I'd stabbed her. She had the shape, and the hair, and the voice, and the ribs my knife passed through were human ribs, stretching wide beneath her skin to give a human form to her back. I'd been present for the deaths of several people, but I'd only ever killed two of them. Now the number was three. Most law-enforcement agencies used three as the benchmark for serial-killer activity: one kill was a murder, two was a coincidence, but three was a sign of habitual behavior. Kill three people in a row and you were a spree killer; kill them over time, with a period in the middle to cool off, lie low, and decide to kill again, and you were a serial killer. I'd tried to kill Brooke, back when she was Nobody. She would have been my third. Now it was Typhoid Mary Gardner, the nurse who slaughtered children and then comforted their parents.

I'd seen her house. She'd had the same TV I did. I stared at the black screen, a flat stretch of nothing turned slightly gray by the light of the kitchen behind me. I could almost see myself in it, a vague outline not quite human shaped; the chair made me look bigger than I was, wide and hunchbacked and menacing.

I still had the knife. The police had taken it, but it was covered with ash, not blood, and they'd had no grounds to protest when Ostler had ordered them to return it. It was back in its sheath now, wiped carefully clean, sitting in my coat pocket. I hadn't taken the coat off yet. I thought about the knife now, wondering if I should get it out to look at it, to clean the last bits of sludge from the blade. To hold it. I wondered if I should hide it, though I couldn't think of any reason why. I didn't know what to do with the knife, or myself, because I didn't know how I felt about killing Mary. Should I be elated? Relieved? Nathan had said that we couldn't possibly feel relieved at her death, because we'd lost Kelly in the process, but those seemed like completely separate things to me. We could feel bad that we lost Kelly, and glad that we'd stopped Mary, all at the same time. Couldn't we? Did it have to be either/or?

I was avoiding the issue. The knife was just a knife, and her body was ash, and it didn't matter what happened to any of it. What mattered was how I had done it. One stab to kill her was justified—it was "good," in the way that our morality shifted to cover the spectrum of attack and defense. She was going to kill Potash, so I stopped her. But I hadn't stopped myself. I'd stabbed her a dozen times or more after that, maybe two dozen, and there was nothing justified about any of those. I wasn't stabbing that corpse to defend myself or protect a friend or even to avenge the other victims. I wasn't even stabbing because I wanted to, though that would be bad enough. I was stabbing that body because I couldn't stop myself from stabbing it. I'd lost control.

In all my years of thinking and struggling and following rules, in all my study of demons and Withered and their untold millennia of terror, nothing scared me as much as this. I'd lost control.

Boy Dog waddled past me and flopped down on the floor, panting from the exertion. The knife was in my pocket. I didn't dare to pet him or touch him or even think about him. I lifted my legs and braced my feet on the seat in front of me, out of reach, where the dog couldn't lean against them, and I sat in a fetal position, staring at my dark reflection in the TV screen.

I didn't move for almost thirteen hours.

Potash was diagnosed with something called cryptogenic organizing pneumonitis, which his doctors defined as "His lungs don't work right, but hell if we know why." I'm paraphrasing. Whatever Mary gave him—a virus, a bacteria, or maybe even a fungus—got into his lungs in such high volume that it started rebuilding them, and if he'd gotten to the hospital even a few hours later he probably would have died. The lead pulmonologist, a man named Dr. Pearl, joked that the disease seemed almost supernatural, but none of us ever laughed, and he eventually stopped making jokes.

I kept the knife with me everywhere, but I never took it out of its sheath.

With Mary dead we focused all our attention on Meshara, though without Kelly and Potash to help there wasn't nearly enough attention to go around. The police gave us access to their files, which was helpful but actually created more work, not less. They set up a few surveillance details as well, but seemed far more interested in watching us. They didn't trust us, and without Kelly to act as liaison, the relationship was strained. Trujillo redoubled his efforts with Brooke, trying everything he could think of to help control her memories and recall more details about Meshara, but it wasn't going well; Nathan said that Trujillo, on the rare nights he slept in their apartment instead of the office, was wracked with nightmares.

"It must be awful to listen to that stuff day in and day out," Nathan confided in me. "She's got a head full of the sickest, darkest stuff you can possibly imagine."

"Then why," I asked, "do you feel sorry for the guy forcing her to remember it?"

He didn't have a good response to that, but at least he started leaving me alone. His job kept him in the office and the library, looking into every little tidbit Brooke dropped about the Withered, so I didn't see much of him anyway. Diana and I were assigned to follow Meshara in his human identity of Elijah Sexton, who turned out to be a hearse driver for one of the larger mortuaries in the city. I immediately assumed that his "power," whatever it was, required access to the recently dead, but I couldn't know why until we learned more. I could investigate better alone, but Ostler insisted we stay together, so Diana never left my side.

Elijah worked the night shift and seemed to maintain that schedule with adamant zeal; records in the mortuary office showed that when the day-shift guy was unavailable Elijah would go so far as to hire a temp worker out of his own pocket rather than take the day shift himself. Another piece of the puzzle. The most obvious guess was that he couldn't go out in daylight, but our very first sighting of him at Whiteflower had been in the daytime, so that wasn't it. Our next thought was that he had something vital to do during the day—like following us, for example—but after a week of careful surveillance, that proved false as well; he slept during the morning, on the normal schedule of any other night-shift worker, and in the afternoon he went shopping, or he went driving, or he shoveled his sidewalks. He didn't really talk to anybody, but he didn't avoid them as devoutly as Mary had, either. By all appearances he was just a quiet man who kept to himself; we couldn't even find evidence that he'd been communicating with other Withered, which made our entire investigation that much more confusing.

The obvious exception to his solitude was, of course, the man he met with at Whiteflower: Merrill Evans. By all accounts, Merrill was a completely normal Alzheimer's patient, albeit a very young one; he was in his seventies now, but had suffered from crippling dementia for just over twenty years, which meant the disease had struck him earlier in life than most. Elijah had been visiting him the entire time, an average of once a week. Looking solely at each man's publicly available history we couldn't determine exactly how they knew each other—they'd never worked together or lived in the same part of town—but the only way to learn more was to interview the Evans family directly, and we wanted to avoid that as long as possible. Instead we focused on Meshara himself, studying his office when he was at home, and his home when he was at the office. When that gave us nothing, we simply watched and waited.

For six nights Diana and I sat in the car and watched his mortuary, our hands tucked into our pockets, too wary of being spotted to risk turning on the heater. This mortuary wasn't like the one I'd lived in for sixteen years; it was larger and newer, full of offices and chapels and viewing rooms and even a garage in the back. And of course an embalming room, which we'd examined very briefly a few days earlier, under the guise of a murder investigation for an unrelated corpse. There wasn't a real murder, as far as we knew; we just wanted a look at their facilities. Elijah worked in the garage, staying out of the embalming process completely, and our cursory examination had revealed nothing unseemly about anything in the building—but, oh, did I want to go back there. I hadn't been in a real embalming room in too long. The memories of it pricked at my heart in the same way Marci did.

"Hold up," said Diana, staring out the window with sudden intensity. I followed her gaze across the street to the mortuary. A black car pulled up and three people got out; they wore black coats and were mostly indistinguishable at this distance, but one of them stood out for his size—easily a head taller than the others, with the bulk to match.

"It's after business hours," I said, pointlessly, since it was practically eleven o'clock. "They might be from the police, maybe a forensics lab, but they don't look like it."

"Elijah's the only one in the building," said Diana. "They have to be here to see him."

"Four Withered in one place is . . ." I grimaced. "That's a lot."

"We don't know that's what they are."

"Can you see the license plate?"

She raised her small binoculars. "It's too dark," she said, "but I can see the visitors pretty well in the light by the front door. All three are men, well dressed, clean-shaven. Not sure of their ethnicity—darker than you, lighter than me. The lighting's too weird to tell for sure. They're . . . picking the lock. Whoever they are, Elijah's not expecting them."

"Then get ready," I said, and put my hand on the door.

"Don't you dare talk to them."

"Not them," I said, watching as the three strangers opened the door and slipped in, disappearing into the building. As soon as they closed their door I opened mine, looking quickly up and down the darkened street for any sign of movement. Diana hissed at me to get back in, but I ignored her and trotted across the street. I heard her door open as she scrambled to follow me, and then I saw it—two men in black coats, standard-issue police gear, walking toward the mortuary. Our unofficial police escort would try to use the picked lock as an excuse to intervene in our investigation, to see if our bizarre claims were actually true, but if they went in that building they'd be dead in minutes. I ran to cut them off, and Diana caught up just in time. The cops scowled when they saw us.

"Don't go in there," I said.

"Oh, look," said the taller cop, "it's the Murder Boy."

They didn't call me by name, which was good; Ostler hadn't told them who I was, and it looked like they hadn't figured it out for themselves yet. Allies or not, I was already uncomfortable just working with a team—bringing in a whole police department made me feel short of breath, like I was locked in a crowded room.

"Get out of the road," I said, glancing back at the mortuary. I couldn't see anyone watching us, but that didn't mean they weren't. "Let's talk about this out of sight somewhere."

Diana flashed her FBI badge—I, as a minor, didn't have one. "This is part of our investigation, and we ask you to stay back."

"Investigation?" asked the shorter cop. "What exactly are you investigating? I know it's not the boogeyman, no matter what your boss says. So is it smuggling? Drugs? Are they using dead bodies to move drugs around?"

"Get out of the road," I said, but neither side was listening to me.

"We are not at liberty to discuss the full details," said Diana. "We thank you for your assistance but—"

"How are we supposed to do our jobs if you won't even tell us what we're up against?" the short cop demanded. His voice was creeping steadily louder, and I looked back at the mortuary, hoping no one had seen or heard us, wondering what I could do to get these idiots' attention. Murder Boy or not, I was just a kid; Diana didn't take me any more seriously than the cops did. I felt the knife in my pocket, running my finger along the bumps in the nylon webbing. On a sudden whim I turned and walked to the side of the road, not saying a thing, heading straight for the darkest patch of shadow I could find.

"Hey," said a cop—I couldn't tell which one—and I heard three sets of feet following me in a rush, crunching on the ice. "Where do you think you're going?" I stepped lightly over a snowbank and ducked behind a brick wall separating the mortuary parking lot from the small storefront next door. There was a narrow strip of lawn on this side, and I trudged through about eight inches of snow. About five feet into the snow-covered grass I turned to look at them: all three adults were standing on the shoveled sidewalk, watching me. "Get back here," said the short cop.

"Come behind the fence," I said.

"Don't make me come after you," said the tall cop. I sighed and took four large steps backward; they swore and followed me into the snow, until all four of us were behind the wall. "Listen, you little—"

"Thank you for getting out of the street," I said. "Are you ready to stop acting like children?"

"Excuse me?" asked the short cop. "What are you, fifteen?"

"The men you saw breaking into the mortuary are very dangerous," I explained again. "We're not covering anything up, we're not trying to get away with anything, we're not even trying to piss you off, as much as I'd love to. We're following monsters, and you were about to go in after them, and I didn't want you to get killed." Saying this out loud to a stranger felt deeply wrong, like I had just confessed to an intimate secret. These were *my* monsters, my demons, and talking about them out loud like this made me feel naked and hurt. They didn't deserve to hear about them. The demons were mine alone.

The short cop sighed, then glanced at the wall a moment before looking back at me. "What it's going to take to get the real story out of you?"

"What's it going to take to make you believe us?" asked Diana. "And don't say 'seeing a monster in action,' because there's no wood to knock, and I assure you that is the last thing you want your town to see."

"Follow them," I said. "We don't have the numbers to keep eyes on everyone we need to keep eyes on, so let's split it: we watch Elijah Sexton, you follow these three."

The tall cop raised his eyebrow. "Are you joking?"

"I stopped you from *confronting* them," I said. "Following is different."

"You don't give us orders," said the tall cop.

"You want to know what we're doing," I said simply. "If you

think they're drug dealers, follow them and see for yourself. Follow them, study them, do whatever you think is smart, but remember that approaching them *isn't* smart. Don't try to get in their way or you will die. I don't want to mince words on this, okay? They can and will kill you, and we can't stop them yet."

"Yet?"

"We need more information," I said. "Give me enough of that and I can kill anybody."

The cops looked at me with obvious suspicion, but Diana froze us all with a whispered word.

"Quiet."

I heard footsteps on the other side of the wall and the sound of car doors; they were talking, which was a reassuring sign they hadn't heard us. I tried to listen to what they were saying but I couldn't make it out. The car doors closed, the engine revved to life, and we crouched low against the wall as the car pulled out into the road. It drove away in the opposite direction from us, so we never saw it and they didn't see us.

"I got the plate when they pulled up," said the short cop, standing and flashing a small black notebook. "Let's go run it and see what we get."

"You'll let us know?" asked Diana.

"Maybe," said the short cop, and the corner of his lip curled up. "Wouldn't want to interfere with your investigation."

They walked back to their car, and Diana and I stepped back onto the sidewalk, stomping our feet to shake off the snow. "We need Kelly," she said, watching them go. "She could talk to these guys; I feel like I don't even speak their language."

"At least they listen to you," I said. "Do I really look fifteen?"

"Don't worry about it," she said. The cops drove off, and we started walking back to our car. "They don't take me any more seriously than they take you. They didn't listen to a word until you insulted them."

We reached the car, and Diana drummed her fingers on the roof before getting in. Her voice was lower now, more solemn, as the full reality of the situation slowly settled in our minds. "Four Withered."

"We don't know that," I said, though I suspected it was true. "Maybe he's hired some human thugs."

"That's only slightly less frightening," said Diana. "Even three human thugs outnumber us by two thugs. I can't defend everyone at once."

"Then let's hope the cops turn out to be more helpful than they look."

"I thought you didn't like relying on people."

"I hate it," I said. *But I don't mind using them.* I stared at the street for a moment, then opened my door. "I got a dog."

"What does that have to do with anything?"

I got in the car without speaking.

Diana sighed. "Hurt it and I'll kill you myself," she said. She climbed in her side and turned on the car, cranking the heater to full; it blasted us with cold air as the engine slowly warmed up. "Obviously we tell the others about this, but then what?"

"We talk to the Withered," I said, looking back at the mortuary.

Diana paused, one finger poised over her cell phone. "You told the cops that getting involved would get them killed."

"Them, yes," I said. "Tomorrow afternoon, I need to meet Elijah Sexton."

6

I had planned to meet Elijah on the street, arranging an "accidental" encounter in a place we knew he'd be, and trying to start up a conversation—I could be the kid down the street, or the paper boy, or any number of innocuous cover stories. As it turned out, I didn't need any of them.

"He's here," said Trujillo. We were on the phone, and I hated phones; it was impossible to know what anyone was feeling without seeing their face. He sounded . . . excited? Scared? I could never tell.

"What do you mean 'here?'" I asked, walking to the office window and looking out; Whiteflower was just across the street, seeming as peaceful and quiet as ever. Nathan heard my question and stood up, coming closer to hear better. "Is he on your floor? In your room?"

"He's downstairs," said Trujillo. "I told the front desk to call if he ever came in again."

"We need more people," said Nathan. "If we had

him under surveillance like we're supposed to he couldn't sneak up on us like this."

"He's here to see Merrill," said Trujillo, apparently overhearing Nathan's angry protest. "As far as I know, that's all."

"It probably is," I said. "Or that might be a ruse to get past the front desk. Get in Brooke's room and lock it, just in case; I'll come over and try to figure something out."

"Where's Diana?" asked Trujillo. "We need backup."

"She's with Ostler," I said. "I don't know what they're doing."

"Why are we alone?" Nathan demanded, for the fourth time that morning. "The one place the Withered know where to find us, and they leave the two scholars and the kid alone without a single trained fighter—we're dead—we're—"

"I'm coming over," I said, and hung up the phone. "Nathan, stop whining and call Ostler."

"Don't talk to me that way—"

"Stay here and lock the door behind me." I grabbed my coat—the knife safe in the pocket—and walked into the hall, pressing the button for the elevator. No one jumped out when the door opened; I rode to the ground floor, and no one was waiting to eviscerate me when I got out. I crossed the street slowly, trying to scan the area without looking like that's what I was doing; I didn't see anything suspicious, but I didn't even know what I was looking for.

This was always the hardest part about hunting for a Withered: we never knew what they could do. The empty street might hold an invisible killer; the old lady on the corner might be a demon in disguise; the woman at the front desk, who I saw every day, might have been replaced by a shape shifter overnight. We had no way of knowing.

I stood in the lobby, trying to think. I still didn't have a plan. Should I go upstairs and confront him? Should I wait here and catch him on the way out? I didn't even know how to approach him when I saw him. Most of the Withered I'd dealt with didn't even know I was hunting them until it was too late. Meshara already knew everything.

The lobby had a few people in it, mostly residents, a handful of visitors. I sat down in a chair near the wall and tried to think. What could I do?

A moment later my plans became meaningless: I heard a small ding from the elevator and watched as Elijah Sexton and Merrill Evans stepped out. I looked away, watching them from the corner of my eye. Was he looking at me? How would he react when he saw me? If he'd seen me already, he was playing it incredibly cool.

Merrill spoke first, his voice sounding frailer than I expected. "Does this place have a restroom?" He was seventy-something, but fairly healthy looking for his age. Maybe the Alzheimer's sapped his will and energy—or maybe Meshara did. Elijah pointed toward a door in the wall, and Merrill shuffled over to it. Elijah wandered across the room and sat across from me—not quickly, or with any clear purpose of confronting me; he simply sat and looked around. Was this it? What was he going to say? I kept my eyes on the wall, keeping him in the edge of my peripheral vision.

"Here for a grandparent?" he asked. Without looking at his face, I couldn't tell what kind of tone he was taking—was it sarcasm? Feigned curiosity? Either way, it seemed he had decided to maintain the facade of innocence. Maybe he didn't know we'd identified him yet?

I turned to face him, studying his features up close: dark eyes, set deep in his face, with faint dark lines below them. He hadn't slept well. He looked to be in his late forties, I guessed—about the age Forman had been. I searched his face for some sign of deception, but saw only a flat mouth, clear eyes, slightly tilted head. Just a face.

I decided to play along for now, wondering where he was going with the conversation. Was I here to see an old person? Technically yes, since Elijah was older than anyone in the building. "Kind of."

"Kind of a grandfather," he asked, "or kind of a grandmother?"

That was an odd question—if he knew who I was, why probe into an obvious lie? Was he testing my cover story or trying to establish his own? "Friend of a friend," I said. A noncommittal answer, but with a hint that I wasn't here for a relative. I was leaving the door open for him to take the conversation somewhere deeper.

He nodded. "I suppose you could say the same for me."

Was that a reference to Merrill or to me? Or to someone else on the team? I didn't dare say more until I knew where he was steering the conversation. I kept quiet, looking back at the wall, waiting for him for to continue.

"Are you okay?" he asked.

His other questions had been odd; this one threw me completely for a loop. Was I okay? What kind of question was that? He was a demon, and I was a demon hunter, and we'd come here to kill each other, and . . . was I okay? It didn't make any sense at all. I looked at him again, trying to decipher his intentions. Was asking about my feelings a part of some strange game he was playing? Was it a prelude to whatever his powers were—was his curiosity, or his concern, or my feelings themselves, a way for him to sustain himself by killing me? Maybe he didn't need to kill me at all; Cody French only drove his victims insane, and Clark Forman, technically speaking, didn't need to harm anyone at all. He'd felt other people's emotions, but he hadn't needed to hurt them in the process, and he killed only because he enjoyed it. Are you okay? . . . Maybe he fed on suffering somehow? Was that why he'd been visiting an Alzheimer's patient for twenty years?

Merrill was the key. If we wanted to solve the puzzle of Elijah Sexton, we needed to know how Merrill fit into it. I glanced over his shoulder at the restroom door. "Who's your friend?"

His eyes widened slightly, giving every indication of innocent surprise at my question. "Just some guy," he said. "I met him about twenty years ago, right before the Alzheimer's. It's not really Alzheimer's, actually, but it's close enough. He was a good man and I liked him."

"And now you still visit him."

"It's the least I can do."

Twenty years. We'd wondered it before, but it had always seemed too good to be true: was his presence here merely a coincidence? Had we just happened to put Brooke into the one medical center an oblivious Withered visited once a week? Was it really possible he knew nothing about us at all?

Twenty years. The only other Withered I'd seen with that kind of long-term loyalty to anything had been Mr. Crowley, my next-door neighbor, who'd settled down and stopped killing completely for nearly forty years. The mental association surprised me, triggering a sense of familiarity with the man, and I fended off the sudden flare of emotion with a joke. He'd said it was the least he could do, so I responded reflexively: "I'm sure you could do a lot less if you put your mind to it."

He laughed softly, but the humor never reached his eyes. "You'd be surprised how little of my mind there is," he said, shaking his head. "Another few years and I'll end up like Merrill, more than likely. Just a . . . hollow man. An organic machine, going through the motions."

"So is it worth it?" I hadn't intended to say it, or even to think it, but it came out too fast to stop.

"Is what worth it?"

"Coming here," I said. His words had hit so close to home, and I thought about Brooke upstairs, too lost to even remember me. I thought about Marci and my mom, and wished I could lose those memories as easily as Brooke did. "Caring about someone who doesn't care about you," I said. "Who couldn't care about you if he tried. Making connections with people who are only going to disappear."

Elijah shook his head and looked down at his lap. He was carrying Merrill's coat over his arm and seemed to stare it, or at nothing, for a long time. I sat quietly, embarrassed by my outburst, wondering what he would say in response. I waited for his answer.

And waited.

It seemed like ages later when Merrill emerged from the restroom. The sound seemed to rouse Elijah from whatever reverie had taken him and he stood and turned to greet the old man.

"All set?"

"Well look who's here," said Merrill, as if he didn't remember that Elijah had been waiting for him.

Elijah offered him his coat. "You still want to go for a walk?"

"I can't go for a walk, have you seen the snow outside?"

"There's certainly a lot of it."

They chatted for a minute about the snow and who shoveled it, and then walked back toward the elevator, their reason for coming down here either abandoned or completely forgotten.

That, or Elijah's sole purpose had been to see me, and now he was done. Walking in here this morning, that would have been the only explanation I'd have believed, but after the conversation we'd just had . . . . I am a very experienced liar and I can tell when other people are saying something that doesn't fit. Nothing Elijah Sexton said made any sense to me, but it had made sense to him. It fit for him.

I pulled out my phone and walked outside into the cold. Agent Ostler answered on the second ring.

"Hello, John."

"Elijah Sexton isn't hunting us."

"You're sure?"

"Not a hundred percent," I said, "but probably ninety-nine. I just talked to him and I'd swear he had no idea who I was. I think he visits Merrill Evans because they're genuinely just friends."

"Would you bet your life on it?"

I hesitated, not because of the question itself, but the way she phrased it. This was more than just asking me if I was certain. She was worried about something, and I knew Ostler well enough to know that she was never worried by abstract concepts. Something new had happened.

I walked toward the street. "What's wrong?"

"Get Nathan and Trujillo," she said, "and come to the police station. There's been another killing."

A dozen questions flooded my mind, but I focused on the one that concerned me most. "That would leave Brooke alone."

"She's in the secure wing of a dementia facility, surrounded by trained personnel."

"Medical personnel," I said, stopping on a windswept corner of the intersection. "If the Withered come for her, they'll be no help at all."

Ostler let out a long, slow breath. "After what I've seen today, none of us would be any help. If you swear Elijah's not hunting us—"

"You asked if I'd bet my life on it," I said. "Betting Brooke's is different."

"I'm asking you to examine a corpse," said Ostler. "Cut the pretense and get down here; you're wasting time."

She hung up, and I stood on the corner, staring at the flurries of fallen snow the wind picked up and swirled across the asphalt. I didn't want to leave Brooke, but Ostler was right. The chance to examine a body was something I'd been waiting for ever since I'd joined this team. I could complain and argue and stall as long I wanted, but eventually I'd go. I wanted to stay away on purpose, obstinately, for that reason alone, but I couldn't. My feet were already crossing the street, as far beyond my control as Brooke's hand, writing invisible notes to no one on her bedspread.

"His name is Stephen Applebaum," said Ostler, "and somebody must have really been mad at him." Our whole team, minus Potash, was gathered in a pale-blue room in the morgue, looking down at a metal table containing a man-shaped thing under a sheet. The police had stepped out, giving us a moment of privacy. The once-sterile sheet was caked here and there with dark brown bloodstains. It was all I could do not to reach out and touch one. "Forty-two years old, Caucasian male, found in the Dumpster behind the Riverwalk Motel. They offer both nightly and hourly rates, so you know it's classy. His clothing was with him, though most of it wasn't on him at the time."

"Sexual assault?" asked Trujillo.

"Nothing that simple," said Ostler, and she grabbed the edge of the sheet. "We think the clothing was removed because it made it easier to do this." She pulled back the sheet and the others gasped. I leaned forward, fascinated by the carnage. The body was pocked with holes—not stab wounds, but shallow gashes, a couple of inches wide and some of them up to two inches deep. They were mostly bloodless, as was typical for a body already cleaned and examined by a forensics team, so instead of red the wounds were brown and purple. Bruises and rotting meat. They covered the corpse like nightmare polka dots.

I was home.

"What? . . ." said Nathan, trying and failing to form a cogent question.

I pulled on a pair of latex gloves and prodded the nearest wound, feeling the ragged edge of skin around its rim. I'd grown up in a mortuary, spying on my parents as a child, watching them work on corpses through the crack in the door, and as I'd grown older they'd started giving me little jobs to do: bring me a drink; hand me that cleanser; hold this just for a second. By the time I was a teenager I was working full time as an apprentice embalmer, and there were few things I loved more in the entire world. Now that Marci was dead, maybe there was nothing.

"What could have done this?" asked Trujillo, apparently more inured to the sight of death than Nathan was.

"Teeth," said Diana. She'd been with Ostler all morning and had apparently already been briefed. I ran my finger gently along a pair of sharp ridges jutting up from the muscle tissue, imagining a row of teeth making just such a mark. It made sense, and I nodded while Diana continued. "It took the local forensics guy a while to figure it out,because the bite marks are obvious but the bite shapes are all wrong. They get dog and coyote attacks in this area every now and then, but those leave a longer wound because that's how a canine muzzle is shaped." She made a puppet-like motion with her hand, chomping at the air. "These bites are wider and shallower."

"A bear?" asked Nathan.

"Human," I said. "Look at this pattern of tracks." I pointed to the ridges I'd been studying and bared my teeth, clacking them together to demonstrate. I pointed at each ridge in the flesh. "There's the incisors—a bigger one, then a smaller one—and then a deeper track on the side for the canine. Those are exactly the tracks a human mouth would make biting through the meat."

"It's disturbing that you know that," said Nathan.

I shrugged. "One of many reasons I'm a vegetarian."

Ostler looked at me. "Have you encountered anything like this before?"

"Forman left bite marks in some of his torture victims," I said, shaking my head, "but they barely broke the skin. Whoever did this was after the meat." I probed one of the deeper wounds on the body, a large chunk missing from the outer thigh. The attacker had taken several bites from the area, digging in and ripping off flesh until the bone itself was exposed. The surrounding muscle hung into the wound in ragged, ropy strands.

As violent as the attack had been, I felt a kind of stately reverence for the body. The cannibal had attacked, the victim had fought back, flesh had ripped away in a bloody spray, but that was all done now, and we were looking at a pale, bloodless effigy. It was like a marble statue, carved in commemoration of an ancient battle. I raised a clean finger and smoothed its hair, doing my part to honor the dead.

"Why wasn't his face damaged?" asked Trujillo.

I frowned, and looked at the body's face. It was completely free of the wounds that covered the rest of it; in fact the whole head seemed practically untouched. Why hadn't I noticed that before?

"There's not a lot of meat on a face," said Nathan.

"You've never eaten sheep in Afghanistan," said Diana.

"Meaty or not," said Trujillo, "the face is a prime target for a cannibalistic assault. Lunge at a person and what does your own face contact first? People reflect each other; our arms grab theirs, our face meets theirs."

"But cannibals don't attack people face to face like that," I said. If he wanted to play serial-killer trivia I could give him a run for his money. "Human cannibal attacks are premeditated and careful, like Jeffrey Dahmer or Armin Meiwes. They carve up the body almost like a—dammit." Trujillo was right. As soon as I started talking about the classic cases, I realized what Trujillo already had: that this one didn't fit the pattern. "*Most* cannibals carve up the body like a butcher," I said. "They incapacitate the victim, take it home, store the parts . . . . This guy didn't do any of that."

"Even without knowing the details of the initial attack," said Trujillo, "the body makes what happened after that fairly obvious. Our killer fed on the victim soon, perhaps immediately, ripping out bites like a feral predator. He took time to remove some of the clothes, but that appears to be the only humanlike behavior; the rest is very animalistic. When he was full, or at least sated, he hid the body in a Dumpster—he didn't save it for later and he didn't even carve off a piece. All the wounds are caused by teeth, and if they weren't human teeth, this would have virtually no hallmarks of a human attack."

"What about the face?" asked Ostler. "You started this whole topic by mentioning the face."

"Because that's the part that doesn't fit," I said. Now that I saw what Trujillo was talking about, I could tell exactly what he was thinking. "The nature of this attack suggests—though again, we don't know for sure—that it was a face-to-face assault, possibly with bare hands. Serial killers who treat dead bodies this wildly tend to attack living ones with the same attitude. But this one didn't." I turned back to the corpse, picking up the right hand and searching it for marks. "Not only would an attack like that damage the face, it would leave some clear defensive wounds from when the victim fought back: scrapes or cuts on the knuckles, ripped nails, that kind of thing. I don't see any of those, either. Did the forensic examiner mention anything like that?"

"No," said Diana. "We assumed it was a more careful attack, so the lack didn't stand out."

"This is why we have a criminal psychologist on the team," said Ostler. She looked at Trujillo. "So this attack was abnormal, that much seems obvious. What does that mean?"

"I'm not sure," said Trujillo. "I'm still getting used to the idea that the killers we're chasing are supernatural, and that changes literally everything. There might be a deeper psychological reason for an attack like this, or it might just be that the Withered who did it eats human flesh, and got hungry."

I'd been so enthralled by the body that I'd missed the significance of it—all the little clues that I should have seen and didn't, and it embarrassed me that Trujillo had seen them so easily. I'd felt even worse when Ostler asked Trujillo for advice, and hearing him admit that he was out of his depth gave me a small, almost petulant thrill. Now it was my turn.

"The first thing we know is that this is probably one of the new guys who showed up at the mortuary last night," I said.

"Really?" asked Nathan. "You got a good look at their teeth, did you?"

"If it had happened in town before, the police examiner wouldn't have been confused by it," I said. "Plus, the killer hid the body in a place no local would have bothered with."

"It was a Dumpster behind a trashy motel," said Diana. "That's such a common place to hide a body it's practically a cliché."

"Most trashy-motel Dumpsters are," I said, "but not this one. I assume the body was found by a homeless guy?"

"It was," said Ostler. "How did you know?"

"Because I've seen the Riverwalk Motel before, when we visited the homeless shelter looking for one of Cody French's victims. The motel and the shelter are barely three blocks apart. That Dumpster probably gets picked through all the time, and a local killer as experienced as a Withered—who has to kill regularly just to survive—would know that. He would have a system in place to hide his victims, and he wouldn't change that system out of the blue to hide a body in such a risky place."

"The change might not be out of the blue," said Trujillo. "An attack this violent could represent an escalation, or a reaction to something that angered him. We did just kill two Withered; they may have been his friends, and the loss pushed him over an edge."

"But that's why the face is important," I said. "That's why this body doesn't make sense: because it doesn't look premeditated, but it is. There's no damage to the face or head, there's no defensive wounds; this was not a feral assault in an alley somewhere." I relished talking about this with people who understood me, who didn't think I was freak. I looked at Diana. "You read the report: did the forensic guy find the wound that killed him?"

Diana scoffed. "Any of those wounds could have killed him."

"But the examiner couldn't tell which one, right?" She hesitated, but nodded, and I knew I was on the right track. "They couldn't find a death blow, and they couldn't find a point of incapacitation. No blunt trauma to the head that knocked him unconscious, no needle mark where he was injected with a sedative. The killer ate him like an animal, but not until after he was rendered helpless so carefully that we can't find any evidence of it."

Nathan surprised me by filling in the next detail before I could say it. "So we're dealing with a Withered who can stun people," he said. "Or . . . hypnotize them or something. Some kind of mental thing that doesn't leave a physical mark."

"Elijah Sexton works as a night driver for a mortuary," I said. "He has more contact with dead people than living ones. Whatever his thing is, it doesn't involve mind control. It's got to be one of the new ones."

Ostler sighed. "I was hoping Elijah's mysterious visitors weren't Withered. That hope is fading fast."

"We need to do our research," said Nathan. "Find out if this kind of attack has been reported anywhere else. If we can tap into some investigative work that's already been done, we'll be a lot closer to an answer."

"That's the kind of thing we need Kelly for," said Diana.

"I have some police contacts of my own," said Trujillo. "I'll see what I can dig up."

"No, we need you talking to Brooke," said Ostler, shaking her head. "If we describe this attack to her it might spark a memory and give us a better sense of what we're dealing with."

"What we're dealing with is a war," said Diana. "Every Withered in the world is descending on this damned town, and it takes us months of planning just to kill one of them. Now there's two at least, probably four, and maybe even more than that. We can't fight this, even with police assistance."

"You want to back off and regroup?" asked Nathan. "I second that idea wholeheartedly."

"So do I," I said. I was responsible for too many deaths already—all the people I couldn't save, the friends I'd endangered. Nathan accused me of getting Kelly killed, and as much as I hated to admit it, he was right. I'd rushed us in to Mary Gardner without knowing all the details, and now Kelly was dead and Potash was in the hospital. It had been a risk worth taking, but it should have been my risk, not theirs. "We're killing too many Withered, and too fast, and of course they're fighting back. We organized, so they had to organize to keep up. This war is our fault."

"They've been killing all along," said Ostler, piercing me with her eyes. "Whoever ate Applebaum would have eaten somebody else in some other town, whether we were hunting Withered or not. Don't get soft on me just because the bodies are piling up in one place."

"He's not saying we stop," said Nathan. "He's saying we should pull back and find a new plan."

"That's not what John's saying at all," said Ostler, still staring at me, and I knew she'd guessed exactly what I was planning. "He wants to run away and do this on his own: no team, no rules, just John Cleaver stalking and killing like the good old days."

Not completely alone, I thought. *I'm not leaving without Brooke.*

"Forget what John wants," said Nathan, "he's crazy. But this *is* a war, and we're on the front lines in a dangerously exposed position. Two of our team got taken out by a nurse, for crying out loud, and that was before the terrifying, mind-control cannibal showed up. We need to run away, straight back to headquarters, and figure out a new way to fight these things because this way is suicide."

"Don't get soft on me," Ostler repeated, her voice as hard as steel. "What did you think you were getting into? I told you the truth when I offered you the job. I told you exactly what we were up against and what we'd be doing, and you knew the risks. You knew there were monsters, and that we were throwing ourselves directly in their path, and if you didn't think that would put you in this kind of danger, you're not as smart as I took you for. Of course this is a war, and of course we started it, and of course people are dying. But we're winning, and they're scared. If they could hurt you, Mr. Gentry, they would, and it would be your body on this slab, and—"

"Is that supposed to make me feel better?" asked Nathan.

"Only if you're clever enough to see it," snapped Ostler. "If we're in so much danger, why is Stephen Applebaum dead and not us? Why have the only times they've hurt us been lucky hits in an attack *we* initiated? Either they don't know who we are, or they can't reach us, and either way, we still have the upper hand. We can do this, but not if we back off."

"I'm willing to keep going," said Trujillo, "but how? Even if the Withered's plan is just to wait for us to come to them, how is that not an incredibly good plan? Mary Gardner was ambushed by a special forces assassin and she still put him in the hospital. We don't have a new Potash to spend on every Withered that comes along."

"The attack on Mary Gardner was reckless," said Ostler, and I felt a pang of guilt—and another pang of anger. "We thought we knew how she worked, and we were spooked by the revelation that we were being hunted. Taking her out quickly was smart, but we weren't thinking clearly, and we weren't ready. I take full responsibility for that."

"So that's the plan?" asked Nathan. "Just keep doing the same thing we always do?"

"But do it better," said Ostler.

I could do it better alone. No one to help me, but also no one to attract attention and get in the way. But with my photo on the Internet, could I ever truly sneak up on a Withered again? My methods were simple: make friends, find their weakness, and kill them. How could I make friends in secret if they all knew my face?

"Dr. Trujillo," said Ostler, "I want you to talk to Brooke and see what you can get out of her: tell her about the corpse, about the three men, anything that might help her to remember something new."

"I can embalm the victim," I offered.

Ostler looked confused. "Why would we need you to embalm the victim?"

It was a long shot anyway. "Then I'll talk to Brooke," I said. "She knows me, and I know what to ask about."

"Trujillo is the expert," said Ostler.

"Trujillo is also the only one left with police contacts," I said. "He's investigated serial killers before, and someone he's worked with is bound to know something about an unsolved cannibalism case."

"You don't make the assignments," said Ostler.

"Brooke doesn't even like him," I said. "She'll talk to me."

Ostler thought a moment before nodding. "Take Nathan with you."

"She won't like him either."

"Hey," said Nathan.

"Half of what Brooke talks about happened thousands of years ago," said Ostler. "Nathan can interpret that data better than you can.

"I've kept notes on everything Brooke's said so far," said Trujillo. "They're not transferred to my computer yet, but—"

"I prefer paper anyway," I said quickly, trying to think of a way to avoid a partnership with Nathan; the thought of him asking Brooke questions made my hands shake with anger. I pressed them into fists and hid them behind my back.

"My notes are all back in the office," said Trujillo. "You're welcome to any of it."

"I'll continue to work with the hospital," said Ostler, "and coordinate with the rest of you as necessary. Dr. Pearl found a steroid treatment that seems to be helping Potash a lot, but don't expect him to bail you out of trouble any time soon. You're all armed?" Nathan, Diana, and Trujillo each patted a concealed gun; I held up my knife. Ostler raised her eyebrow at it. "You don't want a gun?"

"He's not comfortable with them," said Diana.

"Too easy to hit the wrong target," I said. *And not nearly personal enough when you hit a target you really want to kill.*

7

"Four of them," said Brooke, sitting on her bed in the dementia ward. She was more lucid today than she had been in a while, and we were making as much use of that clarity as we could. She looked at me with worried eyes, but I watched as her expression shifted into a sly smile. Even lucid, there was a lot of Nobody mixed in with Brooke. "Four Cursed in one place is dangerous."

"Do you mean the Withered?" asked Nathan. "Or is this a new group?"

"They are Withered *and* they are Cursed," said Brooke. Her voice changed abruptly, sounding almost like a different person's—small and weak and scared. "They used to call themselves the Gifted, and some of them still do, but Nobody never did. Sometimes Nobody did. Only when Kanta was around to hear it. He still believed in the old days, but not me; I hated them all."

She was shifting in and out of memories, sometimes speaking as Brooke, and sometimes speaking as Nobody. I felt a tight pain in the center of my chest, listening to her, fearing again—for the thousandth time—that Nobody wasn't really dead, that some part of her survived in Brooke's bloodstream, talking through her and controlling her. Worse than the fear was the guilt, knowing that I was responsible for what had happened to her, and all I wanted was to make that feeling go away. I wanted to make everything go away, to take Brooke and take myself and just disappear somewhere—as if solitude could miraculously cure us both. I didn't because I couldn't. There were demons here, and I was the only one who could stop them, and every day I wasted was another day someone else could end up like Brooke. I pushed away my fear and my guilt and locked them up tight, where no one could ever know they were there, and I looked at Brooke with cold, emotionless eyes. If she thought she was Nobody, that was good; we needed Nobody's memories. I told myself it was true. I glanced at Nathan and let Brooke speak.

"Kanta wanted to unite us all," Brooke continued, "to bring us all together like a club or a secret society. Club's not the right word: cabal. He said we were stronger together, and I guess that's turning out to be true." She pointed at the photos I'd brought of Applebaum's chewed-up corpse, turned face down on the little bedside table because she didn't want to look at them.

"Did Kanta unite them?" I asked. I knew the Withered stayed in touch now and then, which was why Mr. Crowley had caused so much concern when he'd stopped communicating completely. But it had always been a loose group, and the idea that they were actually organized was frightening—it implied focus and direction, and direction implied movement, even if it was only metaphorical. What were they moving toward, and why?

"He only united some," said Brooke, and she folded herself into a haggard ball, drawing her knees up to her chin and hugging them tight with her thin, bony arms. "The ones who thought like he did. Rack was the worst."

"Rack," I said quickly, catching onto a memory. "Mary Gardner said something about Rack."

"Mary Gardner?"

"Agarin," said Nathan, using Mary's Withered name.

"Agarin said something about Rack when she was standing over Agent Potash," I said. "She said she'd wanted to leave him for Rack, but she didn't have time so she'd have to kill him herself."

"You don't want to be killed by Rack," Brooke whispered.

"I don't want to be killed by anyone," I said, looking through Trujillo's page of Withered identities. "Who is Rack?"

"The king," said Brooke.

I glanced at Nathan again. "Rack's not in Trujillo's notes. Have you ever come across the name before?"

"It might be a title," said Nathan. "It's not similar to any names like Meshara or Hulla, but it's awfully similar to 'rex' and a dozen other words like it. Most Indo-European languages have a word for 'king' that's at least partly related to 'rack.' "

"You have it backwards," said Brooke, more confident now. I wasn't sure if Nobody or Brooke was the more confident personality. "Rack didn't get his name from their titles; they got their titles from his name."

Nathan stared at her a moment, then frowned and made a note. "That is a very disturbing thing to think about."

"Are you saying that Rack is so old," I asked, "and so influential, that our word for 'king' is just his name?"

"Not our word," said Nathan, "just . . . a lot of people's words. The strange part is that Sumerian isn't an Indo-European language, so that relationship isn't as strong as I'd like. But the name Kanta is Hindi, which is obviously Indo-European, which suggests that the different Withered might have come from a single point and then spread out. But it would have to be an incredibly long time ago—"

"How long?" I asked.

"To predate Indo-European language?" asked Nathan. He whistled, looking at the ceiling as he calculated. "I'd guess early Neolithic era, maybe even before. Ten thousand years at least, and possibly more."

"They say they used to be gods," I said. "With these abilities, at the dawn of human civilization, how could they not be?" I looked at Brooke. "Was Nobody that old?"

"I was a goddess," she said, staring at the window. "The goddess of beauty and love, and women would come from all over the world to see me—though of course the world was smaller in those days. Just a valley."

Nathan looked queasy. "I'm not comfortable with the idea that an ancient god ate a man's leg behind a cheap motel."

"Rack didn't eat him," said Brooke, suddenly very serious. "Rack doesn't eat legs. He doesn't even have a mouth."

I leaned forward. "What do you mean he doesn't have a mouth?"

She pressed her lips tightly together, then covered the bottom half of her face with her hand. "No mouth," she mumbled, barely intelligible through her fingers. "No nose, either. Just eyes and soul."

"A soul?"

"Black tar," she said. "Ash and grease." She put one hand on the bridge of her nose, and the other at the base of her sternum, sectioning off about twelve inches of her body. "He doesn't have a face because he doesn't need a face. The dead speak for him, and his soul takes whatever it wants."

"The dead speak for him?" asked Nathan, but I focused on the latter statement.

"What does he want?" I asked. We had to know what he was missing to figure out what he had.

She emphasized the hand on her chest, as if showing how much of her rib cage was above it. "He doesn't have a heart."

I sat silently for a moment, trying to imagine what such a person would look like. Eventually I just shrugged and made some notes in one of Trujillo's heavy binders. "Mary—I mean, Agarin—said she didn't have time to wait for Rack. That means he's probably not here yet, which is the only good news we've heard in weeks."

"But he's coming," said Nathan.

"One monster at a time," I said. "First we have our cannibal; let's deal with him before we have to deal with him and Rack together."

"We're so dead," said Nathan, shaking his head.

"Think back," I said, catching Brooke with my eyes. "Think deep back into all those memories, into everything you know about the Withered, or the Cursed, or whatever you want to call them. Which one eats people?"

"I don't know."

"You have to know," I said, and held up the picture again. She shied away from it, scared or disgusted or both, but I kept it up where she'd be forced to see it when she stopped averting her eyes. *I'm so sorry, Brooke.* "Look at the picture again, Nobody." I hoped the other name would shock her deeper into the Withered's memories, forcing her to remember more. "What does it remind you of? Where have you seen this before?"

"You're freaking her out," said Nathan.

"She's half demon," I said, trying to feel as cold as I could, "I'm not showing her anything she hasn't seen before."

"Just . . . knock it off," he said, and pushed the photo facedown on the table. "Let's go through the names instead. What can you tell us about Meshara?"

"He remembers," said Brooke.

"You've told us that before," said Nathan. "What does it mean? Can he read people's minds—maybe remember other people's memories?"

Forman—or Kanta—had possessed a kind of mind reading ability; he could feel other people's emotions. But the downside was that he couldn't turn it off. Maybe Meshara was similar, constantly thinking other people's thoughts? That could explain why he isolated himself so completely from the rest of the world, working a lonely night job surrounded by the dead. No competing thoughts to get in the way of his own. It might also explain why his only friend was an Alzheimer's patient—maybe Merrill Evans didn't have enough of his own memories to intrude on Meshara's.

But then he would have read my mind as well, I thought, *and he'd have known that I was hunting him, and nothing he asked me would have made any sense.* My brief conversation with him had convinced me that Meshara wasn't hunting us. I still believed that—the other three might have been, but not him.

"What about Djoti," asked Nathan. "That's a name you've used a few times, possibly Egyptian in origin. What does Djoti do?"

Rack doesn't have a heart . . . . I thought.

"We're asking the wrong questions," I said suddenly. Nathan looked at me in surprise. "Forman said the Withered were defined by what they lacked: Crowley didn't have an identity, Forman didn't have his own emotions, Nobody didn't have her own body. They see what humans have and they want it for themselves."

"She has a body now," said Brooke.

"You said Rack doesn't have a heart," I told her. "What does Meshara not have? What is he missing?"

"He can't remember," said Brooke.

I frowned. "You just said he can."

"Maybe she's flipping into a new personality again," said Nathan, and he leaned forward, speaking slowly and loudly. "We want to talk to Nobody—to Hulla. Is she in there?"

"Wait," I said, slowly piecing it together, "she said it right: Meshara can't remember, *and* he can. He doesn't have his own memories, so he remembers your memories instead."

"He was the god of dreams," said Brooke.

"Does he dream other people's memories?" I asked.

"He takes them," said Brooke. "Straight out of your head—boop—like a refrigerator."

"The Sumerian god of dreams was Mamu," said Nathan. "He was the child of the sun, and shifted between genders."

I gave him a sidelong glance. "You just know that off the top of your head?"

"Kid, I've written two books on Mesopotamian mythology; why do you think I'm on this team?"

"Well," I said, looking back at Brooke. "I'm glad we're finally figuring *that* out. Can Meshara change genders?"

"He has one body," said Brooke. "A million minds."

"That might be the same thing," said Nathan. "Or he might have been some other god of dreams in some other culture. Ten thousand years is a long time."

"But why does he work in a mortuary?" I asked Brooke. "Why work at night? Why avoid people? Why visit Merrill Evans?"

"Why do you avoid people?" asked Brooke.

I blinked, staring at her for a moment, then nodded. "That's a fair point. Maybe he's just . . . introverted. There doesn't have to be a supernatural explanation for everything."

"There was another Mesopotamian god named Zaqar," said Nathan. "He was the moon's messenger, and he communicated through dreams."

"We're getting too far out into tangents," I said, shaking my head. "We don't need to write papers on these people, we just need to find them. Let's stick with the basics: who else is in Trujillo's notes?"

Nathan leaned over one of the binders. "In their talks together, restricting the list to Withered we haven't found yet, Brooke has mentioned Djoti four times, Yashodh three times, Gidri three times, Nashuja twice—that one's Minoan, kind of cool—and

Husn, Dag, Skanda, and Ihsan once each." He looked up. "That's quite a list."

"Start with Djoti," I said, turning to Brooke. "What does he lack?"

"Eyes," said Brooke.

I raised my eyebrows. "That's . . . pretty straightforward."

"Does he steal other people's eyes?" asked Nathan. "Wasn't there a serial killer who stole eyes?"

"Make a note and come back to it," I said. "We need to find our cannibal first."

"What about Yashodh?" asked Nathan. "What does he lack?"

"Yashodh is weak," said Brooke, her voice suddenly contemptuous. "Even weaker than Nobody."

Nathan nodded and started writing. "So he lacks strength?"

"Nobody wasn't physically weak," I said, putting out my hand to stop him. "That comparison implies something else—mental weakness, maybe? Emotional?"

"People love him," said Brooke. "Even today. It's not fair."

"If he takes people's love that means he . . . doesn't have any of his own?" I struggled to wrap my mind around the sheer strangeness of the Withered's existence. "He doesn't love, or . . . he doesn't love himself. He lacks self-respect. That certainly fits with Nobody's psyche, but it doesn't tell us much about him."

"It doesn't make him sound like a cannibal," said Nathan.

"A lot of cannibals eat people they want to be like," I said. "Everything from South Pacific tribesmen to . . . Catholicism."

"Excuse you?"

"Catholics are a great example," I said. "They want to become more Christlike, so they eat the flesh of Christ."

Nathan stiffened. "As a Catholic I'm deeply offended by that characterization."

"Sorry," I said, shrugging. "The trouble is, in our case it's backward: usually the one who loves is the one who eats, but Brooke said *they* love *him*. Why would eating people make them love him? Though if he can force people to love him before he eats, so much that they don't fight back, that could explain why Applebaum died without a struggle."

"Don't change the subject," said Nathan, setting down his pen and cocking his head aggressively. "Are you honestly equating the Eucharist with cannibalism?"

"I read an article on cannibalism a few years ago," I said. "You can look it up later—we don't have time to argue about it now."

"Because you're going to get eaten," said Brooke. Her eyes were wide and bright, like she was happy and just trying to be helpful.

"Tell us about Gidri," I said, thinking back to the next Withered on Trujillo's list. "What does he lack?"

"He wants to be king," said Brooke.

I glanced at Nathan. "Isn't Rack the king?" Back to Brooke. "Are there opposing factions vying for control?"

"That's a common enough theme in a lot of mythologies," said Nathan. "The tradition of intrapantheon squabbles might be a reflection of infighting between the Withered who inspired those mythologies."

"If they've been fighting for ten thousand years you'd think they'd have worked something out by now," I said. "Or just killed each other, with only one person left standing on each side of each conflict."

"They could have new conflicts," said Nathan. "I mean, look at them—the Withered are a mess. They used to be gods, and now Meshara works as a night driver in a mortuary. Any glory they used to have is gone. Maybe Gidri's decided that Rack's not doing his job as king, and wants to take over."

"Maybe we'll get lucky and they'll kill each other," I said. "Or maybe we'll get really lucky and the war they're starting doesn't involve us at all."

"I don't want to be trapped between two armies of warring demons," said Nathan. "Your definition of 'really lucky' is not the same as mine." I started to respond, but the door opened behind us, and I looked over my shoulder to see Diana come into the room with a paper in her hand.

"Hello, Lucinda," said Brooke. "Have you milked the cows yet?"

Diana pursed her lips. "Looks like it's been a fun day in here. Anything useful?"

"Plenty of good info," said Nathan. "Probably useful in the long term, but nothing that's going to help us not get murdered tonight."

"Don't get murdered!" said Brooke, her face suddenly lined with grief.

I stared at Nathan just long enough to make him look away, then turned to Diana. "What's up?"

"Two things, actually," said Diana. "Good news first: the security camera at the mortuary got a clear look at one of our mystery men."

"You're supposed to start with the bad news," said Nathan.

"Trust me," said Diana. "Let's get this out of the way first."

I took the paper from her hand. It was a still image from a

camera feed, black and white and poorly lit: one man stood hunched by the door, picking the lock, and beside him was the tall man, but neither's face was visible. The third man, however, was looking out at the street, as if scanning it for trouble, and the camera managed to catch his face perfectly. He was younger than Elijah, late twenties maybe, with a face so handsome it was almost pretty. I studied it a moment, then handed the image to Brooke.

"Do you recognize him?"

She sneered. "Gidri."

Nathan sat up straighter. "The king guy?"

"The Withered have a king?" asked Diana. "That's great news."

"Gidri's not the king," I said. "He's the one who wants to be king." I looked at Brooke. "Are you sure that's him?"

"Can't you tell?" demanded Brooke. Her face was curled up in an angry glare, practically snarling at the paper. "Just look at him."

"What does he lack?" I asked.

"Nothing," Brooke spat.

"Then . . . what does he have?" I asked. "What can he do?" It seemed like there were some bad feelings between Gidri and Nobody—she didn't like any of the Withered, but I'd never seen her this riled up before.

"He's gorgeous," said Brooke. "I hate him. I hate him! I hate him!" Without any warning she tore the photo to shreds, and while I was still trying to figure out what had made her so mad, she leapt forward, snatching Nathan's notes and shredding them as well. He swore and grabbed them back, taking what he could and staggering backwards, knocking over his chair in a desperate attempt to get out of reach. "I hate him!" Brooke shouted, and leapt for Trujillo's binder, which I'd been looking through. Diana pulled it away at the last second, and I pushed past her to grab at Brooke's arms, trying to stop her. She screamed in a rage, no longer capable of coherent sentences, and Diana ran for the door while Nathan stooped down to salvage what he could of his torn papers.

"Security!" Diana shouted, banging on the locked door and pulling on the emergency cord. I managed to grab Brooke's wrists and hold them apart, but she lunged at me and snapped with her teeth, missing my face by millimeters. I stumbled backward, trying to avoid her, and lost my grip on her left arm; her fingers raked across my cheek and eye, and suddenly the door burst open and the room was swarming with nurses, catching her and holding her and bearing her backwards, forcing her down onto the bed as she thrashed and howled. I backed against the wall, breathing heavily.

"She's crazy!" shouted Nathan. "She should be in chains!"

The fact that I didn't kill him on the spot is perhaps the greatest testament to my self-control.

"Guess she doesn't like Gidri," said Diana.

"You think?" asked Nathan. He swore again, looking at the fistfuls of ripped paper he'd saved as if he didn't know what to do with them.

"There's no way your bad news beats this," I said.

"Don't be so sure," said Diana. "We got a letter from the cannibal; Ostler wants the whole group to gather at the office."

I shot her disbelieving stare. A letter from the killer would be teeming with clues. "That's bad news?"

"You tell me," said Diana. "He mentions you by name."

To Mr. John Cleaver, and his Esteemed Colleagues,

I assume I need no introduction; you don't know my name, but you've seen my work and you know what I am—"what" seems like a much more appropriate word than "who" in this instance, as I'm sure you'll agree. But seeing my work and understanding it are two different things, and that is why I am writing to you. I do not take these actions lightly. I want you to understand them.

First, the proof, so that we are entirely clear: the man in the morgue is named Stephen Applebaum, and you found him behind the Riverwalk Motel. He sustained multiple wounds to the legs, arms, and torso, numbering into the midthirties; I won't bother with an exact number, as there is likely to be some variance in our counting methods. His stomach contents, as I assume you've been informed, will have included two slices of pizza—I was too far away to see the toppings—and a chocolate frosted donut. I assure you that his dietary habits helped make my own meal well-marbled and succulent. To help remove any lingering doubt that I am the one who killed him, I bit off the smallest toe on his left foot, then put his shoe back in place; this detail will not be public knowledge, and will be known only to the medical examiner and, I assume, your team. I am not a poseur, claiming credit for another's work. I am the one you are seeking.

Now for the explanation. Do not assume from my desire to explain myself that I am on some kind of crusade; I did not kill Applebaum to punish him, and if he was a sinner against some pale set of standards that is none of my concern. I did not kill him because I was righteous, or angry, or vengeant. I did not kill him for something he did or saw or knew. I did not kill him because he needed to die.

I killed Applebaum because I was hungry. I am a predator, and he was my prey. To deny this is to deny the order of nature itself.

You will struggle against me because it is in the nature of prey to do so. The antelope will always run from the lion. I don't blame you for this or even warn you against it, nor will I waste your time with trite glorification of the thrill of the hunt. You will do your part and I will do mine. All I ask is that you remember this: the only animal safe from a lion is a lion.

Find what the lion fears, and you will have found everything.

"There is no signature," said Agent Ostler, lowering the letter and looking at us. "It's written by hand, in what I suspect is a fountain pen. I'll make a photocopy as soon as this meeting's over, and overnight the physical letter back to Langley for handwriting and DNA analysis. In the meantime, we need to figure out exactly what the hell this means."

I stood behind the others, thinking. How did it know my name? Had Forman or Nobody contacted another Withered before they died? Had Meshara really read my mind and discovered my identity? Or were Nathan's worst fears true?

Was Brooke communicating with the Withered?

"Obviously it's a warning," said Diana. "He said it wasn't, but how stupid does he think we are?"

"Practically every sentence was a threat," said Nathan.

"I don't think it's that simple," said Trujillo. "What we perceive as a threat, the man who wrote the letter might perceive in a totally different context."

Nathan snorted. "What possible context could make comparing us to prey not a threat?"

"The very context presented in the letter," said Trujillo. "A lion doesn't eat an antelope because he hates it, or because he wants to scare it, or because he feels superior. A lion *is* superior, *because* he eats antelope."

"Lions don't send letters to the antelope's friends," said Ostler. "He wanted us to know something, or he wouldn't have communicated. This is not just a courtesy call from a helpful serial killer."

"Don't worry about what he wanted to tell us," I said. I was still embarrassed by my poor analysis of the body, so I was determined to analyze the letter as well as I possibly could. "We can figure that out later, when he sends us another letter. First we need—"

"How do you know he's going to send another one?" asked Nathan. "Or do you have some kind of inside knowledge we don't?" He turned more fully toward me. "Why was your name on the letter?"

I didn't flinch away from his stare. "I don't know."

"How does he know who you are?" Nathan pressed. "Or does he know you personally?"

"Easy, Nathan," said Diana.

"If I knew who he was I'd tell you," I said. "I want to find him just as much as you do." *Almost certainly more,* I thought, but I didn't say it out loud.

"Why wait for a second letter?" asked Ostler. Her authority cut through Nathan's accusations, and I started speaking again.

"I'm not saying to abandon analysis completely," I said. "Dr. Gentry didn't let me finish. First we can look at the clues we have: not what he's trying to tell us, but what he's accidentally telling us without intending to. This letter is like a window into his psyche—what does it tell us about him?"

"He's obviously very formal," said Trujillo, diving into the profile immediately. He'd probably been planning the same suggestion, but this time I'd said it first. "He uses elevated language and vocabulary, complicated sentence structure, and an almost . . . scholarly politeness."

"Contrast that with the nature of the attack," I said. "The wounds were vicious—you described them as 'feral'—but this letter was deliberate and intelligent. He obviously has a plan: he figured out where we are, so he could send us a letter, and he figured out who I am. This is not the kind of man who jumps people in alleys and tears them apart with his teeth."

"Except obviously he is," said Diana. "Half of that letter was proof that he's the killer."

"And why is it so important for him that we know that?" I asked. "He knew we'd doubt it, and he wanted to make sure we didn't. Is he bragging? Did he write to us because he needs . . . what? Recognition? Credit? Fear? Don't think about what he wants to tell us, think about what he wants for himself. What does this letter get him?" It all came back to the same thing. "What did he do that he didn't have to do?"

Ostler looked at me grimly. "Dr. Trujillo will figure that out. I know you've done this before, but he's a professional."

"I can do this," I said.

"You'll still be studying them," said Ostler, "but I want you on Elijah Sexton. You'll be assisting Diana."

"I can get more done alone," I said.

"Elijah went to a grief counseling meeting," said Diana, ignoring my protest. "We don't know why. The cops' surveillance team showed up at the same place, tailing the three mystery Withered, who were apparently tailing Elijah."

"He's not a part of their group," I said again. "If the new Withered are following Elijah in secret, that's just more proof that they're not allies."

"Brooke suggested there might be two factions," said Nathan. "We think this Gidri is leading one of them, so maybe he's trying to recruit Elijah to his side?"

"Could be," said Diana. "If we knew what the two sides wanted we'd have a lot more to go on."

"Why would a Withered go to a grief counseling meeting?" asked Trujillo. "I can't get over that—it feels like such abnormal behavior based on what we know of them."

"The counseling group is my assignment," said Ostler. "I'll talk to the police and learn what I can about it; Dr. Gentry, you stay with Brooke."

"What about Potash?" asked Nathan. "I'm not going back into that room without an armed guard and a license to kill."

"She's a teenage girl," I said, feeling anger surge up inside of me, but Ostler ignored the comment.

"If all goes well they'll release Potash in two days," said Ostler. She picked up the letter. "You have your assignments; go."

8

Potash got out of the hospital three days later; they gave him a cane, and refused to let him leave unless he used it, but he threw it out the car window almost as soon as we turned the corner. Diana told him to grow up, but she didn't backtrack to get it.

"I'm fine," said Potash, who was sitting in the backseat. I had expected him to have an oxygen tank or something, but he was breathing fine on his own; he had a hefty prednisone prescription, but that was it. "I was in there two and a half weeks," he said. "If they can't cure me in that time, what are they even doing?"

"You'll be weak for a bit," said Diana. "I've seen this with injured airmen—they spend a few days in the hospital, they neglect their fitness, and they think they can go right back to full capability the first day."

"I know what I'm doing," Potash growled.

"Do your exercises," said Diana. "Push yourself,

but don't push yourself too far. John, you make sure he doesn't work himself into a relapse."

"What makes you think I have any control over him?" I asked. "Let's send him to your place so you can do it."

Diana rolled her eyes, keeping her hands on the wheel. "Please stop arguing about this—he's staying with you, and that's Ostler's orders, and that's final. All his stuff's at your place anyway."

"He doesn't have any stuff," I said. "Four changes of identical clothes, and some blankets that have been officially ceded to Boy Dog."

"You went through my stuff?" he asked.

"I was making sure you didn't have any weapons," I said. *Which is code for "I was trying to find weapons."*

"Don't touch my stuff," said Potash.

"If you lived somewhere else I wouldn't."

"John . . . ," Diana growled.

We fell into an angry silence, and I thought about Elijah instead. How did his powers work? What was he doing? Why was he going to grief counseling, and visiting Merrill Evans, and everything else? What did he do that he didn't have to do?

He surrounded himself with death and darkness—the night shifts, the mortuary, the grief thing—and I could understand that. He lived the kind of life I'd love: no entanglements, no crowds, just peace and quiet and bodies to take care of. But I knew that I was different from most people, and most people don't like those things. Why was he so much like me? Is that why I wanted so badly for him not to be hunting us—for him not to be the bad guy? Because I wanted him to be like me?

"Diana," I said, "why would you surround yourself with death?"

"That's . . . kind of a deep question. Are you asking why I became a sniper?"

"No, I mean if you were Elijah. Or maybe, I don't know. Why did you become a sniper?"

"Don't pretend like you suddenly want to talk about me," said Diana. "If you just want to brainstorm that's fine, you don't have to get all awkward about it because I misunderstood you."

"I'm not pretending," I said. "I just want to know why someone would live like that—is he damaged? Is he scared? Maybe your feelings would help explain his; I'm just grasping at straws."

"So I'm damaged now?" asked Diana.

"*You* surround yourself with death," said Potash to me. "Why do *you* do it?"

"That's different—"

"Why?" he demanded.

I hesitated. "Because I enjoy it."

"Maybe Elijah does, too," said Diana. "He 'remembers' right? That's his power? Well, maybe it's like a memorial thing—he likes the solitude so he can pay his respects to the dead people he 'remembers.' You told me that was a big part of the job for you when you worked in your mother's mortuary."

"That doesn't hold together," I said. "If he liked death for the same reasons I like death, he wouldn't be at grief counseling."

"Because you don't get sad?" asked Diana.

"Because death is quiet," I said. My heart sped up, like I'd gotten a burst of adrenaline from somewhere, but I was just sitting in the car. "Death doesn't move, and it doesn't talk, and it doesn't . . . make noise." I almost said "yell," but that seemed so on-the-nose, it made me grimace just for thinking it. It wasn't even the full reason. Marci never yelled at me, and she was dead, too, and that didn't make me happy at all. My dad never yelled anymore, at least not where I could hear him, and he was still completely alive. The answer wasn't that easy. I mumbled for a minute, wondering what I'd even been talking about, trying to regain my footing in the conversation. "Grief counseling is a thing you do with people," I said at last. "They're alive, and you listen to them talk. I would never do that. He's not like me."

"Those counseling sessions are where people talk about the dead," said Diana. "They remember their loved ones. Maybe for Elijah it's something more—maybe he *needs* to remember, in order to survive. It's all about what they lack, right? So he needs other people's memories because he doesn't have his own. Maybe counseling helps keep those memories . . . fresh, or whatever."

"Except he's only done it the one time," I said. "We've been watching him for weeks, and he's only gone there once." And then there was the answer, just staring me in the face. "He's not remembering the dead," I said. "He's remembering the living."

"That's not grief counseling," said Diana. "That'd be some other therapy group."

"That's not what I mean."

"Nobody goes out of their way to remember the living," said Potash. "Not unless they're lost, like with the MIA memorial. The rest of the time we just remember the dead."

"We remember the dead because we're alive," I said. "Maybe for dead people it's the other way around." I felt my eyes grow hot as I spoke, threatening tears, but I gritted my teeth and blinked them away. "And that's who Elijah spends all his time with: dead people."

There was silence in the car for a moment, and then Diana began to nod. "Dead people from this community."

"Who else was at that grief session?" asked Potash.

"Exactly," I said. "If Elijah is absorbing the memories of the recently dead, those grief counseling sessions would be full of people he knows—or thinks he knows. He might be there to meet one in person, which is why he only started going recently. He's meeting someone related to a very recent death."

"I'm driving," said Diana, "one of you call Ostler."

"I'm already dialing," said Potash. We waited a moment, then heard him speak. "This is Potash. Do you have the notes from the police about that grief meeting?" Pause. "Read me the list of everyone who attended that night. Hang on a second, I'm writing them down. Delaney Anderson. Rose Chapman. Jude Feldman. Jared Garrett. Susan Roman. Is that all?" Pause. "We're just following up a lead. I'll call you if it goes anywhere."

I already had the mortuary number tapped in and ready to go. I hit send and waited while it rang.

"Good afternoon," said a woman's voice, "and thank you for calling Cochran Mortuary. How may I help you?"

"I need to talk to Mr. Cochran," I said. Like most mortuaries, this was a family business. We'd talked to Rudolfo Cochran before, in our official capacity as FBI; he knew we were investigating something, but he didn't know it was an employee. He'd promised not to tell anyone, thinking it was a matter of high security, and I hoped he'd kept that promise—if Elijah got word that we were investigating him at all, and especially if he knew we were this close, he might run. We didn't want to lose him.

A minute later the call transferred to another line, and rang a few more times before Cochran picked it up.

"This is Rudolfo Cochran speaking."

"This is John Cleaver from the FBI, we spoke last week."

"Yes," he said, "you were the young man?"

"Yes. We have some follow-up questions if you don't mind, and I remind you that this is of the utmost secrecy." Potash handed me his list, scrawled on the back of one of his hospital release forms. I read the names in order. "Have you had any business lately with a Delaney Anderson?"

"Let me pull up my records," he said. I heard a few mouse clicks through the phone, and some tapping of keys on a keyboard. "Delaney?"

"Correct."

"Nothing," he said.

"How about Jude Feldman?"

More keyboard clicks. "We have a Feldman in our system from two years ago, but it's not Jude."

That might mean something. "How about Rose Chapman?"

Click click click. I heard a soft musical beep as the search command was sent, and then Cochran gave a small "Oh." His voice grew more distant as he read the data. "Yes, we did a funeral about six weeks ago for a William Chapman, and Rose is on file as his wife. All the sales transactions were conducted through her."

I felt a surge of excitement. *I was right.* "Can you give me her contact information?" He read it off and I copied it down, and then, just to be thorough, I had him search for the last two names on the list as well. There was another almost match, from nearly ten years earlier, but that was it. I thanked him and hung up. "He was there to see Rose Chapman," I told the others. "He has her husband's memories." I gave Diana the address, and she changed course immediately. I did a search on my phone, finding a massive list of Rose Chapmans, and slowly narrowed it down to the one in Fort Bruce. I found her Facebook page and swore when I saw it.

"What's wrong?" asked Diana.

I showed her the screen, but she glanced at it only for a second before shaking her head and looking back at the road. "I can't look, just tell me."

"Let me see," said Potash.

I held the phone toward him. "I recognize her," I said. "She showed up in our surveillance photos, in the set we shot at the grocery store."

"The woman by the produce," said Potash.

"Exactly," I said. "He doesn't talk to anyone, ever, but he had a three-minute conversation with Rose Chapman in the produce section."

"He's stalking her," said Potash.

"He has her husband's memories," I said. "For all we know he thinks he *is* her husband."

"If he stalks dead people's families, why has that never shown up in our surveillance before?" Diana demanded. "This is the kind of thing that we're supposed to catch, dammit."

"Maybe it's new," I said. "Maybe he . . . I don't know. Maybe he has rules."

"Hurry," said Potash, and started another phone call.

"What do you mean, 'rules'?" asked Diana. "That doesn't have anything to do with it."

"Rules to keep himself from hurting anyone." I said. Did it

really make as much sense as I thought it did, or was I seeing reflections of myself where there weren't any? "After fifteen-something years at the mortuary, taking a new corpse's memories every I-don't-know-how-often, he's bound to have personal connections to half this town—he's somebody's father, he's somebody's mother, he's somebody's brother and son and best friend. He's literally surrounded by people he remembers being close to. But we've never seen him stalking anyone, except maybe Merrill, depending on your definition, and I guarantee that's because he makes rules for himself to avoid contact with people he knows." I thought about Marci, and what I'd do if some random person claimed to be her, returned from the grave. "He can't talk to those people without freaking them out, so he keeps a night shift and never talks to anyone."

"We need to check on Merrill," said Diana. "Maybe Merrill had a father or a brother or something who died right before Elijah started visiting him. But . . . why Merrill and Rose and nobody else? Why are they worth breaking the rules for?"

"I . . . don't know," I said. "Something's still not fitting." I closed my eyes, trying to remember as much of our surveillance info as I could. "We've never seen him hurt anyone. We've never seen him attack anyone, we've never found a body or a crime scene we can connect him to, we've never found anything 'bad.' "

"He gets his memories from dead bodies," said Diana. "If we're right."

"If," I said. I thought for a moment, listening as Potash gave the police Rose's address. *We're still missing something important.* I looked at Diana. "So what does Elijah do that he doesn't have to do?"

"You mean the grief counseling?"

"I mean everything. Like how his powers work. If we're right, he gets his memories from the corpses in the mortuary, but why?"

"Because he has to," said Diana. "Getting your memories from dead people means you'd be constantly filling up on the memories of actual death. He'd remember dying of old age, dying of cancer, dying in car accidents. If they've been around for ten thousand years he might remember dying a hundred thousand times—why put yourself through that if you don't have to?"

I hadn't thought of that, and it disturbed me that I hadn't. "That makes sense," I said slowly, "but that's still something he has to do. The question is what does he *not* have to do? Needing corpses isn't the same as needing the mortuary, because let's be honest: corpses are pretty easy to make. But he goes out of his way to use bodies that are already dead. He doesn't kill."

"Neither did Cody French," said Diana. "He was still a monster."

"Cody French drove girls insane," I said. "Elijah Sexton doesn't hurt anyone at all."

"He's not a good guy," said Diana. "He's a Withered—we kill the Withered, John, that's our whole job. It's our whole life."

"What if he's different?"

"He's not," she said harshly. "You heard Ostler: don't get soft. You're talking about a creature who's preyed on humanity for ten thousand years—"

"You don't know that."

"We don't know anything!" she said. "We're blind, even more so than when we hit Mary Gardner, and she killed Kelly because of it. If you go after Elijah Sexton with anything less than straight-up hatred you'll be dead, okay? He'll kill you and probably the rest of us with you, just like every other Withered has killed every other person they've ever messed with."

"Not everyone is evil," I said, almost irrationally desperate to convince her—or myself. "Just because you think someone's bad doesn't mean they are. And even if he was bad he could change."

"You're wrong, John," said Potash, hanging up his phone. His voice was cold and hard. "I just talked to the police, and when they put her name in her system they instantly hit a flag: her sister filed a missing-person report this morning. Rose Chapman's disappeared."

We were already most of the way to Rose Chapman's house, and thus arrived before anyone else. A car was in the driveway, though it and the sidewalk were covered with about an inch of snow; that was probably just from the previous night's storm, and it was far from the only snow-covered car on the block. More telling were the footprints leading from the curb to the porch—someone had pulled up, walked to the front door, then walked back out and driven away. I wasn't a good enough tracker to tell if the prints leading from the house were any different than the prints leading to it—like if the person was carrying a body, for example—but I was fairly certain there was only one set. Had Elijah come here, and kidnapped the woman he thought was his wife? I wanted to believe it wasn't him—that it was the three mystery Withered—but then why only one set of prints? I made a careful footprint of my own in the snow next to them, studying the comparison as Potash and Diana walked past me toward the door. The footprints were small—maybe it wasn't a Withered at all, but the sister who'd reported Rose as missing?

I want you to be good, Elijah. Please be good.

"Whoever walked up here went inside," said Potash, squatting by the front door. "They stomped the snow off their shoes onto the welcome mat, and then stepped in the pile on the way back out."

"How can you tell?"

He shrugged. "You get a feel for these things."

Diana rang the doorbell, and I trudged up the porch steps to join them. We waited a moment, rang again, then banged loudly on the door. Nothing.

"I'm declaring probable cause," said Diana, drawing her sidearm. Potash already had his out. I put my hand in my coat pocket, feeling the grip of the knife handle; I hadn't been without it in weeks. Diana looked at us, nodded, and kicked the door in.

The entryway showed no sign of a struggle, though it did have a few wet patches where someone had tracked in snow. The door didn't show any sign of forced entry, beyond Diana's kick. Whoever had come here had let themselves in peacefully, which meant they'd had a key. That implied it was the sister, and the condition of the tracks suggested she had come this morning, after the snow. The lack of any other prints meant Rose Chapman had disappeared before the snow, and without her car; probably a day or more before the snow, since the police didn't usually accept a missing-person report within the first twenty-four hours.

If the sister had been here and found nothing, we could probably move through the house safely, but after our experience with

Mary Gardner not one of us dropped our guard; Diana and Potash kept their guns up, and I pulled my knife silently from the sheath as we moved deeper into the house. I felt better with a knife in my hand, as if my hand had always been incomplete without it, and I'd only just now become whole. The front door opened directly into a living room, where the walls were hung with landscape paintings and a photo of what I assumed were Rose and William Chapman. Had she joined him in death? Was Elijah Sexton remembering both of their lives now?

Beyond the living room was a kitchen, and a short hall leading back into the rest of the house. We walked through each room slowly, checking behind doors and furniture, clearing each space as we went. A bathroom. A laundry room. A hall closet full of musty cardboard boxes. A master bedroom on one side of the hall, and a guest room on the other. There was no one in any of the rooms, living or dead. The master bedroom had a large sliding door leading out to the backyard: a small lawn on one side and an extended driveway on the other, leading back to a garage—but the snow back there was far deeper than in front and completely devoid of prints. It looked like no one had been back there all winter. Potash checked the last closet and shook his head.

"Nothing."

"Most houses in this town have a basement," said Diana, "but I didn't see an entrance anywhere. Maybe it's outside?"

"We would have seen tracks in the snow if anyone had used it recently," said Potash. He glanced outside, breathing heavily. "It's worth checking out, though." He unlocked the sliding door, but Diana put a hand on his arm.

"I'll go, you just got out of the hospital." She opened the door and stepped out. "I'll call you if it looks sketchy. See what else you can find, but don't leave any fingerprints." She closed the door behind her.

"Of course I'm not going to leave fingerprints," Potash grumbled. "Am I an idiot?"

I ignored him and started looking through the piles of stuff on the nightstands and dresser, using the knife to move things without touching them directly. People who were kidnapped tended to leave key personal items behind, the kind of things they were usually never without: keys, wallets, purses, phones. If we could find one of those, we might also find some personal info we could use, like a schedule or a contact list of people she'd talked to recently. A smartphone would be a gold mine—depending on what settings she'd turned on or off, we could know not just who she'd called, but when she'd done it and where she was standing at the time. I found a few papers that might be useful later, funeral receipts and so on, but nothing that helped me now. I turned to go down the hallway, heading back to the living room to continue the search, when Potash's phone rang. I turned back to listen.

"This is Potash." Pause. "We're inside now; there's no direct evidence of kidnapping, but the car's in the driveway and it's pretty clear nobody slept here last night. That's not damning, but it's definitely suspicious."

Diana opened the back door, kicking the snow off her feet before coming inside. "Nothing in the basement but a furnace and some storage." She batted at her hair with a grimace. "And every spider within ten miles."

I nodded at Potash. "He's on the phone with Ostler, I think."

"Bad news?" asked Diana.

"Do we ever get good news?"

"We'll be right there," said Potash. He hung up and looked at us. "Cops'll be here in about five minutes; we'll let them take over the crime scene while we head back to the morgue."

"Rose?" asked Diana.

Potash shook his head. "No, but still bad. Another cannibal attack." He looked at me. "And another letter for John."

To Mr. John Wayne Cleaver, and his Esteemed Colleagues,

Hello again. It is, as always, a pleasure to write to you, though I admit I haven't given you much of a chance to respond since my previous letter. Worse still, I haven't given you the means to respond, and for this I am truly sorry. Only a churl would be content with a one-sided conversation, and I assure you that I am not such a boor as to talk and talk about myself without ever letting you respond.

In light of that, let me suggest a number of options that might facilitate a more interactive discussion. The option you are considering first is simply to capture me, but I assure you that this is ridiculous. You will neither catch me nor even find me. Option number two is equally unlikely, but in the opposite direction: you could simply communicate in kind by killing a victim of your own and leaving a note pinned for me to find. While I can promise you I would find such a note, I imagine your superiors would be displeased with the manner of its delivery. Until such time as you no longer care what they think, we must find another way of communicating.

Option three, then, might be one to consider: you could publish a letter in the newspaper. It would not be the first time the police have sent messages this way. This method has some sub-options, as you could choose to be brazen about the message—my unfinished meals are already headline news, after all—or you could couch it in secrecy, burying it in a coded letter to the editor in which only every second word counts. Title it something about lions and antelopes, if you do, so I'll know where to look.

But in the end, why bother with all of this rigmarole? If you've been paying attention, you know who I'm going to kill next. Slip a note in his pocket, and I'll have something to read while I eat.

Yours,
The Hunter

P.S.—I was extremely gratified to learn that Mr. Potash is recovering so quickly. May his restored health bring him as much happiness as possible before the end.

"*Dios mio*," said Dr. Trujillo.

"Where's the body?" I asked.

"Still in the autopsy," said Ostler, gesturing at the police station's examination room behind us. "Barring any shocking discoveries, though, the story's the same as last time: a middle-aged person, female this time, found mostly naked with her body covered in bite wounds. Head and neck undamaged. The note was pinned to her chest."

"Pinned?" asked Nathan.

"With a safety pin," said Ostler. "Keep in mind, she wasn't wearing a shirt."

"The weirdest part of this job," said Diana, "is that none of that counts as a shocking discovery."

Potash sat down, breathing in slow, controlled breaths.

"Why does he keep addressing them to John?" asked Nathan. "I want to know what that's all about."

"He mentioned Potash, too," I said.

"But they're *to* you," said Nathan. "When he said he wanted to start a conversation, he was talking to you specifically. When he suggested that we murder somebody, that was also to you."

I looked at Potash, and found him staring at me. He was still the only one who knew about my brutal stabbing of Mary Gardner.

He didn't say anything.

"He used John's name because he was trying to show off," said Trujillo. "Everything about these letters—the tone, the vocabulary, even the message itself—is a deliberate attempt to exert control over us by showing his superiority. Not just showing it, but hammering it home with all the subtlety of an oversized cartoon mallet. He wants us to be afraid of him, and part of that is showing what he knows about us: John's name and Potash's health."

"Well it's working," said Nathan. "Once again, I humbly request that we pack the hell up and leave this town ASAP."

"You've never done anything humbly in your life," said Diana.

"All he's really showing us are his limits," I said. "He knows my name because my picture was on the Internet, and he put it together and knows who I am. He knows Potash's name because it's on record at the hospital. Those are the only two members of our team with an easily researched identity—even Brooke is registered under an alias at Whiteflower. The only things he knows about us are the things anyone could know about us."

"Maybe there's more to come," said Ostler. "He could know everything, and just be rolling it out slowly, one snippet at a time."

"That's going to mean a lot of chewed-up corpses before he finishes," said Diana.

"I don't think so," I said. "I think he's actively researching us while we're researching him. Read the header again."

Ostler looked at the paper: " 'To Mr. John Wayne Cleaver, and his Esteemed Colleagues.' "

"He used my middle name," I said. "He didn't do that before."

Nathan sniffed. "So your evidence that he's not revealing information one piece at a time is that he's revealing information one piece at a time?"

"I'm saying that it isn't new information," I said. "Dropping Potash's name at the end was a shocker, but did any of you flinch when he said my middle name? Did any of you even notice? We already knew that he knew who I was—revealing my middle name doesn't change that. So either he knew the name before and forgot to mention it, which isn't exactly menacing, or he just figured it out and he's showing off. If it's the former, who cares? If it's the latter, then we know he's figuring this out as he goes."

"The next letter will tell us more," said Trujillo. "If he mentions Brooke's alias instead of her real name, we know he has flawed information. If he mentions Ostler's name, we know he has a connection to the police, since they're the only ones who know her. If he mentions any of the rest of us, it'll be more troubling, but it will still be something to go on to trace his information back to the source."

"Unless he can read minds, like we discussed before," said Nathan. "Then he could know everything, and any information trail we think we see would be an illusion."

"I don't want to find any more letters," said Ostler firmly. "He says we should have him figured out by now—that we have enough clues to know who the next victim is. So let's figure him out and stop him."

"Who was the victim this time?" asked Trujillo.

"Valynne Maetani," said Ostler, and she held up an evidence bag with the victim's ID. "Her wallet was still in her purse. I made some calls while you were en route, and she works at a software company. Project manager, if that means anything."

"The first victim worked in a hardware store," said Diana, and she looked at Trujillo. "What's the link?"

I felt a small pang of anger that everyone continued to ask him these questions instead of me, but at least it gave me the time to think about the letter in more detail. Was the killer just using my name to scare us, or was he really talking straight to me? If he'd looked me up he'd have found my connection to Crowley and Forman, and if he knew anything about the wider Withered community, he probably knew about Nobody as well. He knew that I'd killed people. And now he was asking me to kill again.

"The occupation of the victims probably has nothing to do with it," said Trujillo, looking at the bagged ID. "Serial-killer brains don't really work that way, though I admit there are exceptions to everything. It's also unlikely that he's targeting a specific demographic, since so far he's killed both genders, and two different races—Maetani was Asian."

My head snapped up. "Really?"

"Do you have a problem with that?" asked Nathan.

"I have a problem with Ostler holding back key information," I said. "If he really does know us as well as he claims, then killing an Asian woman might be a reference to Kelly." I looked at Potash. "And if killing a white guy was a reference to Potash, we might have a pattern."

"Great," said Nathan. "So he's consuming us all in effigy? Does that mean the next victim's going to be a black research professor, or will any black guy do?"

"Don't jump to conclusions," said Trujillo. "It's far more likely that he's just taking targets of opportunity when and where he can. It's hard enough finding a victim he can kill without being seen—never mind complicating it with races and genders and who knows what else. The simplest explanation is that he has a specific hunting ground—one location or one type of location—and the victims all come from there." He looked at Ostler. "Was the body found anywhere near the first one?"

"Opposite sides of the city," said Ostler. "And she was dumped by a train crossing instead of stuffed in an alleyway Dumpster. That's not much of a link."

"A train crossing will have a camera," said Potash. "There might be footage of the killer, or at least the car."

"The police are already looking into it," said Ostler.

I was staying silent because I didn't know how to feel—or I

guess you could say I was feeling too many things at once. I was angry that Trujillo had shot down my idea, but impressed that his own idea made so much sense, and then angry again that he would dare to be so good at something I considered my own personal domain. And then I was embarrassed for feeling so petty about it, and I was worried if I was right, and I was frustrated we hadn't found anything solid yet, and I was mad at Nathan, and scared for Brooke, and fascinated by this new killer—and all I wanted to do was get out, and away, and be by myself, even if it was just for a minute. Even just half a minute. Maybe just forever.

Trujillo tapped his chin. "Let's consider that where the bodies were dumped might have nothing to do with where they were killed. He might have pulled them from the same area and then scattered them around the city to stay hidden, or simply to throw us off."

There had to be more than that. I knew it. The killer had written us two letters—he had to have given us a clue, even if it was only by accident.

"We didn't see an obvious link between their home or work addresses," said Ostler, "but maybe their commutes take them along a similar path? Or they cross at a specific point? I'll have the police look into it, but we need something stronger. I won't let this man eat anyone else."

Eating. It was right there all along.

I dug in my pocket for my copy of the first letter, now worn smooth by my pocket, and sharply creased along the edge. "What were the new victim's stomach contents?"

"You think those matter?" asked Nathan. It was a typically snarky question from him, though his face seemed more confused than confrontational. "Is that really a thing—a killer that targets people who eat the same foods?"

"Not the same foods, but at the same places," I said. I pulled out the letter and unfolded it, bending the creases backward to help it lay flat. "In the first letter he told us Stephen Applebaum's stomach contents, to prove he was the real killer, but then he also mentioned that he watched him eat. Here it is: 'His stomach contents, as I assume you've been informed, will have included two slices of pizza—I was too far away to see the toppings.' He picked a mark, watched him eat, and then killed him after. Probably very soon after. These letters are constructed so carefully—that's got to mean something."

Ostler considered this a moment, then walked to the examination room and opened the door. "Excuse me, gentlemen, but have you examined the stomach contents yet?" I heard murmuring, but couldn't make it out. "And what were they?" More murmuring. "Thank you." She closed the door and turned to face us. "Pizza. Diana, I want you to get in Detective Scott's face and find out exactly where both victims ate dinner the night they were killed."

"Yes ma'am." Diana left immediately, and Potash stood up. Ostler walked slowly back to our misshapen circle.

"We can't monitor every person who eats at a pizza place for the next several weeks. It's impossible."

"We can put someone on the restaurant itself, though, right?" asked Nathan. "I mean, that's better than nothing. At the very least we can watch for anyone eating there who matches our team's demographics."

Ostler looked at me. "What else does this letter tell us?"

It took all my willpower not to glance at Trujillo, gloating in petulant triumph that she'd asked me instead of him. "He's given us the biggest clue yet," I said. "He named himself."

"We already know his name," said Nathan. "Or . . . maybe. We don't know if the cannibal is Gidri or one of his thugs, but either way the name's not going to help us."

"His real name wouldn't," I agreed, "not with Brooke still too upset about Gidri to talk to us. But this letter has something even better: he picked a name for *himself.* He could call himself anything in the world, and he chose The Hunter. That speaks volumes."

"And that's meaningful how?" asked Nathan. "It's just the same old metaphor about lions and antelopes."

"In that metaphor he called himself a predator," I said. "A hunter is different. Whether he intended to or not, he's telling us that the hunt itself is important—not just eating the victim, but finding them, chasing them. Matching wits with them. He sees himself as a hunter."

Nathan raised his eyebrow. "And his quarry is a bunch of slobs at a pizza place?"

Trujillo's voice was grave. "His quarry is us."

"I think we can get more specific than that," said Ostler. "If the demographic theory holds, the two victims so far represent two of the three people who killed Mary Gardner." Her eyes fell on me. "You were the third, and he already knows your name."

9

There was an old park on the outskirts of Fort Bruce—a wide lawn and a little playground, now piled with snow and empty for the winter. The picnic area held a few tables and pair of state-sponsored barbecue grills: thick metal boxes, rusted orange with age, each one sitting on a rusty metal pole. The boxes were open on the top and the front, with a heavy metal grill that could fold up and down. Snow sat on top of them in lumpy drifts, sagging into the gaps between the grill bars. I set my box of store-bought firewood on a snowy picnic table and used a broken plank to clear the snow from the nearest grill, pushing it away in long, even strokes, and then rattling the board between the clanging metal sides.

Boy Dog whined and crawled under the picnic table, crouching in the cavelike hollow that had formed where the snow couldn't reach.

"Stop being such a wimp," I told him. "You're a

dog in a park—go chase a squirrel or something. Eat a bunny rabbit. Reclaim your birthright as a wild animal." He growled pitiably and dropped his head on his paws.

"Yeah," I said, just to have something to say. I tilted up the grill, which let out a metallic squeal, and started to build my fire. There are plenty of ways to build a fire, but I tend to use a method called the log cabin: thin sticks, laid out in a square, with larger and larger sticks on top of them to build up the walls. I wasn't supposed to light fires, but that was just a self-imposed rule: there was no law against it. The city had built these stupid metal boxes expressly to light fires in. There was nothing wrong with it.

Except that I'd told myself not to do it, and now here I was.

I built the log cabin about four inches high, and then built a larger one around it. The flames would start on the smallest sticks at the bottom of the center, and then slowly spread up and out until the entire thing was on fire. I had nothing against a good accelerant, of course—sometimes you needed a good dose of gasoline or lighter fluid to save time—but if you built it right, all you really needed was the wood and a single match. I prided myself on doing it right. I studied my layout, crouching down to see inside, choosing exactly where I'd place the match, and when I was satisfied I pulled out a matchbook and ripped out a single cardboard stick. I folded the book backward, pressing the bulbous chemical head between the starter strip and the outer flap, and ripped them apart. The friction ignited the chemicals, which flared to life in a sputtering yellow flame. I cupped it in my hands to keep it safe.

"Think I can do it in one match?"

Boy Dog gave a noncommittal whine.

"You've never supported me in my dreams, Boy Dog," I said. "I could have been the best arsonist there ever was, but you wanted me to go to law school." I leaned in close to the log cabin, and gently held the match to the prime lighting spot I'd made out of twigs and splinters; it caught, and I dropped the match and watched the yellow flames turn orange as they found more fuel to burn. The metal was still wet from the snow, but as the fire heated up, the damp disappeared—it didn't hiss or steam, but seemed as if it simply ceased to exist.

This was my pressure valve. When everything else was just too much to take, and all my . . . rage, I guess. Confusion. Energy. When all of the emotions I'd never known how to deal with finally built up so high that I thought I would burst, I lit a fire and let them out, and everything was good again.

Except it wasn't working.

Ostler thought I was the next victim, but I knew I wasn't. The letters were addressed to me—he wanted me to kill. I had a copy of both letters now, and pulled them out to read again. They weren't written to the team as a whole, but directly to me. The key was in the middle of the second one: "I imagine your superiors would be displeased with the manner of its delivery. Until such time as you no longer care what they think, we must find another way of communicating." It was one thing to ask for a corpse as a message; it was another thing completely to suggest that the only thing stopping me from doing it was the approval of my "superiors." He was implying, or perhaps suggesting, that without Ostler and the others keeping me reined in, I'd be out there killing, just like him. Was that true? I'd managed to get by for sixteen years without any of them controlling me and I'd never killed anyone. Except the Withered, of course. If I didn't have the team, would I be out there killing Withered? Of course I would. Nobody else's Marci would ever have to die if I could do something to stop it. Technically, I was killing the Withered even with the team, but I was sick of having them around and I knew I could work better without them. What had the team gotten me so far? A bunch of running around, my picture on the Internet, and almost zero new info about the cannibal or Elijah or anyone else. It was nice to have access to the forensic files now that I didn't have my own mortuary to examine the bodies, but frankly I'd have been a whole lot happier with the mortuary. I found myself envying Elijah, and not for the first time. He was alone, and he had the dead to keep him company. It was the best of both worlds.

"Until such time as you no longer care what they think." Did I care what they thought? They didn't care what I thought. I had to fight just to make myself heard in our meetings; I was the child prodigy, brought in as a specialist, but they never let me do anything. Not the way I wanted to do it. I worked by getting to know the Withered, by slipping in the back door of their lives and listening while they talked. That's what I'd done with Cody French and Mary Gardner, but we couldn't do it now. I'd met Elijah once, but I'd never found a way to speak to him again; the few times he'd come back to Whiteflower I'd been out on other assignments, coffee runs, stakeouts of empty buildings, and stupid things that anyone else could have done—but I was the kid so why not send me? And forget about getting to know The Hunter. Gidri and his mystery companions had an uncanny knack of giving the slip to police surveillance, and we had no idea where any of them were. It was hard to disguise yourself as the boy next door when you didn't know what door to be next to.

Brooke had lived next door to me. I'd watched her through her window at night, watched her sleep. Now she was trapped in that room, and I was trapped out here, and I just wanted to—

One, one, two, three, five, eight, thirteen, twenty-one.

"Until such time as you no longer care what they think, we must find another way of communicating." It was a message for me, I was sure of it. So why not send one back? I couldn't kill someone, obviously, but I could do a letter to the editor. What would I even say? "Hi, this is John, tell me about yourself." I was hunting him, not dating him. And, of course, as soon as I put a letter in the paper the others would know it—the protocol was laid out right there in his note: the headline and the code phrase and everything. I couldn't talk to The Hunter without Ostler and Nathan and everybody else freaking out. I was hemmed in. They wouldn't let me work, they wouldn't let me talk, they wouldn't let me do anything. I crumpled the letter in my fist, only to growl at the sheer uselessness of such a gesture.

The fire was mewling, even more piteously than Boy Dog. A fire was a thing of chaos, the ultimate expression of life and freedom, and in this tiny metal box it had nowhere to go, nothing to do, nothing to eat but the little I gave it. It made me sick to look at it, so anemic and wasted, and I used another plank of wood to lever it out, dumping it on the ground to watch as the flames hissed against the snow and sputtered and died, too disorganized to maintain their heat. I kicked a pile of snow over the blackened patches of wood and then suddenly I was stomping on them, jumping up and down, screaming in a wordless rage at the sheer wrongness of the entire world. It didn't work, it didn't make sense, it didn't do anything the way it was supposed to. The way I wanted it to. Boy Dog waddled out of his table cave and howled, with me or at me I couldn't tell, and I jumped and growled and stomped on the boards, but they didn't have anything to break against, and after a while I collapsed onto a snowy bench, exhausted. I didn't know if the tears in my eyes were from sadness or the bitter cold.

I had a heart now, but I didn't know how to use it.

Boy Dog barked a few more times, his hidden stores of energy not yet spent, and then shuffled toward me and put his head on my leg. I put my hands on my head, like I was being arrested, too worried that if I touched the dog I'd try to hurt it, to break it like I hadn't been able to break the wood. I closed my eyes and the tears came faster.

I needed to talk to Brooke. She couldn't help me and I couldn't help her but she was all I had, the only hint of the life I used to know. I stood up as gently as I could, dislodging Boy Dog as gingerly as possible, and fished in my pocket for my phone. I'd turned it off when I'd slipped away from Potash—he was supposed to stay with me like before, my babysitter again now that he'd gotten out of the hospital. But he'd been in a meeting with Ostler so I'd slipped away, with nothing but a text message to let them know I hadn't been kidnapped. I saw The Hunter's letters on the ground, trampled in the ash and snow. I picked them up and wadded them into a ball, waiting while the phone booted up. There was no sense leaving any evidence that I was the one who'd been here.

My phone chirped hysterically when it connected to the network, and I glowered at the thought of how many angry messages I was sure to have. I scrolled through the list—thirteen texts and twenty-one calls. They must really be pissed. I started dialing Trujillo's number, to tell him I was coming in to Whiteflower, when suddenly my phone rang. It was Diana.

"Hello?"

"Dammit, John, where the hell have you been?"

"Secret dance lessons," I said, "what's going on?"

"Get to the mortuary immediately—as fast as you can. We found Rose."

I looked at my car, a hundred feet away through the snow. "What? At the mortuary?"

"Are you running?" she demanded.

"Yes," I said, and broke into a run. Boy Dog followed, panting with exertion. We still didn't know who had kidnapped Rose, but finding her at the mortuary meant one of two things: either Elijah had taken her there, or she'd shown up the way most people show up at a mortuary. "Is Rose dead?" I asked. "Did Elijah kill her?"

"Elijah's not even here," said Diana. "Gidri's gang showed up about forty-five minutes ago, with Rose slung over their shoulder—we haven't dared make contact so we don't know what condition she's in."

So Gidri kidnapped Rose? But why? Did Elijah tell him to? Was Elijah the leader of the whole wretched group?

We could figure out why later—first things first. "Don't make contact," I said. "Every human in that building will die."

"That's the problem," said Diana. "The cops won't believe us—they still think this is some kind of drug ring and they're gathering at the gas station around the corner."

"Gathering?"

"Armed and armored," said Diana. "They're going to go in."

I screeched to a stop on the edge of a crowd of cop cars, their lights turned off in the hope that the mortuary half a block away wouldn't know they were there. I left Boy Dog in the passenger seat, hoping that he'd be okay—would I be back soon? Would he freeze? I couldn't hurt him or allow him to be hurt; I had to follow my rules. I hovered a moment in indecision, then ran toward Agent Ostler.

"Where have you been?" she snapped.

"Selling cigarettes to children," I said. "Have they gone in yet?"

"Do they look like they've gone in?" She pointed to the massing crowd of police in armored vests and helmets, clutching assault rifles as Detective Scott gave them a final briefing. Fort Bruce was too small for a real SWAT team, but in every situation they typically encountered, this group would be enough. This was not a typical situation.

I counted them as quickly as I could. "Looks like eighteen guys? Against four Withered?"

"And all four are here now," said Diana, walking toward us. She had a bulletproof vest of her own, with a small radio handset clipped to a strap on the shoulder. "Elijah drove up right after I talked to you. That puts him twenty minutes late to work, if that means anything."

Ostler sneered. "It's a miracle he didn't drive past this . . . bonehead parade. Surprise might be our only real weapon here, but it's better than nothing."

"Are you going in, too?" I asked Diana. "That's a death trap in there."

Detective Scott approached with a frown, his handheld radio squawking. "This is your last chance to be straight with me," he said. "We're not going to let that woman die, but that'd be a whole lot easier if you'd just tell me what my men are going to find in there."

"I've told you before," said Ostler. "They are ancient creatures we don't even begin to understand—"

"They are not vampires!" Scott hissed. "They're not ghosts or goblins or whatever other lies you keep insisting on telling me. I have eighteen good men, with families at home, and if you can't stop this charade long enough to tell them the truth—"

"Don't send them," said Ostler. "If you refuse to believe anything else I say, at least listen to this: anyone you send in there will die, and you will not blame me for being anything less than clear about that."

Boy Dog howled from my car, lost and primal.

"You're not a part of this community," said Scott. "You can waltz around here and watch our people get killed and kidnapped and then you can leave, but we have a responsibility here. We have to get up every morning and tell our neighbors we're doing everything we can to protect them, and if that means going in there, then that's what we do. It's eighteen on four, with no sign of heavy weapons on any of the suspects. We have to take this chance."

"Send them in," I said.

"He doesn't have the authority to give you that permission," said Ostler quickly.

"And she doesn't have the authority to stop you," I said. "You go, you do your thing, but you remember what she told you."

The detective's voice dropped, and he spoke through clenched teeth. "What is this?"

"It's a war," I said. "It's been in the shadows for centuries—for millennia maybe—but if you're determined to start the first real battle, we can't stop you."

Scott looked back and forth among the three of us, then stormed off with a snarl. "Bunch of freaks."

"What are you doing?" Ostler demanded.

"Communicating," I said bitterly. "The Hunter wants a corpse, and the police are determined to die. It's a win-win."

"I'm going with them," said the radio on Diana's shoulder, and I realized it was Potash's voice, rough with static.

"Stay in the car," said Diana. "You can barely breathe."

"No," said Ostler, "I'm sending you both—first in the door, since you're the only personnel with any experience fighting Withered. If we can save even one of these idiots' lives, we will."

"Yes ma'am," said Diana, and she ran off with her rifle—not her long sniper, but a short automatic that would be better in close quarters.

Ostler handed me a radio. "If you have any brilliant insights, now's the time to let them know. They're the only people who can fight these monsters, but you're the only person who can think like one."

I looked at the radio in my hand, then back at Ostler. "No radio silence?"

"The cops are going to be broadcasting the whole time anyway."

"All right then." I paused. "Do you and I get vests, too?"

"You're not going in there," she said firmly.

"And you're so sure that what's in there isn't coming out?"

She frowned, but walked to her car and opened the trunk, revealing an array of armor and weapons. I took off my bulky coat, shivering in the night air, and pulled on a vest. Ostler did the same. I clipped the radio to a strap on the front and switched it on.

Words hissed across the radio channel like ghosts.

"Team One in position."

"Team Two move to the back entrance." It sounded like Detective Scott, but I couldn't be sure. "Team Three, stay here to cover the retreat."

"Potash," said Diana, "you need to hurry it up."

The only answer from Potash was labored breathing and the sound of boots in the snow.

"Form up along this wall," said Detective Scott. "Weapons hot."

"Shoot anything that moves," I said. "Chairs, shadows, cats, I don't even care. Anything you don't kill will kill you."

Ostler scowled. "That's your great advice?"

I laughed dryly. "If you thought the raid on Mary Gardner was reckless and stupid, you ain't seen nothing yet."

"You're broadcasting," said Diana.

"Go team," I said. "We're all out here cheering for you."

I should be in there, I thought. Not part of this raid, but the only one on the raid, and instead of a raid it would just be quiet, unassuming John Cleaver, picking up a night job to make a few extra bucks. I could learn about the hearses, dazzle Elijah with my knowledge of mortuary life, and over weeks and months find the cracks in his armor. I could kill him if they gave me time.

But there was never any time anymore. The war had started and this was its future: terrified men without a hope of survival, future corpses lining up for The Hunter to eat.

Elijah absorbed memories from the dead. The Hunter ate people and possibly controlled their minds. Gidri we had no idea about, and we didn't even have a name for the final man. I had nothing I could tell the team.

"Go," said Diana, and the hiss of the radio was joined by the click of a lock opening, of a door swinging wide, of weapons being readied. Boots thumped and spare magazines jangled.

"They're arguing," Diana whispered. "No, they're fighting. Something's gone wrong."

I heard crashes and a loud, feminine scream that was probably Rose, followed by an inhuman roar whose origin I could only guess at. Seconds later the channel erupted in the sound of gunfire, and I heard Diana shout "Potash, fall back!"

What could I tell them that could save their lives? That Elijah should have been good? That kidnapping Rose felt like a betrayal I didn't even understand? I heard Potash's ragged breath and something that sounded for all the world like an axe biting into wood. The woman screamed again, and then I heard Diana's voice, her words short and clipped.

"I have one still alive in here but I can't hit him without hurting the woman."

"So try harder," I said, but something didn't feel right. She'd said she had "one still alive." Were all but one of the cops already dead? But I could still hear them shouting over the radio. Was she talking about a Withered, then? Did she have one of them already dead and another alive but not killing her? How was that even possible? Unless they weren't Withered at all.

"I need backup," said Diana. She sounded like her teeth were clenched tightly shut from fear. "He's healing."

So they were definitely Withered. What was going on?

"Please don't shoot us," said Rose, barely audible through Diana's radio, and I froze. *Don't shoot us.* She'd said "us." One of the Withered was still alive, so close to Rose that Diana couldn't risk a shot. And now Rose was pleading for his life.

I started running.

"John, come back!" shouted Ostler, but I ignored her and sprinted to the mortuary, shouting into the radio: "Don't hurt Elijah!" I'd been right about him: he was good. He wasn't working with Gidri and he hadn't kidnapped Rose. She was defending him. The only way the other Withered could have already fallen was if Elijah himself had attacked them.

He was good.

"Officer down," said a man on the radio. "Repeat, officer d— no, two down!"

So there was at least one Withered still up. I had to go carefully. I ran past Team Three, ignoring their warning as I dashed through the door. The hallway inside was a chaos of light and dark, and far at the end I could see Potash and a group of police locked in combat with what looked like a thick, spiny rosebush. Halfway down the hall was a bright doorway, yellow light spilling out into the corridor, so that's where I ran.

It was Elijah's office and it was devastated. Furniture was smashed and overturned and blood and ash covered the floor. Elijah stood in the far corner, his chest sliced open; blood and soulstuff spilled out in thick rivulets, greasy and black. Behind him was Rose Chapman, covered with cuts and bruises, staring out in wide-eyed terror, and against the opposite wall stood

Diana, her rifle trained on them both. Between them on the floor lay three bodies: the first I recognized as Jacob Carl, Elijah's counterpart on the day shift; he sprawled against the wall with his eyes wide open and his head twisted nearly backwards. Beside him was the tallest of the Withered, completely inert, and closest to me lay Gidri—young and handsome and still as the grave. I stepped toward him, feeling the familiar rush at the sight of a corpse—but no. His chest was moving. He was alive. I looked at the other Withered and saw the same. They didn't have any visible wounds. I stooped over Gidri to examine him closer. How had this happened?

But of course there was only one answer.

"You drained them?" I asked. Elijah moved his mouth but no sound came out; the slash across his chest must have damaged his voice.

"He can only drain dead bodies," said Diana.

"Obviously not," I said. I touched Gidri's throat, feeling his pulse. "If they were dead they'd turn to ash. That means he incapacitated them, and draining their minds is the only weapon he has." It looked like he'd drained so much of their memories they couldn't even think anymore, couldn't even stand. They were infants—worse than infants. They were hollow shells.

"What are you talking about?" asked Rose.

Potash appeared in the door behind me, covered in blood and grease and splinters. His machete dangled from his fingers; he didn't try to speak but simply gasped for breath. Beyond him the police were calling for medics, and I knew they'd won their fight. That shouldn't have happened—we should have all been dead. But Elijah had turned on his own kind, and turned their four-monster army into a lone, desperate runner, and suddenly the odds were in our favor. We'd won because of Elijah.

Diana seemed to be thinking the same thing, but it hadn't convinced her. "Protocol says we kill him anyway—"

"Protocol can wait," I said, and I looked at Elijah. If he could drain the living, why didn't he? What was stopping him from draining my memories, or Diana's, or Rose's? He could drop us in seconds, and we'd never even remember that he'd gotten away. But instead he stood there and watched me, and his face didn't show fear or determination or anything else I would have expected in a battle scene. The corners of his mouth turned down, his brow wrinkled over his eyes. He was sad.

We'd thought he was forced to use dead memories because no one would ever take them if they could take living ones instead. We'd had him completely backwards—he could take living memories just fine, but he chose not to. What were we missing? What made a living man's memories so much worse than a dead one's? Why should he be so sad about a living man with no—

And then everything made sense.

"These aren't the first people you've drained without killing," I said.

His face, already sad, collapsed into a despair so deep it seemed to draw me down with it. "I never want to kill," he said. His voice sounded ragged and raw, as if the gash in his chest were only half healed inside. "I thought I could . . . sustain myself without hurting anyone, but it was all wrong. I never meant to hurt him."

"Who?" asked Diana.

"Merrill Evans," I said, and Elijah closed his eyes. How had it happened, I wondered? Some night, twenty years ago, when Elijah's mind was fading and he was desperate for more memories to fill it. The only sustenance he really needed, but not a body anywhere to take it from. Perhaps he'd gotten sloppy? Perhaps he'd let it go too long? And then he was stranded, without a mind to call his own, and there was Merrill Evans. "It isn't really Alzheimer's," he'd told me that day in the lobby. Elijah had broken a man's mind, and that knowledge hurt him more than any death ever could, because he'd done it himself.

I didn't know how a lot of things felt, but I knew what it felt like to fail someone.

Elijah sank to his knees.

"I have a shot," said Diana.

"Wait," I said fiercely. Elijah couldn't die here—not like this. I looked at Rose. "We're with a special branch of the FBI and we're here to rescue you. We have an ambulance outside." I pointed at Diana. "Will you go with my friend, here?"

"Will you tell me what's going on?" asked Rose.

I nodded. "Outside." She hesitated, probably still in shock from the last few hours. But after a moment, she stepped around Elijah and took Diana's hand. She led Rose out, casting me a glance halfway between hope and fear, and then they disappeared into the hall.

"How did you know about us?" asked Elijah. His voice was better now; he was healing quickly.

I wanted to trust him but I was still too cautious to tell him everything right up front. "We have what you might call an informant."

"Another Withered?"

Close enough. "Friend of a friend."

He nodded, as if this made some kind of satisfying sense. "Who are you?"

"My name's John Cleaver," I said. I realized that this was the first time I'd introduced myself to a Withered—the first time, maybe, that any official overture had been made between the groups. I wanted to add more circumstance to the occasion but I didn't have any authority or even a title . . . and then a sudden whim took me and I couldn't help the small smile that crept into the corner of my mouth. "Professional psychopath."

He studied me a moment before speaking. "Why didn't you kill me?"

"The war I assume Gidri warned you about is real," I said. I pointed at the carnage in the room, at the blood and ash and destruction. "I take it you didn't like his offer, so I'd like you to hear mine."

He closed his eyes. "I don't want to kill them."

"You didn't kill these."

"Just wait." He paused, and I wondered what he was thinking about. "They're my brothers," he said at last. "Not literally, but . . . we're the same."

"Don't insult yourself," I said.

His silence stretched out, broken only by Potash's labored breathing in the background. After what felt like ages, Elijah spoke again, and his voice was soft and distant.

"We had such dreams, you know. Back in the beginning. I don't even remember it all now, it was so long ago, but I remember the excitement—the thrill and the power, the dreams of immortality. We were going to rule the world. I guess we did, for a while." He swept his hand across the cramped, bloody room. "Now look at us."

"They're organizing," I said. "Counting these two and the one in the hall, we've stopped five in this city alone, and that's set them back, but there are others. You know that better than I do. They're out there and they're killing, and we need to stop them. You don't even have to do it yourself, just tell us what you know." I looked at Gidri and his comatose companion. "Which one was the cannibal?"

"Cannibal?"

"One of them was sending us notes," I said, "pinned to his half-eaten victims."

"Neither of them eats people," said Elijah, and pointed at the Withered in turn. "Gidri steals youth, and Ihsan steals skin. They've always gotten along."

I frowned, fearing the worst but not daring to say it yet. "The thorny guy in the hall?"

"I don't think he eats at all," said Elijah.

Potash's voice was a ragged whisper. "Looks like we're not done with this town yet."

10

"I don't remember everything," said Elijah.

"Great," said Nathan. "Two inside sources and they're both broken."

"Quiet," said Ostler.

Nathan shrugged. "He can't hear me."

We were sitting in the police station, watching Elijah through a one-way mirror. He was alone in the interrogation room, manacled hand and foot and chained to a hook in the floor. Volunteer or not, he hadn't earned anyone's trust yet.

The cameras and voice recorders had all been disabled at Ostler's request. Nothing we said would be recorded. She thumbed the button for the microphone and asked him our first question: "Tell us about Rose Chapman."

"She's a . . . mistake," said Elijah. "I do my best to avoid any contact with the people in my memories, but this is a small city. I saw her first by accident, and it was . . . " He closed his eyes. "It was so hard. That's no excuse, but you have to understand. I have every memory of her that her husband ever had. I couldn't help but love her. I should have stayed away but when Gidri showed up, I knew the city was about to get more dangerous and I convinced myself I had to protect her. I saw her again, on purpose this time, and Gidri figured it out."

"The grief-counseling session," said Ostler.

Elijah nodded. "He wanted me to join their war, and when I said no he looked for leverage to convince me. He followed me to the session, saw my connection to Rose, and took her."

"Rose's story to the police corroborates that," said Diana.

Ostler hit the microphone button again. "Thank you, Mr. Sexton. Or should we call you Meshara?"

He looked up in surprise, but after a moment he sagged back down in his chair. "I suppose I shouldn't be surprised that you know that name. Who's your informer?"

"Just tell us about yourself," said Ostler.

Elijah sighed and nodded. "They call me Meshara, though I don't think it's my original name. I think we're older than that. My memory fades without a constant source of new ones and over the years I've missed too many times, lost too much of what I used to be. A lot of that, I admit, was on purpose. I've done a lot of things I was happy to forget."

Detective Scott had joined us to listen, his opinion of our wild boogeyman stories somewhat altered by the man-shaped tree who'd injured four of his men before dissolving into sludge. Two were in critical condition but none had died. Yet.

"It started, I think, in a city," said Elijah. "We were all from the same city mostly, though there were a few from other places around the valley. Rack and Ren were the ones who brought it to us, but I don't remember where they came up with it—and when I say 'it,' I don't mean an object, I mean the idea. Eternal life. We could become so much more than we were. We could be gods."

"They're human?" asked Diana.

"Or at least they started that way," said Ostler.

Nathan was taking notes at a furious pace, his fingers clacking on the keyboard of his notebook computer.

Potash's oxygen tank beeped. It reminded me of Darth Vader.

Elijah started tracing something on the table, and I craned my neck to see. There didn't seem to be any pattern to it, just a nervous tic. "There was a ritual, I guess," he said. "I don't remember the details, but I suppose that's to be expected. We had to give something up—something deep, some part of ourselves that defined who we were. It was a way of giving up our humanity, I guess, so we could move on to something bigger, but that might be my own opinion on it, after the fact. It's hard to separate my original motives from the ten thousand years I've had to reconsider it. Giving it up was a freedom, Rack said—the only thing we were losing were the limits that held us back. I guess I believed him because why else would I choose to give up my memory?"

His face darkened. "I've wondered, a lot, what horrible thing I must have gone through to make me think that forgetting everything would be a release. I was just a dumb kid I guess—probably a city elder, honestly, if you think about the life expectancy we must have had back then. But still, a kid in comparison. Ten thousand years is a long time to look back on one decision. It didn't take me long to replace whatever I'd been trying to forget with a thousand new experiences every bit as terrible. A lot of them worse. The human race is truly, truly evil." He paused. "And unimaginably good."

I watched him as he spoke, trying to read his face. Trying to see in him some element of Crowley, or Nobody, or Mary Gardner. Who were they, really? Back in the beginning, if there was one, who had they been?

"I don't remember where that city was," said Elijah. "There was a mountain nearby, though I know that doesn't help much. I went east, I think, but eventually I went everywhere. I've lived all over the world. I live here now because it's quiet, and because I have a steady source of memories I can use without hurting anyone." He went suddenly quiet. "Except . . ." He paused again, as if warring with himself over how to say the next thing, or whether he should say it at all. I wondered what he was struggling to confess—we already knew about Merrill Evans—but when he finally spoke again it was a question. "Is Rosie okay?"

Ostler looked at Trujillo, then leaned forward and pushed a button. "She's fine."

Elijah's face looked pained. "Does she . . . know? About me?"

"No, she doesn't," said Ostler. "She's talked to the police and to a trauma counselor, and now she's safe at home."

"Thank you for that." He leaned back in his chair, his head down. He looked deflated, as if all the life had gone out of him.

"Ask about The Hunter," I said.

Ostler pushed the button again. "Can you tell us about the cannibal?"

"I don't know anything," said Elijah.

"You have the photos in front of you," said Ostler. "Does any of it look familiar?"

Elijah sighed, then leaned forward to look at the images. "This definitely isn't any of the three who came to me. Ihsan flays his victims—he was going to flay Ted if I hadn't stopped him last night."

"Who's Ted?" asked Ostler into the mic.

"I'm sorry, Jacob," said Elijah, shaking his head. "Jacob Carl. I forget his name all the time."

Ostler frowned. "How long does your memory last before you need to drain another person?"

"A few weeks at most," said Elijah. "Honestly, that was just a bad habit just now—my memory is sharper than it's been in . . . forever, maybe. I'm used to drinking humans with seventy or eighty years of good memory, at the most. Last night I drank two Withered with ten thousand years each. I've never done that before. It might last me for months."

"Then why can't he remember the cannibal?" asked Diana. "You'd think that kind of thing would stick in your mind."

"Ask about The Hunter," I said again. "Use that name, see if it means anything to him."

Ostler nodded and pressed the button again. "Do you know of any Withered who calls him- or herself The Hunter?"

"I don't think so."

"Perhaps the name 'Hunter,'" she asked, "as first or last name, or maybe part of an alias?"

He thought, then shook his head. "Not that I can remember."

"Ask about ancient hunters, then," I said. "Ten thousand years ago his society had to include hunters, right? Was there anyone in the group who hunted for a living?"

Ostler relayed the question, but Elijah just kept shaking his head. "I'm sorry, I just can't remember. There are too many holes in my memory."

"There's an easy fix to that," said Potash. "Bring him one of the victims and let him go to town."

"You can't ask him to do that," I said immediately.

"Why not?" asked Nathan. "It's the most perfect thing ever. Do you realize how easy it would be to catch killers if we could just ask the victim: 'who killed you?' "

"You're asking him to remember being eaten alive," I said.

Nathan shook his head. "We don't know that the victims were conscious—"

"Would you risk it on yourself?" I asked. "If you could experience everything a murder victim went through, but it had to be you doing it, would you still think it was such an awesome idea?"

"When did you get so empathetic all of a sudden?" asked Nathan.

"I'd risk it," said Potash, and looked at me. "And I know you would, too."

I glowered at him. "If I did it, it would be specifically because I didn't want to make anyone else do it. I can be responsible for my own suffering—that's why we're on this team in the first place. So we can do the hard stuff and no one else has to."

"He's on the team, too," said Ostler, looking at Elijah through the glass. "He said he'd help us, and this might be the best way to do it." She pushed the button for the speaker. "Mr. Sexton, it is vital that we learn as much as possible about this killer. Since your memories of him are incomplete, would you be willing to . . . 'drink' the memories of one of his victims?"

Elijah furrowed his brow, and the sides of his mouth drooped down in a mournful frown. "Do you realize what you're asking?"

"I do."

He took a deep breath. "Okay, then, but . . ." He glanced at the photos. "Is Valynne Maetani the most recent?"

"She is," said Ostler. "Is that a problem?"

"I have to get them fresh," said Elijah. "Twenty-four hours at the most. This thing that I do isn't designed for dead brains; the memories start to degrade, I guess you'd say. I don't think I can help you until he kills again."

"That's still good," said Nathan. "Better late than never, right?"

Sure, I thought. Unless you're the one he kills.

Stephen Applebaum and Valynne Maetani had both eaten at Pancho's Pizza the night they were murdered; Ostler wanted to keep that detail secret, to avoid ruining the restaurant's business completely, but Trujillo insisted that warning people was the best possible thing we could do, even if it meant driving The Hunter away and losing one of our only leads. My thoughts were somewhere in the middle: the pizza place was the ideal way to send this guy a message.

I would have to be extremely careful about the way I contacted him, not just because I was worried about him finding me, but because I knew Ostler would be furious. Any contact our team made with a Withered was supposed to be approved by her and open to the group; everyone knew everything. After the deadly police raid on the mortuary, I was done working like that; I would do this my way, and no one would get hurt but me.

The first step was to get away from Potash, which was harder than it sounded now that he was out of the hospital. He was a special forces assassin who'd been running surveillance on people since before I was born—he knew how to follow people, and he knew how to do it right. He was also dying of a lung condition, though, so I used that to my advantage. He slept at night with a CPAP machine on his face, which was basically a giant oxygen mask that forced air into his lungs. It didn't restrain him as much as I'd hoped, but it was relatively loud. Asleep, with that on, and with my bedroom door closed, he could barely hear me at all. The first night after we questioned Elijah, I stayed awake reading and waited for him to fall asleep. Around two in the morning I slipped out my back window, shimmied down a power pole, and ran off into the darkness.

I preferred this time of the night. In a big city there might still be a lot going on in the early morning—nightclubs or parties or who knows what else—but in a small town like I'd grown up in, and even a smallish city like Fort Bruce, the entire world was asleep. The bars had already closed, and the early morning businesses hadn't opened yet. I saw a car here and there, but always in the distance, and only for a moment. The world was silent and empty, and it was mine.

I had a few hours to kill before the thrift store opened—the first step in my plan—so I went to Whiteflower and watched Brooke's window. She was on the third floor, the highest in the building, so I couldn't see anything, but it was comforting to watch it. I used to stalk her like this back home in Clayton, watching her possessively. This was different. I didn't have to dream about her thinking of me, or wanting me, or relying on me, because she already did in real life. I was her actual protector, and my motives weren't creepy but laudable. Besides, I wasn't in love with Brooke anymore.

I was in love with a dead girl.

Even though she was gone, I still thought about Marci all the time. I thought about the way she used to look at me, like I was puzzle with one piece left and she just had to find where to put it. I thought about the way she smiled, and the way she talked to her siblings—little twins, a boy and a girl—and the way she used to be more proud of the money she'd saved finding a great deal on some hot new outfit than she was of the outfit itself. She looked good in everything; the savings were the real accomplishment. I thought about the way she'd helped me track a serial killer, and the way she'd seen clues that I would never have seen in a hundred years. The way she'd put the pieces together. The way she'd grounded me to a reality I'd never experienced before.

The way we'd danced and the way we'd kissed and the way she'd died, all alone in a dark bathroom, while the demon called Nobody made her slit her own wrists.

I stood up and started walking, feeling the energy in my hands and feet like a vibrating engine. I thought about Marci all the time, but I shouldn't. It always made me too excited—too angry. The sheer injustice of it, the wrongness, the powerlessness that I felt reliving a night I wasn't even there for . . . . I wanted to punch the light post as I passed it on the corner, but I didn't. I couldn't let that rage get loose. I twisted my hands in my pockets and gripped the knife in its nylon sheath and clenched my teeth and thought about nothing. Of darkness. The empty city. The calm streets. The numbers, one by one in my head.

One, one, two, three, five, eight, thirteen.

Twenty-one.

Thirty-four.

I stopped and put my hands over my face, breathing deep. I wanted to start a fire, a real one, not that fake nonsense in a tiny metal box. But I couldn't. Not tonight. Tonight had to stay completely hidden from everybody.

I checked my pocket again for money, pausing to count it. Fifty-four dollars and eighty cents. I crouched by a snow bank and scrubbed the coins with snow, removing any trace of my fingerprints that might be clinging to them. When the thrift store opened at five in the morning I bought a used coat, a hat, some thin gloves, and a pair of sunglasses. I walked around the streets in these for another hour, and when the copy center opened at six I bought thirty minutes of computer time and wrote an incendiary flyer about how Pancho's Pizza was run by the cannibal himself, and that for all we knew the pizzas were topped with finger sausage and people-roni. I was pretty proud of that last one. I signed up for two free e-mail accounts and put one of them on the bottom of the flyers, then printed a hundred copies and distributed them all over Pancho's neighborhood, an east-side borough called The Corners: shoving them into mail slots, sticking them under windshield wipers, even taping them to windows. I stayed away from Pancho's itself because I knew the police were watching it. When I was done I took the bus to another part of town, wrote my second e-mail address on my last remaining flyer, and buried it under a small tree in a quiet residential neighborhood. It was just after seven, and no one had seen me. I memorized the location of the tree, made an X in the bark with my knife, and cleaned the blade of sap. I walked four blocks to another bus, rode to the far side of town, and dumped my new clothes in a donation bin. I rode a different bus away.

No one had seen my face, and nothing I'd touched had my fingerprint on it. No one could possibly trace the flyers back to me.

I wanted to stop by an Internet cafe and check the first e-mail address, but I knew it was too early. Even if The Hunter read the flyers and guessed that they were a message, there was no guarantee he would send an e-mail. He was clever, though, and meticulous, so he probably would. Probably. I just had to hope that he read the flyer, guessed what it was, and decided to write me before Ostler caught wind of it and had the e-mail account closed—or, worse, had it monitored remotely. Either way, any conversation that started on that e-mail account would have to move somewhere else immediately, hence the second account. I could give The Hunter the location of the tree, and as long as he got to it first, there'd be no evidence left for whoever tried to follow him. We'd have our own private conversation, with nobody the wiser.

But first I had to wait.

It was nearly eight in the morning, and almost time for Whiteflower to open. I used my last bits of change for one more bus, and walked the final few blocks to the rest home. I was the second one in the door.

Potash was waiting for me.

"Busy morning?" he said.

"You know how it goes." I sat on the couch opposite him in the lobby. "The carpe doesn't diem itself."

"You have those backwards."

"The eprac doesn't . . . me-id . . . That's hard to say, are you sure?"

Potash didn't laugh or sigh or roll his eyes, he just stared. I relied on a very specific set of facial cues to help me figure out what people were feeling, but Potash never seemed to feel anything.

"I had a sausage biscuit on the way over here," he said. "Three of them, actually. They're cheap."

I didn't know where he was going with this. "Good . . . for you?"

"Just letting you know I didn't eat them at the apartment, per your wishes."

Aha. "Thanks." I still wasn't sure what we were talking about. Anyone else on the team would have bawled me out for insubordination by now.

"I know you better than you think," he said, and lowered his voice as he leaned forward. "You take life more seriously than any seventeen-year-old I've ever met, but that's never obvious from the outside. You try so hard to look like you don't care about anything."

"I care very much about not caring about anything," I said. "Thank you for noticing."

"I think the difference," he said, "is that you only care about death. If something can kill you or someone you know, you take it seriously. With everything else, you pretend like it doesn't matter. It's time for you to take me seriously."

That sounded incredibly like a threat, and I felt my throat begin to close in nervousness. I deflected without thinking. "Does someone need a hug?"

He put his hand on the coffee table between us, palm down, fingers loose, and I swear no hand motion in history has ever been so menacing. "You will take me seriously because I can and will kill you. You are a sociopathic murderer, and I've seen what you're capable of, and we tolerate you on this team because you're good at what you do, but you are not the only one who can do it. I do not share whatever maternal attachment Ostler may feel for you. I am not bound by the ethical concerns that inhibit others' behavior. If I deem you to be a threat, to this team or to anyone else, I will kill you, and you will not see it coming."

It occurred to me suddenly that Potash had probably killed more people, up close and personal, than any criminal I'd ever studied. Hit men were considered by many psychologists to be serial killers. Why not government operatives?

I nodded slowly. "Thanks for letting me know."

He stood up and walked to the elevator. "I assume you're here to talk to Brooke. Let's go say hello before we head to the station." I rose and followed him, saying nothing.

I keep two lists in my head: enemies and everyone else. There isn't really a friends list, just people I can't hurt, and people I can.

Potash just changed lists.

11

The hardest part about checking an e-mail address you know the FBI might eventually be watching is figuring out where to check it from. Whatever hotshots they had working in their cybercrimes division would be able to trace the IP address the e-mail was sent from and figure out exactly where I was and when. Using my own laptop was completely out of the question, along with all the other computers in our office or the police station—even if no one saw me using them, the fact that I was in the same building at the same time the e-mails were sent would simply be too suspicious. A public computer would be ideal, which was why I'd originally planned on a library or an Internet cafe, but now that Potash was following me more closely, there was no way to get to one without raising suspicion.

So I dropped my phone out the window the next time we drove on the freeway.

"Crap."

"Was that your phone?" asked Diana.

"Crap," I repeated. I was never a very emotional person to begin with, so I didn't bother acting too bothered about the loss. I craned my neck around to look at the road behind us, but we were already hundreds of yards away.

"Why do you even have the window open anyway?" asked Diana.

"I told you," I said, "Potash smells like dog."

"It's your dog," said Potash.

"I was trying to find a spot where the sun wasn't glaring off the screen. It slipped right out of my hand."

"Ostler's not going to buy you a new one," said Diana.

"Ostler's going to flay you for losing it," said Potash. "That phone had sensitive information on it."

"There's no way it survived," I said. "That semi behind us looks like it ran right over it." I had, of course, waited for a semi to come up behind us before I'd dropped it. I turned back around and looked out the front window. "You think they sell phones in the hospital?"

"Probably not," said Diana. "Not good ones, at least."

"I don't need another smartphone," I said, "just something I can call you guys with."

She shrugged. "We'll check when we get there."

We were going to the hospital because the two comatose Withered were "degrading." Dr. Pearl was unclear on what that meant. It wasn't his area of specialty, really, but to be fair, Withered biology wasn't anyone's area of specialty. We worked with Pearl because the FBI had cleared him when he worked on Potash, and he was the only one in the hospital we trusted. After all the weird crap we'd put him through, I can't imagine he trusted us anymore.

The hospital gift shop had a small selection of prepaid phones, just barely smart enough to handle text-based e-mail. I bought one—cash again, of course—and started setting it up while we went upstairs. Pearl met us at the elevator with his eyes red and his thinning hair mussed.

"Thank you for coming," he said, and gestured down the left hallway. "Do you want to tell me what's going on now, or do you want to wait until we see them?"

"They're vampires," I said.

He hesitated for barely a second. "That only explains one of them."

"The other one's a werewolf," I said. "Keep your nurses away, they'll fall madly in love with—"

"He's kidding," said Diana. "Let's go see what's going on."

Pearl nodded, then glanced at Potash. "How's the breathing?"

"Still using the CPAP at night," said Potash. "Don't even need the oxygen tank during the day."

"That's great," said Pearl. "Let's hope we can cure these two as quickly."

Gidri and Ihsan were being kept in a secured upper wing of the hospital, with police guards and a small, carefully vetted staff. Potash nodded to them as we walked by, and I wondered if they were the same ones who'd worked with him as well. How much had their lives changed, just by being on call in the ER the day we killed Mary Gardner?

I checked the dummy account I'd set up and found more than

thirty messages. Not bad for about five hours. Most of them would be random people off the street, asking about the flyers or yelling at me for causing trouble; at least one of them was guaranteed to be from Pancho's Pizza itself, demanding to know who I was so they could sue me for libel. I'd have to read each one carefully, trying to see whatever clues The Hunter had left so I could figure out which one was him. If he'd written me at all.

"In here," said Pearl, and he tapped a container on the wall beside the locked door. "We advise masks, because whatever those guys have you definitely don't want to catch it."

We strapped on paper masks—they didn't seem like they'd do much good, but whatever—and pulled on nylon gloves. There was a whole custodian's rig outside the door as well, including a bucket of water, a mop, and an army of bottled cleaning chemicals. I wondered how often they cleaned this hallway, just out of paranoia. Pearl checked our masks and then led us inside. Gidri and Ihsan were laying side by side on parallel beds, hooked up to what looked like every machine the hospital could fit into the room. The root of Pearl's worry was instantly obvious, and I realized that the word "degraded" was both surprisingly correct and woefully inadequate. Ihsan, the big man, looked like he had leprosy; his skin was pocked and splitting and sliding off, almost like it wasn't connected to his body at all. Gruesome as he was, Gidri was even more shocking—his formerly supermodel-worthy face had wrinkled and bloated and sagged, his limbs twisted, his bones curled like old paper in a fire. He looked not injured but deformed, so hideously I could barely imagine—even having seen him before—how his body had ever looked normal.

Potash looked at the screens as if trying to make sense of the various numbers and charts and blinking alerts, but Pearl waved him away. "Don't bother," he said. "None of it makes sense. Not a single one of the readings have any bearing on what we think might be happening—except for the handful that do, which only make us more confused. Their heart rates are wrong, but not in the way their conditions suggest that they should be wrong; the same goes for their temperature, their white cell count, their oxygen saturation—pretty much anything you care to name. We've biopsied their tissue and found all sorts of problems, just not the ones we expected, and none of our treatments create the kind of response we're hoping for. We even took a sample of this one's bone tissue"—he pointed at Gidri—"and it started shriveling under the microscope. I didn't even know bones *could* shrivel. You told me to take care of them, but without some specialists in here to help figure out what's wrong with them, they're going to die in a matter of days. At the most."

Diana touched one of Gidri's limbs; I expected it to move when she did, like a floppy foam noodle, but it was rigid.

Potash looked at me. "You're the expert."

Sure, the one guy who recognizes my skills is the guy who thinks I'm a psychopath. I suppose he's not wrong, but it still hurts.

Fortunately, I knew exactly what was wrong. "They're malnourished."

"We've got them on the best IV supplements in the hospital," said Pearl.

"These two are nourished by a very specific set of things," I said. "Things you don't have, and which we are *really* unwilling to provide."

Pearly looked at me intently. "If there's something we can do to save them—"

"Can you give us a minute?" asked Diana.

"I need to know whatever it is you're not telling me," said Pearl.

"Just give us a minute," said Potash. "We'll fill you in after we discuss it."

He shrugged and let himself out. When the door locked Diana looked at me with her eyebrows raised. "You think they need to feed on somebody?"

I nodded. "Whatever they need—skin, maybe, or beauty—Gidri looks like the kind of Withered that steals youth and beauty from people—they can't get it while comatose. The Withered eat food, as far as I can tell, and they support their bodies with the same basic physical materials that the rest of us do. They don't want to starve to death any more than you do. But their human shape is sustained by other things, and they can't get those things like this, and no amount of food or vitamins is going to make up for that."

"So what do we do?" she asked.

"And what do we tell Pearl," said Potash. It was a question, but he wasn't asking it—it sounded like he was correcting Diana for not having asked it. Had he always talked that way or was I just seeing problems now where I hadn't before?

"We need to learn what we can," I said. "They won't live, so cut them open and figure out as much of their biology as possible. We might never get another chance at an incapacitated Withered."

"As soon as we start an autopsy they'll die," said Potash. "They'll turn to ash before we learn anything."

"That's why we keep them alive," I said. "Treat it like a surgery, hook them up to every form of life support we have, and work fast."

"I'm calling Ostler," said Diana, pulling out her phone.

"They don't have the facilities for that here," said Potash.

"We don't have doctors we trust here, either," I said. "They're going to have to fly the bodies to Langley and hope they survive." I pulled out my new phone and scrolled through the list of Pancho's Pizza e-mails, looking for a likely candidate.

Oh. How about the one that says: "Hello, FBI."

"Agent Ostler," said Diana, "we have a situation at the—no, I hadn't heard. Let me ask." She lowered her phone and looked up at us. "Have either of you heard about the pizza thing?"

So Ostler knew about the flyers. "I could go for a pizza," I said. I tried to keep my voice even and forced myself to breathe calmly. If my face went red, they'd know I knew something.

Potash looked at me. "What pizza thing?"

Stay calm.

"Looks like the victims' link to that pizza place got leaked," said Diana. "Someone spread a bunch of flyers all over the neighborhood." She looked at us, so I shrugged. She put the phone back to her ear. "We haven't heard anything. Probably one of the cops—that station's the most gossipy group of grown men I've ever met." Pause. "I'm not being flippant about it, I'm saying this is exactly why we didn't want to bring them in in the first place."

Potash was still staring at me.

I raised my eyebrow. "You're not in the mood for pizza? We could go to a different place."

He looked away, and I went back to my phone. Was this message from The Hunter, or from Ostler?

"Hello, FBI. I must say I'm impressed with your cleverness; it's not every day one finds a secret message plastered across an entire neighborhood. I'm disappointed there's not a corpse, though. Maybe next time."

That was the entire thing—no identifiers, no new information, not even a signature at the end. Whoever it was had mentioned a corpse, which was a direct reference to The Hunter's second letter, so I knew it wasn't just a person on the street; it was someone with inside knowledge. But who? I was still worried it might be Ostler, trying to pretend she was The Hunter in order to trap me—or to trap whoever she thought had written the flyer. She might have a suspicion it was me but she didn't have proof. Lies within lies, in so many layers I could barely keep track.

The Hunter had always addressed his letters to me, and this one had not. That made it look like this wasn't from him . . . but I wasn't so sure. If Ostler was trying to emulate The Hunter's style, she'd use every trick she had: she'd address it to me, she'd get verbose in her language, she'd probably throw in a mention of lions or antelopes. She'd even sign it with his name. She'd do all the things she'd know I'd notice. But if the real Hunter was trying to contact me—not just the FBI, but me personally, like I suspected—he'd recognize that this might be an attempt at a private conversation and keep my name out of it to help maintain that privacy. It might be him.

Of course, if he'd really wanted to prove that it was him, he could have told me to look for a certain keyword and then carved it into the next victim's chest. It wouldn't be hard to prove himself. Instead he was forcing me to trust him.

I just didn't know if I could.

"Ostler's calling headquarters," said Diana. "We'll see if they care enough to come pick these bodies up. We're supposed to tell Pearl to keep them alive as long as he can."

No more mention of the flyers then. Ostler was either playing it cool, or the bodies were a bigger concern. Or she hadn't sent an e-mail at all.

How cool could Ostler even play it, even if she wanted to? The e-mail hadn't asked for a response—if Ostler was fishing for a suspect, wouldn't she have prompted me to write back? I wanted so hard to believe that this was really from The Hunter.

Diana walked to the door and knocked to get out. While we waited for a response, she looked at me. "Does that phone do web?"

I tried not to look guilty. "Not well, why?"

"The flyers about the pizza place had an e-mail at the bottom. Ostler wants us to look into it, see if we can figure out who the leak comes from."

She wouldn't ask me to investigate myself, I thought. This probably isn't her. "I can do better back on my laptop," I said. "Let's go back to the office." Pearl unlocked the door, and I keyed in a single line response to the e-mail:

286 Penelope Road, under the third tree. I hit send.

"You going to tell me what this is about?" asked Pearl.

"Keep them alive," said Diana. "The FBI is coming to transfer them to a larger hospital."

"When?"

"As soon as they can get here," said Potash.

"But you have to tell me what's going on," Pearl demanded. "What have I exposed my staff to? What precautions do we need to take? How can I keep them alive if I don't even know what they—"

My phone dinged, telling me the message was sent. I dropped it in the mop bucket. The three adults all turned to me in surprise.

"Damn," I said. "I'm really clumsy today." I looked at Potash. "I should get more sleep."

I bought another prepaid phone then spent the afternoon with the rest of the team, poking and prodding at the mysterious Pancho-hating e-mail address. We couldn't determine anything and ended up sending that job to FBI headquarters as well. It bothered Ostler to send two things upstream in the same day, as if it were a sign to her bosses that she couldn't do the ridiculous job they didn't believe in anyway. I told her not to worry: once they got hold of those two bodies and they melted into ash right there on their operating tables, the FBI might finally be convinced. Ostler nodded gruffly but didn't look remotely comforted.

That night, when Potash was on his CPAP and Boy Dog was snoring loudly on my floor, I used my new phone to check the e-mail address I'd buried under the tree. There was one message:

To the Esteemed John Wayne Cleaver,

I assume you're the only one reading this. It was clever of you to build a double-blind message system, but the only reason to do so is to hide from both sides: mine and your own. You're right not to trust them. I've been dealing with the FBI for years, probably since it was created. It may have been created specifically to search for me, in fact, but don't put too much stock in it when I say things like that. When you're as old as I am, and you've spawned as many kingdoms and religions, a single government agency is all too easy to claim credit for, deservedly or not.

I also think you're right not to trust me, but only because I approve of caution. I am not an immediate danger to you, though I won't promise as much for any of your friends. But I suppose "friends" is the wrong word, isn't it? Your acquaintances. You've fallen in with a bad crowd, and if your mother was alive, she'd be very disappointed. Her little darling, consorting with thugs. And yes, knowing who you are means that I know about your mother, and of course your aunt and your sister. I know where they live. I've been in their homes, though they didn't know it; I advise you not to tell them, either, as it would only disturb them unnecessarily. Let this stand as my first promise to you: that I will not hurt your family. Whatever trust is to exist between us, let us build it on that.

Because you are more like me than you admit, John Wayne Cleaver. I know about the Gifted you have killed. I know about the deep, driving need you feel to find us. You are a hunter, like me, and you feel in your bones the same primal instincts, stronger than any choice or moral. You catch the scent of blood on the air; you follow it with a single-minded dedication; you take away your prey's defenses and destroy them utterly. It's not the death that thrills you, but the power. The glorious secret knowledge that you are the one who did it, that nobody helped you and no one could stop you. That within your sphere of control you are absolute.

I know you, John Wayne Cleaver. I only wish that I can be there when you finally know yourself.

12

"Tell me about the other Withered," I said. I was in the same room as Elijah this time, no mirrors or microphones to get in the way. He was still in a cell, of course, and probably would be until Ostler was convinced beyond all doubt that he was truly on our side. I didn't know if that would ever happen. I wanted to apologize to him, for promising him partnership and then being stuck in a lie when Ostler made him a prisoner. I wanted to apologize but instead I planned. This wouldn't happen if I were working on my own.

Potash was outside, waiting. As soon as I left, I'd be stuck with him again.

Elijah looked morose, but that was nothing new. Even before we'd recruited him, when we were still merely watching him from shadows and street corners, he'd been quiet and melancholy. He had nothing in his life but memories, and most of them were regrets.

"I need to visit Merrill," he said.

"He's fine," I told him.

Elijah started to protest. "He'll . . ." He stopped himself, and sighed. "I guess he won't miss me. But I miss him. I owe him. I'm the one who put him in that living tomb—the least I can do is say hi once in a while."

"Doctor Trujillo checks on him every day," I said. "I can ask him to stop by and chat for a bit too, if it would make you feel better."

"When he's visiting your 'friend of a friend'?" asked Elijah. We still hadn't told him about Brooke, but his recent memory was whip sharp at the moment, thanks to the effect of the two Withered minds he'd drained, and he could remember our first conversation with startling clarity. I nodded.

"He spends most of his time there," I said. "Visiting Merrill might actually be a relief."

"It should be me," said Elijah, and I could see the determination in his face: nostrils slightly flared, his mouth a grim line. "I'm the one who did it, I should be the one who pays for it."

I thought about Brooke, completely alone in her medical cell, and nodded. "I know how you feel."

"No you don't," he insisted. "Your mind isn't a sieve—when you do something wrong you try to forget it, because if you don't it will stay in your dreams forever. I don't have that luxury."

A broken mirror, covered with blood. "Haunted dreams are a luxury?"

"Nature's way of making sure you don't make the same mistake twice," said Elijah. "I visit Merrill because what I did to him was horrible and I have to remember that—I can't ever stop remembering that—because if I do I might hurt somebody else the same way."

"He won't live forever," I said. "You have to stop sooner or later."

His gaze grew even more intense. "Then you understand why I have to hang on to him as long as I can. How many times in my ten thousand years do you think I've drained a living mind, forgotten about it, and tried it again? How many times have I left someone a hollow shell? How many times have I rediscovered the horror that I'm capable of?"

A burning car and an ear-splitting scream.

"The one day I didn't wake up to horror," I said. "The one day I woke up without thinking about Marci—without remembering her face, without dreams of her dead body still fogging up my eyes—that was the worst day of my entire life, even worse than the day she died, because I walked to the refrigerator and saw that little fish magnet she used to have, the one I asked her mother for before I left town, and then everything Marci had ever done or said or been came rushing back and I knew that I had failed her. All I had to do was think about her, the easiest thing in the world, and I hadn't. For twenty whole minutes."

I stopped talking abruptly, as if I'd only just noticed the fact that I was talking at all, and wanted to hide it. I didn't know why I'd told him that. My therapy sessions with Dr. Trujillo—which we hadn't had in a while, to my great delight—had taught me that sharing my feelings was important, not because it accomplished anything or achieved any great purpose, but because the sharing itself was important. Maybe that's why I told him. Maybe I just needed to say it out loud.

Or maybe I wanted to know if he was like me. Maybe I just wanted to see some recognition, for once in my life, that I wasn't completely alone. If I had to get that from a demon, then . . . that sounds about normal for me.

"It gets easier," he said. "Losing people."

"I guess you do that a lot."

"Millions of times," he said. "But it's never the millions that get to you. It's the ones. That one person you can't ever be without, and then you are."

"People like Rose Chapman?" I asked.

He closed his eyes for a moment, then opened them and nodded. "People like Rose. I built my whole life around two things, you know: taking new memories and avoiding everyone in them. It's not the easiest life to maintain. Mistakes like Rose—like meeting her in the supermarket, talking to her again, going out of my big stupid way to see her again—they happen. This one ended poorly, but they can be so much worse. Rose can go on her way now and imagine that I'm some creepy weirdo she got mixed up with for a week or two, that got a little obsessed and put her life in danger, but I can live with that. Because she can move on from that. Her memories of me—of the Billy Chapman part of me that cares about her—those are undamaged. She can remember Billy Chapman, without any of this baggage, for the rest of her life."

"I can't say that," I said. "You lost living people—mine are all dead."

"You think I haven't lost dead ones, too?" His eyes practically flashed with anger. "You think I've never been in a car accident that killed my wife and children along with me? You think I've never been in a murder suicide? Because I have, from both sides." He leaned forward. "You think I've never been a sweet little old lady dying of old age, so excited to wake up and see her husband again on the other side—married for fifty years, separated for ten, and now at last on the verge of a joyful reunion in heaven? And then I wake up and I'm me. And he's nowhere. And all I can think about is that it's not over and I'm tired and I'm ready to go, but I'm still here and I have to do it again and again and again." He leaned back in his chair. "You think about that before you tell me I've got it easy."

I stayed silent a while before speaking. "So why don't you end it?"

"Suicide?"

"If your life is such a hell," I asked, "why bother? Why go through it again and again and all those times?"

"Because of . . ." He stopped and looked at the ceiling. After a moment he shrugged. "Because of children," he said. "Because of smiles and sunshine and ice cream."

"You've got to be kidding."

"You don't like ice cream?" Elijah shook his head. "It's the best. Imagine how excited I was when someone finally invented it."

"Sunshine and smiles don't make all that other stuff go away," I said. "This isn't a fairyland."

"No," he said, "it's the real world. And the real world is the most amazing thing any of us will ever experience. Have you ever climbed a mountain? Walked through a garden? Played with a child? This isn't exactly a revelation, John; people have been praising the simple pleasures since even before I was born, and that's a very long time."

"You don't do any of those things."

"But I have my memories," said Elijah. "Sometimes. And I have even simpler things: music. Food. Everybody likes bacon."

"I'm a vegetarian."

"Asparagus, then," said Elijah. "Roast it in a pan, a little olive oil and a little salt; you get the most incredible flavor, almost like a nut, but deep and rich and the texture is just perfect."

"I've tried it."

"The world is more than sadness," said Elijah. "I have a hundred thousand memories in my head—I can't remember all of them, or maybe not even most of them, but they are so much happier than sad. For every dead mother or brother or child there are a hundred breezes, a hundred sunsets, a hundred memories of falling in love. Have you ever kissed anyone, John?"

"I don't see how that's any of your business."

"A first kiss is incredible," said Elijah. "Most people only get one, but I can remember a hundred thousand of them. How could I give that up?" He shook his head, smiling for the first time. "The world never gets old, John."

I thought about Cody French and Clark Forman, so weary of the world they could barely stand it. "The other Withered would disagree."

"They only see it through Withered eyes," said Elijah. "You're human, so you can see it any way you want to."

I said nothing for long time, just sat staring at him and thinking. There was no way it was that simple, no possible way that the darkness and the horror and the half-eaten bodies of the world could all just be brushed away with nothing—with the laughter of a child. That's not how the world worked. All light does is cast more shadows.

But I wanted to believe him. Even if it's all I ever did, I wanted to take what he knew and give it to Brooke and make all that darkness go away.

But it doesn't go away. I said it again, out loud so he could hear it. "The darkness doesn't ever go away."

He nodded. "No it doesn't. For every time I've fallen in love, I've eventually lost a loved one. That's how it works."

"So how do you do it?"

"Find the good in the bad—in the places that they overlap. Bittersweet might not be very sweet, but it's not pure bitter, either." He paused. "What music do you listen to?"

"I'm not really a music guy," I told him.

He shook his head. "You can't tell me the world isn't worth it if you haven't even bothered to experience what's here."

"So what's your favorite music?"

"Irish," he said.

"Why?"

His smile faltered, just a fraction. "Because all their love songs are about death."

I was starting to like Elijah and that worried me. I didn't like anybody, not even my mom when she was alive, not even Max, the kid I used to hang around with. See? Even in my head I didn't call him a friend. They were all just people, and sometimes they got in the way, and sometimes I could get things from them, and sometimes they wanted things from me. But that's as far as it ever went, until Marci. Marci I talked to because I liked talking to her—because I liked hearing what she said, and how she said it, and why. In the beginning all I wanted was a sounding board, and Marci's father was a cop so she had inside information. She was a means to an end, just like everybody else, but over time that changed. Maybe not even while she was still alive. I don't know. She became more to me than just an informant, or an acquaintance, or a piece of the scenery. She became a person I cared about.

I couldn't care about Elijah because he wasn't Marci. It was an insult to her memory that I should even pretend to feel a kinship with anyone after I'd felt one with her. I left the interrogation room in a confused, angry haze, not talking to anyone.

I was downright relieved when the new body was discovered a few minutes later.

The police brought it in through the basement, trying to keep the new death quiet as long as possible; the general public still had no idea it was a supernatural killer, but tensions were high just the same. I thought they were just delaying the inevitable, but nobody asked me. The victim this time was Kristen Mercer, a short, blond woman who looked nothing like anyone on our team. There went that theory. Obviously The Hunter was choosing his victims by some other formula; now we had to figure out what it was.

There was no note this time. We called for Elijah, and the police walked him through the hall with a pole-and-collar restraint, the kind they use for the most dangerous inmates. Nobody wanted to get close enough to touch him.

He stood before the body, which was fresh from a highway underpass, where a homeless man had found it; it hadn't been cleaned or examined and blood still seeped from the gaping bite wounds. One upper arm was chewed down to the bone, and on her other side, the shoulder and back were missing giant chunks of meat. Her chest was nothing but a bloody hole, and bite marks dotted the rest of the corpse like a pox. You could feel the violence of the attack just by looking at it, and Elijah hesitated.

"Are you sure this is the only way?"

"To talk to the victim directly?" I asked. "We could ask her questions all day if you want, but I'm pretty sure this is the only way she's going to answer."

"I thought you were against this," said Diana.

I looked at Elijah, feeling again that unbreakable knot of confusion and hatred and guilt. It was wrong not to hate him. I needed to hate him. "This is the only way," I said, and immediately hated myself for echoing Elijah's words. "I don't have to like it for it to be right."

The coroner was a pale woman named Hess; she looked up from her inspection of the body to address Ostler. "It's a few hours old at the most. Probably died this morning, but I'll have to do a full exam to be sure."

"Then we can wait," said Elijah. "I have until tonight at least—"

"Do it now, please," said Ostler.

"Can't we at least clean her up?" asked Elijah. "Or cover her, or something? This is a human being!"

"Like you care about that," said Nathan.

"She's a human being that I'm about to become," said Elijah, his face growing fierce. "When I drain her I'll have all of her memories—everything she's thought, everything she's felt—not just her death but her life, her family, her wedding, her dreams of the future. I will care about her more than anyone in this room."

"The sooner you do it the sooner we can find her killer," I said. "It's just a few hours old—we're right on his heels this time." He looked at me, and I looked back coldly. "Stop stalling."

Elijah took a deep breath, and closed his eyes. Ms. Hess backed away, and we all braced ourselves for whatever was about to happen. How did he "drink" a mind? Would it be gruesome, or violent, or traumatic? How long would it haunt our nightmares?

He put his hand on her forehead, and as we watched, his arm began to tremble.

"No," he moaned. Nathan stepped back.

"My son!" Elijah shouted, staggering away from the body on the table. "Is he okay? Has somebody checked on him?"

"Where did you leave him?" asked Ostler.

"He's at the neighbor's," said Elijah, tears streaming down his face. "I left him there to go shopping, I . . . I don't think I made it."

"Tell us the last thing you remember," said Ostler firmly. Elijah hid his face, wailing into his hands.

"My husband," he cried. "He doesn't know."

"Help us catch the man who did this," said Diana. "Please."

"I was . . ." He clutched his head, turning to the wall and crouching down into a fetal position. If it had been anyone else, someone would have run to him by now with a blanket or a comforting arm, but the Withered suffered alone. "I was on my way to go shopping and I got a flat tire. Somebody stopped to help. I remember . . . a sharp pain, in the back of my neck."

"A bite?" asked Ostler.

"No." Elijah shook his head, as if trying to shake the thoughts right out of it. He put his hand on his shoulder. "It was like a stab, barely more than a pinprick. It's the last thing I remember."

"A needle," said Potash. "He injected her with something."

"The back of the neck doesn't show any signs of damage," said Hess, rolling the body on its side and peering closely with a light. "Some blood, but it's all from other areas."

"Not the neck," I said. "He *said* neck, but look where he's holding himself: on the shoulder."

Hess looked up; Elijah was clutching the spot where his neck met his back, just over the right shoulder behind the collarbone. Hess looked back at the corpse. "That part isn't even here anymore."

"He ate the wound," said Diana. "That's why we couldn't find any cause of death on the other bodies—The Hunter ate the evidence."

"Something will show up in the toxicology report," said Ostler. "Ms. Hess, I want your report immediately."

"Yes, ma'am." Hess signaled to a member of her forensic team, and they wheeled the body into the exam room.

"This doesn't make sense," I said. "Why would he hide the method of death?"

"Because he doesn't want us to know," said Potash.

"Yes," I said, "obviously. But why not? Start asking the right questions."

"Somebody find my son!" yelled Elijah.

"Get him back into interrogation," said Ostler, gesturing brusquely to a nearby cop. "Find out where Mercer's car broke down and get someone on the scene ASAP."

"And check to see if her car was tampered with," I called after them as they left the room. Diana looked at me quizzically.

"Maybe The Hunter sabotaged it," I said. "He's not the kind to leave things to chance."

"Get Dr. Trujillo on the phone," Ostler snapped to another officer. "He'll need to update his psych profile with this new information."

"This destroys the profile," I said. "Nothing we thought we knew about The Hunter makes any sense anymore."

"He's meticulous," said Ostler. "He's precise. That all still holds. Trujillo's profile even theorized he was a doctor or a scientist, and this injection story corroborates that."

"The only thing we have to change is the method," said Nathan. "We thought it was mind control, now we know it's not; that's only one detail—"

"That's everything," I said again. "We thought we were looking for a Withered who stunned people and ate them. Standard predator behavior, regardless of the method itself. Now we're looking for a Withered who's actively deceiving us about his own nature. Why would he do that?"

"Maybe he's trying to spook us," said Nathan. "A needle in the back isn't nearly as frightening as a mind-controlling monster, so he's making himself look more frightening. Everything about his letters was intimidation—this is just one more piece."

"Only if he could predict that we'd guess that he could mind control people," I said. "There's no way he could control any of that; it's too many leaps of logic."

"Unknowns are always more frightening than knowns," said Potash. "The specifics don't matter."

"What did he do that he didn't have to do?" I asked, thinking out loud. "He ate the needle marks because he . . ." I was grasping at straws. "He was ashamed of them because a Withered shouldn't need to sedate people. Or he hated them because he felt guilty for what he did, so he wanted them destroyed."

"The man who wrote those letters doesn't feel guilty about anything," said Ostler.

"I know," I said, "I'm just trying to think."

"Maybe the injection isn't a drug at all," said Nathan. "Maybe it was butter and herbs, like you'd inject in meat before you cook it."

"That wouldn't knock her out," said Diana.

"If that were the case we'd see more signs of food preparation," I said. "A guy this meticulous should be carving off slices and pairing them with wine. If he were doing anything to add flavor, we'd see evidence of it somewhere. Ketchup stains at a minimum. Instead he's just . . . taking bites." I frowned. "Almost at random."

"Maybe the injection is the whole point," said Nathan. "Maybe he's proud of it, like it's a sign of his own power, so he started to fetishize it, and eating kind of grew out of that."

"That's . . ." I paused. *Not bad.* "That's the best idea you've had yet."

"And that's one of the worst compliments I've ever gotten," said Nathan.

"Maybe all of these discrepancies stem from the fact that he's not a cannibal," I said. "Not innately. He's not eating because he's hungry or because he wants to consume the victim or anything like that. Maybe he's eating because it's a sign of power—not his power over the victim, but a symbol of his own ability to act. That would mean he's not trying to hide the wound, he's just making other wounds to commemorate the first one."

"We need Trujillo," said Ostler again.

"This doesn't make sense with the hunting imagery," I said, trying to regain their attention. But the room was already in motion.

A cop handed Ostler a phone, and she started filling in Trujillo on the situation. Nathan hunched over a counter and started pounding out notes on his computer. Diana answered her phone. Only Potash was looking at me.

"Anything else you want to tell us?" he asked.

"You look great in that suit," I said. "It brings out your eyes."

"Cops are en route to the husband and son," said Diana, putting away her phone. "They've got the location of the car, but no one to spare on it."

"Looks like us, then," said Potash. "Come on, John."

I checked my phone as we drove, logging in to the webmail server to look at the dummy account.

"Looks like they found it already," said the e-mail. "I'll send my official correspondence tomorrow. Anything you want me to leave out?"

Was he threatening to expose our connection? It was only the second e-mail he'd ever sent me. Or was he talking about something else?

I logged out of the server, cleared the browser history, and power cycled the phone. I might need to lose this one soon, too.

The car was abandoned on the side of the freeway; Kristin Mercer lived near the center of town, but Elijah had told the cops she drove to the outskirts to shop in the warehouse stores. We parked behind it, being careful of the cars racing by in the next lane, and it didn't take long to find the problem: the front right tire was completely flat.

"The valve stem's been cut," said Diana. "It's not a gaping

slash, but it's bigger than a thorn in the treads would have been. She probably got a few miles before she noticed."

"And The Hunter was following the whole time," I said. He must have slashed the valve stem while she was . . . dropping off her son at the neighbors? How did he do that without anyone seeing him? I looked at the cars speeding past. "The only witnesses here were going too fast to see anything, but we can ask in her home neighborhood."

"He's lucky she stopped here," said Potash. "There's no way to control exactly when a tire will go flat, and even less control over when a driver will stop because of it."

"He had good odds that she'd stop somewhere on the freeway," said Diana. "It's a long drive from one exit to the next."

"Good but not perfect," I said. "But that might be part of his plan, too. If she'd stopped in a better place, he might have just kept going and tried to create another opportunity on another victim." I looked at the wide, flat road, stretching out in front and behind us. "At least now we know a little more about how he thinks."

Diana's phone rang, and she plugged her other ear when she answered, blocking out the sound of speeding cars. "This is Agent Lucas. Okay, hang on." She motioned us toward the car. "It's Hess, they have some blood work back. Get in where we can hear." We climbed back into the car, Potash taking the wheel so Diana could hold the phone. "Okay, Hess, I'm putting you on speaker."

"It's a sedative called etorphine hydrochloride," said the coroner. Her voice was quiet over the speakerphone, and Diana turned up the volume. "We never would have found it if we weren't looking for it—it's a drug that works in incredibly small doses, and there's barely any left in her system. But she was definitely drugged."

"I haven't heard of it," said Diana. "Is it common?"

"Common but restricted," said Hess. "It's a synthetic opium, basically, like a superconcentrated morphine. It's mainly used for large animals, like bear or bison. Makes sense for an attack like this because it works in seconds. Sale is restricted to veterinarians, and it gets used a lot in zoos. Around here it's more likely to show up in the parks service, maybe a ranch—anyone who might need to sedate a moose really, really urgently."

"Glad to know we don't have the weirdest jobs around, then," said Diana. She looked at Potash. "A veterinarian who works with park rangers—that's a pretty good lead."

"It doesn't make sense," I said.

"You keep saying that," said Diana.

"Because it doesn't," I said. "Now we're looking for a Withered who eats people, and sedates people, and ritualizes the sedation wound, and is also a veterinarian and a park ranger, and stalks women who go shopping, and—come on. It's too much. Why go to all that trouble?"

Diana rolled her eyes. "People do weird things, John."

"No, they don't," I insisted. "People do rational things based on normal reasons that we haven't found yet. None of this makes sense, which means we haven't found the right reasons."

"We don't need to find the reasons," said Potash, "just the killer."

"You keep asking the same question," said Diana. "What does he do that he doesn't have to do? Why did he try to hide the injection marks? This is your answer: because they're a massive clue that will help us find him."

"But it doesn't hang together," I said. "Ms. Hess, are you still there?"

Her voice was tinny over the phone. "They're right about this one, John—"

"Why is the sale of this sedative so restricted?" I asked.

"I told you," she said, "it's incredibly potent."

"And how much do you need to knock out a human? Especially a small one like Kristin Mercer?"

She gave a curt laugh. "According to the product specs it takes around five milligrams to knock out an elephant, about three milligrams for a rhino—the closest thing I could find to a human dose is in the safety notes, where it says even scratching the skin with the needle could be enough. There's a huge risk of accidental exposure."

"So think about that," I said, and turned back to Diana and Potash. "This drug is so powerful even touching it could knock a man unconscious, and we're supposed to believe this guy injects it into his food?"

There was a moment of silence, eventually broken by Diana's uncertain voice: "Maybe he's immune. A Withered who can eat anything, like . . . that kid from the comics. Matter-Eater Lad."

"You're stretching," I said. "Anything *might* be correct with a supernatural killer, but the simplest explanation is still always the best."

"I know," she said, and looked back out at the stopped car. "Damn."

"We know this guy's trying to deceive us," I said. "He wants us to think he's killing them one way, when really he's killing them in another."

"It seems to be," said Potash.

"So which is more likely?" I asked. "The cannibal who's feral yet meticulous, who's magic but also uses sedatives, who's a park ranger but also a veterinarian, who defies our profiling attempts at every turn because nothing he does makes sense, who not even our two Withered insiders have ever even heard of? Or a man who's killing people in a bizarre, indecipherable way specifically to throw us off?"

"Start driving," said Diana. "I'm calling Ostler."

13

"He's sent a letter after every victim," Ostler told us on the phone. "We don't have much time before he sends the next one."

We got the address for the Mercer family and joined the cops already on the scene. The father was holding his boy tightly, crying in shock while detectives scoured his home for clues. The boy, about six years old by the look of him, seemed disturbed by his father's crying and by the strangers in his house, but mostly he was curious. They hadn't told him about his mother yet.

"It doesn't look like anybody came inside," Detective Scott whispered. "There's no signs of forced entry, and the attack itself took place on the highway."

"We'll start talking to the neighbors," said Diana.

I checked my phone again, but The Hunter hadn't written back.

Nobody was home at the first house. The woman in the second house hadn't seen anything out of the ordinary and said that the guy from the first house left for work at five every morning.

"Define 'nothing out of the ordinary,'" I said. "Did you not see anything, or did you see the same people you see all the time?" If the killer lived on this street, he might be one of the ordinary things this woman had seen and not thought twice about.

"Who's the kid?" asked the woman.

"He's one of our investigators, ma'am," said Diana. "Can you tell us exactly who you saw this morning, if anyone?"

"Seems awfully young to be a policeman," said the woman. She was older, with her gray hair dyed brown, and wearing some kind of shapeless bag with a floral print. "How old are you?"

"I'm forty-seven," I said.

"You don't have to get sassy about it."

"Please, ma'am," said Diana, "can you answer the question?"

"Do I have all morning to sit and stare out my window?" she asked, her eyes wide with indignation. "Sure, I saw Kristin take her boy over to the Smith place, which I told her not to do because I don't trust the Smith family. Look at their yard! And Mr. Smith was already gone by then, of course, because he works in an office downtown, though I figure he can't make much money from it or they'd fix up their house a little."

"Did you see anything else?" asked Diana.

"The Mexican man in 2107 left to go to his job at eight, but then he came back at nine, or maybe a little after nine, so he may have gotten fired. He left again by 9:30: I know because my show hadn't gone to commercial yet, and it always goes on the half hour."

"Kristin Mercer took her son to Margaret Smith at 10:15," I

said, reading from my notes. "That's the house across the street from you, correct?"

"And just look at it," said the woman, waving toward it disdainfully.

"Did you see anyone near her car while she was inside?" I asked.

"Should I have?" asked the woman. "Has something happened to Kristin? It was that Mexican man, wasn't it?"

"Please answer the question," said Diana.

"No, I didn't see anyone near her car," said the woman. "What am I, some kind of a spy with nothing better to do than watch my neighbors all day?"

"Thank you," said Diana. "We'll get back to you if we need any more information." She closed the door, and we walked to the next house. Potash met us coming the other way.

"They don't know anything," he said. "Nobody does."

My phone rang; I hadn't put any contact numbers in it yet, so I was surprised to hear Trujillo on the other end.

"John," he said, "any luck at the Mercer house?"

"Nothing yet," I said. "Ask Elijah if Kristin stopped anywhere else before getting on the freeway."

"He already said she didn't."

"Ask again," I said. "His memory's terrible."

"I want to talk about your theory," he said. "It's interesting, but it doesn't hold water."

Yes it does. "You think we're chasing a ten-thousand-year-old veterinarian park ranger cannibal scholar who's well-spoken and careful except for when he's not?"

Trujillo sighed. "Is that really any more ridiculous than a ten-thousand-year-old plague goddess who packs a gun she never uses and makes sick kids sicker so she can hide in a hospital?"

"Yes," I said. "Mary Gardner had solid reasons for everything she did. We don't have that for The Hunter."

"We don't have it yet," said Trujillo. "That doesn't mean we never will."

"So how does he not pass out from the sedative?" I asked. "He can't inject it into their bodies and then eat them. Especially not Kristin Mercer—we found her hours after she died, but if he ate a sedative in her shoulder he'd have been too asleep to finish the attack, let alone dump the body."

"We know he injected her," said Trujillo, "and we know he ate her. We have clear evidence of both."

"You don't know it was him," I said, and began to grow excited as I thought more about it. "That would actually explain a lot: what if he has an accomplice? Or a pet, I don't know what you'd call it—someone he brings bodies back to, and then they eat them. That gives us the meticulous mastermind *and* the feral cannibal, in a way that makes sense."

"And then the pet falls asleep instead of the mastermind," said Trujillo, as if mulling the idea over in his head. "Still doesn't work: whoever eats the body will fall asleep before they're finished, unless they're immune to the sedative, in which case we don't need two people, we're back to just one. Simpler is better. And the bite wounds are still too . . . deliberately random. They don't follow a normal eating pattern, the way you'd expect from a feral accomplice like you're suggesting. The best theory is still Nathan's: that this killer somehow fetishizes the sedative—possibly because he's immune to it—and then takes weird bites out of the corpse."

"The best theory is mine," I insisted. "That the reason this doesn't make sense is because it's intended to confuse us."

"But that theory doesn't solve any problems," said Trujillo. "It denies all of our other answers without positing any of its own: it doesn't solve the sedative eating, it doesn't tell us how he slashed the tires without being seen, it doesn't give us anything new we can work with."

"It tells us our other answers are wrong," I said. "We have to give them up and start over."

"I have to go," he said. "Ostler needs something."

I hung up without saying good-bye. Why was he being so stubborn? He was so determined his profile was correct that he wouldn't see any alternatives.

We were back at the Mercer house, and Detective Scott met us at the door. "Good, we were just about to look for you two, we figured you'd want to be here when we questioned the husband."

Two? I looked at Potash and Diana, then down at myself before looking back at Scott. Typical.

"Hey, John," he said, "can you do me a favor? We're going to ask some rough question, it's . . . not good a situation for a kid to be in."

"I'm not a kid."

"I mean the Mercer kid," said Scott. "Can you take him into another room, keep him distracted?"

One, one, two, three, five, eight, thirteen. "Of course," I said. "Get rid of both kids at once, that's a good plan."

"We'll fill you in on everything," said Diana.

"Sure," I said, no longer caring. If they cut me out of this investigation, I was free to start my own. I walked to the father, still holding his son. "Hey . . . buddy. Want to come with me for a minute? We're going to watch . . ." What did kids watch these days? "Dora?"

"I want to watch *PAW Patrol*."

"Of course you do," I said. "Let's go, you can show me how to turn it on."

His father seemed reluctant to let him go but saw Detective Scott and the others looming nearby and apparently realized what was going on. The boy climbed down off his lap and led me into the other room. He handed me a remote. "You turn it on with this."

It looked like it had a thousand buttons, and I grimaced. "Thanks, kid." The power button was easy enough to find, and I was surprised when it actually turned on the TV instead of killing a satellite connection or something. They had the same cable company I had in my apartment, so I was able to search through the channels and find the kid stuff pretty quickly. "Look, *Sesame Street*. I didn't know they still showed that."

"I want to watch *PAW Patrol*."

"It's not on right now, and I don't know how your DVR works. Just . . . watch the puppets, I have to do something." He sat down, relatively calm, and I pulled out my phone. Still no e-mails from The Hunter. I typed one to him:

> *You're the one who wanted to talk. What do you want to say? I assume you're not going to just tell me who you are, or how to find you. So what are we doing here?*
>
> *Do you want me to kill someone for you? Is that what this is about? Because that's not going to happen either.*

I don't care if you're a lion or a hunter or whatever the hell you think you are: I'm not like you.

I sent it, then thought a minute and wrote another one:

Why do you eat them? It's not for food, because you don't treat them like food. You don't degrade them, either, like you're punishing someone vicariously, and there doesn't seem to be any emotion behind it, like you're living out some kind of fantasy. You just take bites, and then give us the bodies.

And then you give us a letter, I thought. *That's the key. What do you do that you don't have to do? You talk to us. That's what this is all about.*

The kid said something, and I looked up, but he was just talking to the TV. One of the puppets was talking back, in a weird kind of one-sided double conversation. I looked back at my phone and hit send on my message.

The Hunter was talking to us—somehow that's what this was all about for him. Was he trying to scare us? Trujillo thought he was trying to taunt us, to show his superiority, and I'd been arguing that he was just trying to confuse us. What if there was something more? We kept trying to describe the killer in human terms—we talked about Withered powers here and there, like the ability to withstand a sedative, but we hadn't talked about Withered motivations. Why would a Withered send us letters? What does he lack, that these letters are trying to make up for? A voice? Brooke had never said anything about a Withered without a voice. I'd have to ask Elijah.

I hadn't logged out of the e-mail server like I usually did, so I was surprised when it beeped softly. The Hunter had sent me a message:

Tell your boss to check the police station courtesy account. She might want to get to it before the interns do.

We had a new letter. Obviously I couldn't tell Ostler to check a specific e-mail account without exposing that I had an alternate line of communication . . . but who knew how long we'd have to wait before someone decided to check the police department courtesy account? If we got to it fast we could stay on his trail, we could find out where he'd sent the e-mail from and go there to look for clues. But I couldn't give myself away. I had to be patient.

I watched the little boy and the puppets talking to each other without ever talking to anyone but themselves.

I was at Whiteflower when the e-mail was finally discovered by a police department receptionist who was manning the phones on the night shift. Apparently she got bored; now we knew who checked the courtesy account. She alerted her superior, who alerted Detective Scott, who called Ostler, who called the rest of us and told us to meet at the old offices across the street. I told Brooke I was sorry to be leaving.

"You'll come back?" she said. "I love you, you know. You need to come back so we can get married and live happily ever after in a little white house."

"You don't love me," I told her.

She looked at the floor, the corners of her mouth sagging. "Do you love me?"

I hesitated, my hand hovering over the door. How could I answer that? I didn't love her, not the way I loved Marci. Not even the way I loved my mom, and at least half of that love was hate. After a long moment I found my voice to speak. "I don't know what that means."

Her voice was pleading. "Then how do you know I don't love you?"

"Because you're alive," I said, and banged on the door in a sudden rage. "The only people who love me are dead."

"You're not going to like this letter," said Ostler. The whole group was seated around the conference room table: six people, and an empty seat for Kelly. Ostler looked at each of us in turn. "None of us are. Know before we read it that I've already contacted headquarters, and they're dispatching people to check on your families."

"Holy crap," said Nathan, "how bad is it?"

Ostler looked at him, put on her glasses, and started to read: " 'To the Esteemed John Wayne Cleaver, and The People He Occasionally Associates With.' "

"Nice of him to include us," said Nathan. Ostler ignore him and continued:

" 'I hope you liked my last gift. The clues are important, and I trust you'll enjoy them, but don't overlook the body itself. Bodies are important. They are what makes you human. Your humanity is a gift, in a very real sense, and so I make a gift of it to you. Do not squander it.' "

Nathan snorted. "This guy's insa—"

"Shut up," said Diana.

" 'Because I am in a giving mood,' " Ostler continued, " 'I offer you another gift: the gift of knowledge. You seek to understand me, but do you really know yourself? Can you be true to what is in you if you don't know what that is? I suggest that you cannot. Your secrets must be opened, to yourself and to the world. You told me you're not like me. It is important to understand that you are.' "

"Hold up," said Trujillo. "We've never communicated with him directly, have we?"

"We have not," said Ostler. I didn't look at Potash, and counted my breaths slowly to keep my face from changing color. Ostler didn't look at me. "His last letter told us to kill someone and leave a note on the corpse. I think 'you told me you're not like me' is a reference to the fact that we didn't."

I said nothing.

Ostler took a deep breath. "This is the part where it gets bad. You each have a file, but I'm sure you've noticed that some of the key details of your lives have been redacted out of them. I did that to keep our focus on the enemy, and not each other, but some of that information is about to come out. Know that none of this information is new to me: I reviewed it all carefully, and didn't recruit anybody to the team that I didn't trust."

Nobody said anything; we just looked at each other in silence, wondering what horrible secrets were about to be revealed. What had Diana done? What about Nathan? I wasn't worried about my own secrets—anything Ostler knew, the others could know as well for all I cared. It was the things Ostler didn't know that I was worried about.

Did the letter really reveal secrets about Potash? How could anyone know that?

" 'Martín Trujillo is a statutory rapist,' " read Ostler. " 'She was willing, by most accounts, but the law does not consider a fourteen-year-old girl to be a reliable witness.' "

I leapt up from my chair. "You let him spend months alone with Brooke! He slept in the very next room!"

"I was nineteen years old," said Trujillo. "That was more than thirty years ago."

"And that makes it okay?"

"He served time," said Ostler. "He's had a flawless record since, with a long history of helping to enforce the law."

"You shouldn't have let him near Brooke," I said hotly.

"I'm not a pedophile, John," said Trujillo, "I was a dumb kid who made a dumb choice. 'Rapist' is a poor descriptor of what happened, but it's the correct legal term and I don't deny it."

"How does The Hunter even know this?" asked Nathan.

"He probably had to register as a sex offender," said Diana.

I felt my left hand curling into a fist, my right hand in my pocket, clenched around my knife. "Dammit, Ostler!"

"He's paid for it, and moved on," said Ostler. "People change—do you want me judging you by your worst mistake?"

"You mean you don't?"

"Just read the letter," said Diana. "It's probably going to get a lot worse before it gets better."

Ostler continued with the message: " 'I've met the girl—she's much older now, of course. Much prettier than his real wife. Maybe that's why the ugly one died so young?' "

"She died in a car accident," said Trujillo, and now his face was as thick with anger as mine. He rolled up his sleeve to display a long scar on his forearm. "I was in the car, too—to even suggest that I would kill my own wife—"

" 'Diana Lucas was drummed out of the air force,' " Ostler read, cutting him off, " 'dishonorably discharged for beating another woman. The victim was sent to the hospital with two broken ribs, several internal injuries, a concussion, and a dislodged eyeball.' "

"Wow," said Nathan. "What'd she do to you?"

"Nothing," said Diana curtly.

"I don't mean injuries," said Nathan. "I mean what did she do to deserve it? What started the fight?"

"She did nothing," said Diana slowly. "It wasn't a fight, it was a . . ." Diana sighed. "Gang initiation. She wanted to join our crew, and that means you take a beating. Same thing I got when I joined."

"They have gangs in the army?" asked Nathan.

"Air force," Diana corrected him sharply. "And yes, every branch of the military has gangs. I was in one before and I was in one there."

"And now?" I asked.

"Now I send a quarter of my paycheck to inner-city schools," said Diana. "Now I volunteer at a Big Sisters program whenever we're in a town big enough to have one. Now I think I've done pretty damn well for myself in paying for that mistake, and I don't want to have to relive it for you all any more than Trujillo wanted to relive his."

"So far these have both been a matter of public record," said Nathan. "Kudos to him for digging them up, but anybody could have done the research. He's not a mind reader."

"He knows about you," said Ostler.

Nathan shook his head. "I haven't done anything like this—"

" 'Nathan Gentry sold cocaine in West Philadelphia for three years,' " Ostler read, " 'and then again in Harvard for two. Most of his customers dropped out, unable to continue school; one of them turned to prostitution to pay for her habit.' "

"I didn't know about that," said Nathan.

"Are you kidding me?" asked Diana.

"I didn't know about the prostitution!" he protested. "Of course I knew about the drugs."

"And you thought that wasn't the same?" asked Trujillo. "I lived with an underage girl who thought she loved me—you destroyed dozens of lives."

"And then tried to hide it from us," added Diana.

"I was never caught or convicted," said Nathan, "I didn't think he'd know about it. I didn't think anybody knew except Ostler, and that's because I'm the one who told her."

"Mr. Gentry has moved on," said Ostler, "just like the rest of you."

"But he didn't suffer for it," said Diana, and I could tell from the curl of her brow that she was furious. "Trujillo went to jail, I was court martialed, and Nathan just skates by?"

"I knew it was wrong so I got out," said Nathan. "Do you know how hard it is to get out of dealing? And I think the fact that I did it voluntarily should say a whole lot more than you're giving me credit for—would you still be gangbanging if the air force hadn't forced you to stop?"

"They forced me to leave the air force," said Diana. "I could have kept banging anywhere I went."

"Arguing about these details gets us nowhere," said Ostler. "I wouldn't even be reading this if I didn't think it would help us catch a bad guy. How did he find out about Nathan? Where is that information available? What kind of person might have access to it? Put the past behind you and let's treat this letter like the clue it is."

I listened to them argue without joining in. Didn't they see that Nathan's crime was different, though? Not just because he didn't get caught, and not just because he only hurt people indirectly—his was different because he did it for different reasons. Trujillo was in love, or at least he was horny, and Diana wanted to fit in. They were both emotional acts, made for social reasons. Nathan's crime was all about himself: he wanted money, so he went out and got some. He sold drugs to get ahead.

As if I needed any more reasons to hate him.

"Okay," said Nathan, closing his eyes. "Who knows about me? . . . One of the other dealers, maybe? The kid who supplied me?"

"Kid?" asked Diana.

"I got started in high school," said Nathan. "We were all kids."

"More likely one of the victims," said Trujillo. "How many people know about the one who started selling herself? That can't be a big group of people."

"I didn't even know about her," said Nathan. "I can't exactly pull up a list of her friends and family."

In The Hunter's e-mail this morning, he'd asked me: "Is there anything you want me to leave out?" Is this what he was talking about? What was he going to say about me?

"Read the rest," said Potash. It was the first time he'd spoken. "It's no use jumping to conclusions until we have all the clues."

Ostler nodded. "The next part's about me." She read in a clear voice:

" 'Linda Ostler is a war criminal.' " She paused, but I didn't know if she was waiting for comments or just steeling her nerve to continue. " 'In 2002 she was assigned to a task force investigating the sale of weapons and explosives across the border from the US to Mexico. She used her position to sell hundreds of automatic rifles to a drug cartel, directly resulting in the deaths of six DEA agents and more than a hundred Mexican civilians.' "

She lowered the letter and looked at us. "Obviously I had my reasons," she said. "And 'war criminal' is a bit of an exaggeration."

"That was you?" asked Diana.

"I sold coke to some rich kids trying to get enough buzz to get their homework done," said Nathan. "You sold guns to drug lords? And they're mad because *I* ruined a few lives?"

"It was a plan that got out of hand," said Ostler. "Nobody wanted to supply the cartels, we wanted to catch the smugglers in the middle. We made a hard call and it was the wrong one."

"That's an understatement," said Diana. She looked around at the rest of us. "Has anybody killed more than a hundred civilians? Is that pretty much the high score for the group?"

Potash raised his hand, and Diana fell silent. The rest of us stared at him. "I'll be very surprised if it's in that letter, though," he said simply.

I'd known he was a killer. I'd known he was the most dangerous one of us. Why did this still feel like a shock? Because he'd admitted it so casually?

Potash hacked a Withered to death with a machete. While dying of a lung disease. Who had I gotten myself entangled with?

Ostler shook her head. "Here's the only line about Potash. It comes at the end, though, after the one about John—"

"Do them in order," I said. "Let's see if he has anything to say about me that the rest of you haven't already guessed."

Ostler cleared her throat: " 'I haven't forgotten about you either, John. I'm sure your friends know about the man you electrocuted; that was in the papers. Do they know about the time you beat your elderly neighbor half to death, and then killed her husband? What about the time you soaked your mother in gas and burned her alive in a car?' "

"Bloody hell," said Diana.

I said nothing, only stared at Ostler.

"No excuses?" asked Nathan. "No tearful explanations of how it all had to happen and there was nothing you could do to stop it?"

"I assume there's more," I said, still not looking at the others.

"How could there possibly be more?" Nathan cried.

" 'You think you're not like me,' " Ostler read, " 'but you're more like me than any of them. They hurt people because that's the way the world works: they want something, so they take it, and hold no pity for the rabble who get in their way. Thus it has always been. You and I are different. We hurt people because we enjoy it. Because the pain and the death are ends unto themselves.

" 'The antelope may crash their horns and call themselves strong, but all of them fall before the lions.' "

I'm not like him, I told myself. *Even if we do the exact same things for the exact same reasons, I'm not like him.*

I just can't explain why.

"In John's defense," said Ostler, "everyone he's killed was a Withered."

"Even your mother?" asked Trujillo.

"She wasn't when I started," I said, and turned to him without blinking. Even thinking about this made me want to scream in rage, but I'd be damned if I was going to let them see me lose control. I told the story in short, even tones. "Nobody possessed Brooke, so I was trying kill her. My mom showed up, Nobody left Brooke to attack her, and . . . she died." I made a small rolling motion with my hand. "Yada yada yada."

"What the hell is wrong with you?" asked Diana, and somehow that was the comment that stung me worst of all.

"The Hunter knows too much about us," said Nathan. "If he has all of this he could have anything—he could have my parents' address."

"People have been sent to your friends and family," Ostler repeated. "The Withered bodies the FBI picked up from the hospital were more . . . enlightening than my superiors expected. I think they're finally taking our work seriously, and that includes this implied threat to your loved ones."

"You still haven't read my section," said Potash.

"It's the conclusion of the letter," said Ostler:

" 'And of course Albert Potash, the Death that Walks. How many people has he killed? What noble justifications did he claim? Let this be the most damning evidence of all: I know everything, and I could find nothing on him. He is a man without a past. In the modern age, nobody loses their past unless someone has gone to very great lengths to bury it.

" 'There are antelopes, and there are lions. And then there is something more. Think carefully about the company you keep.' "

14

When I was a little boy I used to love dinosaurs. Who wouldn't? They were huge, and everyone was afraid of them, and they could eat my parents. I didn't necessarily want them to eat my parents, but I knew that they could; I knew that they had the power to do whatever they wanted, and no one could stop them because they were dinosaurs.

Clayton County didn't have a zoo, but once when I was four we went on vacation to San Diego, and we visited the zoo there, and the lions and tigers and gorillas were great and all but what I really wanted to see were the dinosaurs. I'd been reading about them my whole life, and this was my big chance. Did the zoo have a T. rex? A stegosaurus? My favorite was always the triceratops, don't ask me why. They just looked cool. Do they have a triceratops, Dad?

He laughed, and told me the dinosaurs were dead.

Imagine for a moment that you've gone to a zoo,

excited to see your very favorite animal—let's say elephants—only to learn that all the elephants have died, just before you got there. That's what I thought at first: that the dinosaurs at the zoo had all gotten sick, or been poisoned by bad food, and had passed away in a sudden tragedy. How would you react? How would you react if you were a four-year-old boy? It destroyed me. I wanted to know what had happened to them, and if the zookeepers had tried to save them, and when they were going to get new ones. And of course my parents were both morticians, and I had a vague sense of what that meant, so I wondered if we were going to embalm the dinosaurs while we were there on our trip. I didn't know what embalming was when I four, but I knew the word. I knew it was something you did to dead people, and that it was important. I figured that dinosaurs were important enough to warrant the same treatment.

I don't know if my father understood the depths of my confusion—if he understood what it meant to me—but around this time he figured out why I was confused. No one had ever told me that dinosaurs were extinct—or if they had, they hadn't explained what the word meant. My father laughed again, delighted by his four-year-old's adorable misunderstanding, and told me that all the dinosaurs were dead, in the whole world. That they'd been dead for millions of years. No matter where I looked, or how long I lived, or how hard I wanted to, I would never see a dinosaur anywhere because they didn't exist anymore. All we had were bones, and even those were too old to touch.

Roll that around in your mind a little. The sudden realization that every animal you wanted to see was suddenly and irrevocably killed—sure, it had happened millions of years ago, but for me it happened right then and there. In my head they were alive, billions of them, and then the meteors struck, and the world ended, and they all died in fire and agony. I was a personal witness to a mass extinction. How can a child endure such a thing?

There's a lot of trust tied up in the way we learn about the world. The things we know, and the things we think we know, and the people who tell them to us. The facts we learn for ourselves, and the facts we assume about everyone else. Trust is how we function as a society. Take away the trust, and you take away the function.

I joined Ostler's team because I had nothing else left, and no other clear alternatives. My plan had always been to grow up, get a degree in mortuary science, and work as a mortician. I'd never really wanted anything else. That seems like a weird dream in hindsight, to be so set on following in the footsteps of parents I hated. But the hatred, when I thought about it, was recent, a new development brought on by divorce and abandonment and adolescence. For most of my life they'd been fine: angry sometimes, loving at others. My father beat me up a few times, and he beat my mom a lot of times, but I didn't have the emotional capacity to separate that from the good stuff: the jokes at dinner, and the movies on the couch, and the stories at bedtime. Sometimes he slept on my floor because I was too scared to sleep alone. I don't know if that made him a good dad, but it made him more than just a bad one.

By the time things soured and we all fell apart, my heart was already set on the family business, and no amount of uncomfortable association could change it. Embalming a body—cleaning it, caring for it, giving it that final solemn celebration of the life it used to have—was my greatest source of peace. It's where I went when things got too messed up to deal with, and when my family got messed up. The embalming was all I had.

And then the Withered came, and my mother died, and I ruined Brooke's life, and Ostler had the only key to the only door that looked like an escape route. I'd done a lot of very shady things killing those Withered, and in my final desperation to kill Nobody, I'd done things I couldn't hide. If I worked for Ostler I could help Brooke, forget my mom, and make all my crimes go away. I could leave my life behind.

That's never as easy as it sounds. And now I was doing it again: I was leaving, maybe forever. I'd slipped free of Potash again, and I was ready to disappear for good.

Almost ready.

I was back in the park, holding a new box of wood as I stood before the grill. It hadn't snowed since the last time, and the half-charred logs of my previous fire lay in a wet, cold heap on the ground. I kicked them out of the way; they'd burn, but only when the fire was already big. That wouldn't be a problem today. I was going to make a very big fire.

I started the same as always, breaking the planks into smaller and smaller pieces, bending them with my hands—feeling the wood resist, feeling it bite into my hands as I strained against it, gritting my teeth until the boards snapped with a brutal crack that made Boy Dog yelp. I ignored him; I couldn't allow myself to laugh at his fear, but I couldn't bring myself to comfort him, either. He was simply there, and I was simply next to him, and any interaction we had was an illusion, like the puppets on the Mercer boy's TV. I took deep breaths and stacked the splinters in careful rows, crafting my little log cabin with all the precision of an architect building a world-spanning bridge: piece by piece, bit by bit, this twig here and this wood there and each one exactly where they had to go until I couldn't take it anymore and scattered them with my hands, screaming in frustration. Boy Dog stood up in his spot under the table, looking around for whatever danger had alarmed the weird human boy. I clenched my hands in fists, breathing deep. I had copies of The Hunter's letters in my pocket, all three of them, and I pulled them out now and crumpled them into balls, and piled the wood scraps haphazardly on top of them. It wasn't pretty, but it would burn. I struck a match and lit the paper, watching it turn brown and then black, with a thin line of yellow crackling hot along the edge. A wave of color spreading across the wrinkled surface, leaving a blackened char behind.

The smaller sticks began to smolder, and then to burn with a low, almost invisible flame. I watched the fire carefully, feeding it bigger sticks when it was ready to catch them, and smaller sticks when it just needed fuel. Soon the flames were high, burning hotter than they needed to, so hot they'd burn themselves out before all the fuel was gone, but I didn't care, and when the heat beat against my face I realized I was smiling, and when Boy Dog barked I realized I was laughing, whooping with joy at the chaotic mass of flame. I needed more; this wasn't big enough, the fire wanted to get out of its metal box and burn higher. I looked around, but everything was covered in snow. My eyes lit on my cardboard box of firewood, and I placed it carefully in front of the metal grill and then pushed the entire fire into it; dumping the fire had killed it last time, but now I'd been smarter; I'd moved it into fuel and safety, and after a brief lull it caught again, flames licking the cardboard and lighting up the wood until it seemed to glow with an inner power, as if the wood itself was only fire in disguise, trapped in a painful solid form and yearning to burst free. The flames grew higher, climbing and leaping until they rose two feet out of the box. More than three feet off the ground.

Three feet was high enough to reach the picnic table.

I wanted more.

"Out!" I shouted gleefully. "Get out of there!" Boy Dog looked at me dumbly, but when he saw me shoving the fiery box across the ice toward the mouth of his lair he yelped and ran out. With Boy Dog out of the way, the space beneath the picnic table was a perfect cave of snow-covered wood; the box was almost too hot to touch, the flame eating hungrily at the cardboard sides, but I pushed it under the table with my foot and watched with giddy fascination as the fire began clawing at the table itself.

The fire was going to be free.

The poor ventilation made the air roar as the fire sucked it in beneath the table. Melted snow dripped down between the boards. I found the old, charred planks from the last time I was here, and used them as makeshift shovels to push the snow off the top of the table, and suddenly instead of melting, the snow was evaporating completely, rising into the air in visible clouds of steam. The thick, painted wood of the picnic table started to blacken and burn, and I smiled as the orange flames curled up and around each individual board. The fire had grown and swelled and taken over, leaving its tiny box and going not where *I* wanted, but where *it* wanted. And it wanted everything.

"That's right," I said, watching it, and then shouted at the sky: "That's right!" I looked at Boy Dog, hoping to share my exultation, but he only stared back morosely, unmoved either way. I thought again about the puppets on the Mercer boy's TV, and the sudden juxtaposition struck me as so funny I couldn't help but bring up my hand, flapping the fingers and thumb together like a puppet mouth. "Hey there, Boy Dog, what do you think of this awesome fire?" I made a grumpy face and spoke in a gravelly tone, opening and closing my hand in time with the words: "Well, John, I'm a stupid dog. I have no opinion about anything that isn't food or Potash's blankets." I returned to my normal voice, facing the hand puppet with my most serious expression. "Speaking of Potash, why didn't he follow me? Too busy murdering innocents to threaten my life today?" Back to the dog voice. "I know, it's like he doesn't even care about threatening you anymore. The magic has gone out of your relationship completely. Maybe he's off growling at some other teenage boy he's been threatening on the side. You'll be gone for days before they even . . . notice . . . ."

I stopped talking, but kept moving my hand, opening and closing the fake puppet mouth, staring straight into it. It was the same hand motion I'd done in our first viewing of the cannibal's first victim. I'd been demonstrating the movement of the teeth. I bared my teeth now, clacking them together, and mirrored the motion with my hand.

It was a puppet.

The picnic table snapped loudly, some knot in the old wood popping in the heat. A car drove by in my peripheral vision, along the road on the far edge of the park, and seeing it brought me back to reality with a sudden shock. This wasn't a barbecue or a campfire anymore, it was arson—arson in a public place, destroying city property. I swore and backed away, looking at the scene with a critical eye. The snow I'd pushed away was too obvious: no one would see this as a picnic that got out of hand, but as a deliberate attempt to burn the table. My best bet was to grab Boy Dog and go, to get away before anyone noticed. I called him softly and ran toward the car; he followed, but only in his slow, plodding way. I called again, patting my legs, but he couldn't be bothered to move. I opened the car door, shifting the things I'd packed there in the early morning when Potash was asleep, and Boy Dog picked up his speed a little, shifting from a walk to a slow jog. I looked around. Who was watching me through distant windows? Under heavy branches?

Should I warn the others about the puppet? Would they even take me seriously if I did?

Boy Dog finally reached the car, heaving himself into the foot well on the passenger side. I made sure he was out of the way, slammed the door, and ran around to the driver's side, fumbling for my keys. I threw myself in, sat down and stared at the fire. It seemed thin and ethereal from this distance, in this light, the flames fading into the morning sky beyond. Black smoke was beginning to curl up in dark, angry billows.

I had to leave now. I had to get to Brooke and go.

But if I did, the whole team would die.

I pulled out my phone, dialing Potash's number with one hand while I started the car with the other. I got a recorded alert for a wrong number and wished I'd bothered to put everyone in speed dial. I hung up and dialed again.

Potash answered his phone. "John, why did you leave again?"

"Plausible deniability," I said. "I didn't see you commit any genocides, and you didn't see me not burning down a picnic table."

"Did you burn down a picnic table?"

"I just said I didn't, do you even listen to me?" I shoved my keys in the ignition and turned it on, hearing the engine roar to life. "The Hunter is using a puppet."

"What?"

"He has a skull puppet, probably an actual skull—he cleaned it up, bolted the jaw on, and now he's using it to take bites out of the corpses." I threw the car into reverse and backed up wildly, looking over my shoulder as I shouted into the phone. "That's why he doesn't pass out when he bites the sedated bodies, and that's why the bites are scattered all over instead of concentrated in one spot, and that's why his methods are a crazy mishmash of precision and ferocity: because he's faking being a cannibal. It's all an act, from the bites to the hidden injection marks to the letters he sends us. It's all fake."

"Why would he fake cannibalism?"

"To throw us off the scent," I said, putting the car in drive and heading for the street. The park table was burning brightly behind me now, and it occurred to me that in all my frantic planning, I'd only thought about escape. I'd never even considered the possibility of putting out the fire. I could have, if I'd acted quickly; there was enough snow to smother the whole thing. But it hadn't even crossed my mind. I hate to kill a fire.

"John?" said Potash.

"He's trying to trick us," I said, as I pulled into the street. "He's a Withered and he knew we had Brooke and now he probably knows we have Elijah, so he's hiding his methods. If he'd come into town killing people the same way he always did we'd have figured out who he was and how he worked, and then we could have figured out a way to kill him. He knew we could do that because we'd done it to half a dozen Withered already. So he's hiding his real kills and feeding us a bunch of fakes to keep us in the dark. When he comes for us, we won't know anything about him."

I paused, waiting for him to answer, but all I heard were vague mumbles in the background. After a moment Potash spoke again. "It looks like we're the ones going after him. Trujillo thinks he's figured out where he is."

"Where?"

"Do you know anything about this guy?" asked Potash, ignoring my question. "Anything at all? A cannibal we thought we could deal with—just wear body armor and shoot first. But if that's all an act . . . we need to know what we're up against."

I hemmed and hawed for a minute, trying to piece together the few bits of info that we knew about The Hunter—or the real killer who was using The Hunter as a facade. He was smart. He was careful. He was patient. But we knew all that already. He was taking on an FBI kill team all on his own . . . . "He's confident," I said, slowly putting the picture together in my mind. "He's made a lot of plans, including a lot of interaction, and so far all of it has worked. He's a planner, which means he's planning something big—not just individual kills and messages, but an end game. He's . . ." I shook my head, watching for ice on the road, trying to think as fast as I could—all the more difficult because there was so much I couldn't say without giving myself away. "He's a talker," I said, thinking about the letters. And the e-mails: he'd insisted on communicating with me, but he'd never really said anything. "Words are important to him," I said, "and communication. Something about that means something to him, maybe the exchange of words or thoughts or ideas."

"Maybe he's just an extrovert," said Potash.

"Maybe," I said. "Or maybe he's just a liar. His communication is only important because it's been a method for deceiving us. He planned this entire thing to throw us off his trail, which means . . . which means that his real trail has nothing to do with what he's trying to make us think about."

"So he's not a cannibal," said Potash.

"Maybe he *can't* be a cannibal," I said suddenly. "Are you there with the others?"

"Yes."

"Brooke said something about a Withered with no mouth: someone who couldn't possibly eat our victims because he can't eat anything. A Withered with no mouth is also likely to be obsessed with talking, which could explain why he's been writing so many letters—because written words are the only way he can communicate."

I heard more mumbling in the background and an expletive that must have come from Nathan.

"Potash?" I asked.

"Are you close?" he said.

"Maybe ten minutes."

"And you're sure about this?" he asked. "The puppet, the deception, the whole thing?"

"It all makes sense," I said. "For the first time in the entire investigation we have a single theory that explains all our variables."

"And the Withered with no mouth?"

"I can't be sure until I see him," I said, "but it fits. If you were a monster with no mouth, trying to hide from a bunch of monster hunters, what better way than by tricking them into chasing a fanged, hungry carnivore?"

"Don't worry," he said, "I believe you. Get here as fast as you can, because we're going on high alert. Trujillo's got a lot of notes about a mouthless Withered and it's not good."

"Which one is it?"

"His name is Rack," said Potash. "Apparently he's their king."

15

"The key was in the third letter," said Trujillo. "Nathan and I found the clue last night, but I didn't realize the full significance until this morning. In the penultimate paragraph, talking about Potash, he says he knows everything."

"Just to be clear," I asked, "are we talking about the cannibal or Nathan?"

"Shut up," said Nathan.

"Obviously we're talking about the cannibal," said Trujillo. "He's always gone out of his way to show us how smart he is, but here's the thing: he says he knows everything about us, but he never mentions Brooke."

Of course he knows about Brooke, I thought. *He's knows all about me and where I came from, so he'd have to know about Brooke. Why wouldn't he mention her in the list?*

"Obviously if he knows everything, he knows about Brooke, right?" said Trujillo. "And given that his first letter was delivered in the regular mail, to this office, he obviously knows where to find us. There's no way he could have all of that information and not know about Brooke. Which means Brooke is somehow different in his mind: she's not one of us. Look at the structure of the letter: an introduction and then a paragraph for each member of our team—except there are six team members mentioned by name, and seven paragraphs."

"The last paragraph doesn't have a name," said Nathan. "It's got to be about Brooke—it's the only thing that makes sense."

"It could just be a conclusion," I said.

"Possibly," said Trujillo. "But it doesn't act like a conclusion: we all read it as an extension of Potash's paragraph, but that would make him the only member of the team to get two. It's more likely, I think, that's it's a reference to the seventh member of our team. Let me read it to you." He looked at his computer screen and read: " 'There are antelopes, and there are lions. And then there is something more. Think carefully about the company you keep.' " He looked up. "The Hunter has kept a very consistent pattern with his lion-and-antelope metaphor over all three letters: a lion is a killer, and an antelope is a victim. Him and us. Withered and human. But what does that last bit refer to? Something more? Couldn't this be a reference to Brooke? The amalgamation of human and Withered together?"

"She's not a Withered," I said.

"But she's not really human anymore either," said Nathan. "We're not trying to disrespect her, obviously, but be honest with yourself. She's messed up."

"Maybe she wasn't in the letter because she didn't do anything wrong," I said. "Did you think of that? This nasty little hit squad of rapists and murderers, and the one who suffers the most is the one who's never actually hurt anyone?"

"How does this help us find The Hunter?" asked Ostler.

"We're getting to that," said Nathan. "And it's a direct answer to John, too."

"Brooke's paragraph is different because she is different," said Trujillo, "but also because The Hunter thinks of her differently. He doesn't see her as an enemy—which implies that she's a friend."

"She's not Nobody," I said. "She's Brooke Watson."

"She has more of Nobody in her than Brooke," said Trujillo. "This has been our concern ever since she first recognized Elijah—even before that, frankly, which is why I was brought on the team in the first place. If Brooke feels more kinship with the Withered than with us, she might start to help them."

I wanted to break his skull. "She would never—"

"We searched her room," said Nathan coldly. "Top to bottom. There was a rip in the bottom of the mattress: she was hiding letters."

The room fell silent.

"That's impossible," said Diana.

"The one we found was written in crayon," said Trujillo. "It's the only writing instrument the nurses would give her, because they're not sharp enough to hurt anyone. She ripped the letter out of my hands and ate it before we could learn any more, but one of the nurses confirmed that she'd been passing letters between Brooke and another man for a couple of weeks now."

"I think you could have led with that," snapped Ostler, suddenly angry. "How did this happen? Weren't the nurses briefed on Brooke's situation?"

"We've been keeping them in the dark about almost everything," said Trujillo. "They knew Brooke was unstable, but they didn't know why, and they certainly didn't know she might be contacting a fugitive. In a regular mental institution this might have raised some red flags, but in an assisted-living center it's a different situation. The nurses go out of their way to help the patients interact with people because most of them don't get *enough* contact with the outside. It didn't occur to the nurse that the letters might be bad."

"It's not true," I said, though I didn't feel it. He was right: Brooke was more Withered than human, mentally speaking. She was an emotional wreck. *Think carefully about the company you keep.*

"Did you get a description of the man?" asked Ostler. "Have we found him?"

"His name is Aldo Blankenship," said Nathan. "He lives in The Corners, a block away from Pancho's Pizza."

I stared at Elijah. "Tell us everything you know about Rack."

We were back in the interrogation room, where he'd been led by the restraining collar.

"Rack's not your cannibal," he said, rubbing his neck. "He doesn't have a mouth."

"So I hear," I said. "Sit down and tell me about him."

Elijah blew out a long, slow breath, and sat heavily in the chair across from me. We were the only two people in the room—I was the only one willing to be in a room with him—but the others were listening behind the glass. He looked at me intently.

"Rack is the king," he said. "He's the one who came up with

this idea in the first place, who figured out how to make us Gifted. He is far more powerful, and far more dangerous, than any other Withered you've ever faced."

"What kind of power?"

"Do you believe you have a soul?" he asked suddenly.

I didn't know how to answer. "What do you mean?"

"I mean a soul: an eternal spirit or an inner animus or whatever you want to call it. A special thing that makes you *you,* the thing that goes up to heaven when you die, the thing that gives you conscious thought instead of animal instinct. Some people say it weighs twenty-one grams, some people say it doesn't exist. Whatever you think it is: do you have one?"

My family wasn't especially religious, but we had a funeral chapel in our home, and I'd heard more sermons about the afterlife than most kids have heard sermons. They said the soul left the body when it died, and that made a kind of sense to me because I'd seen Marci after she died, and she wasn't there. Her body was, but *Marci* wasn't. Was that just a superstition? I don't know. Probably. But I wanted to believe that some part of Marci was still somewhere, because otherwise what was I in love with? A cadaver? I guess there are a lot of people who wouldn't be surprised by that at all.

I shook my head. "Are you asking about souls in general, or mine specifically? Because those are going to be two very different answers."

"I only ask because it's a word we use," said Elijah. "I don't know if it's the right word, or what 'right' even means. But the Withered's souls are broken and corrupted—not just metaphorically, but physically."

"You're not just talking about their sense of wonder."

"I'm talking about the black sludge," said Elijah, and I looked at him closely. He nodded. "I know you know it, because you saw it dripping out my chest that night in the mortuary. You've killed Withered before, so you've seen what happens: the body decomposes into a kind of dark muck. Charred grease and gristle. We call that soulstuff."

"Brooke's used that word before," I said. "What is it?"

"Some say it's our souls, which are too corrupted to go to heaven, so they just stay behind and destroy the body. Some say it's our bodies themselves, breaking free from the physical form that confines us, which is why some of us can use it to change shape or move around."

"That's how Nobody worked," I said. "Or I guess you knew her as Hulla—she didn't have a body of her own, just a big blob of ashy grease."

"I remember her," said Elijah, "though not much. She worked with Forman, I think."

I nodded. "Our best guess on the sludge was that it's what happened to the body when whatever power that keeps you alive isn't . . . keeping you alive anymore. That you'd been around so long your body was just a pile of grease that looked like a human, and as soon as the energy or whatever disappeared—the thing behind that human disguise—the real body fell apart."

"Maybe," said Elijah. "I don't know enough to say that's not true, but I can tell you for sure that it's not the only truth. It has a power of its own, like you saw with Nobody. Some Withered can use it for other things. Rack is one of them."

"What can he do?" I asked again. "We need to know, so we can kill him."

"Rack has a normal human body," said Elijah, "all except for one part." He traced a line around his upper chest and lower face, and I remembered Brooke saying something similar. "He has a hole here, where his heart should be, and up through his neck and into his head—there's no jaw, no mouth, no nose, just a hole. It's full of soulstuff, and that's how he kills people: the darkness reaches out, like a tendril, and it goes right down your throat and tears out your heart."

"He eats hearts?" I asked.

"He doesn't eat them," said Elijah, "he uses them. His body needs a heart just as much as yours does, but when we made our pact with the darkness he gave his up. He lives by stealing new ones."

"And you say he takes the hearts through the throat?" I asked. "He doesn't go just straight through the chest?"

"I suppose he could do it either way," said Elijah, "but I've only ever seen him use the victim's mouth and throat. It's . . . actually much more disturbing that way."

"And much easier to hide," I said, and glanced at the mirror behind me, knowing the team was watching and listening. "If he has to sustain himself by eating hearts, there will still be corpses around town that we haven't identified as his victims. We might not have identified them as victims at all—most bodies don't get autopsies, so a mysterious death with no external sign of violence would probably just get rubber-stamped as a stroke or a heart attack. Someone would find the body, the coroner would take a look, and then it's on to the funeral." I looked over my shoulder. "Somebody talk to Rhonda Hess and see if she has any unexplained deaths over the last few weeks."

"You think Rack is here?" asked Elijah. "In Fort Bruce?"

I nodded. "We think he's hiding his own kills and using a

skull puppet to create a fake Withered cannibal, to keep us busy hunting for the wrong guy."

"If Rack was killing people in town I'd know," said Elijah. "I get all my memories from dead bodies, and I don't remember being killed by him."

"There are five mortuaries in Fort Bruce," I said. "Do you each cover a specific area?"

"Not geographically, but yes. Kind of. For random bodies like you're talking about, there are guidelines as to which mortuary handles which cases."

I looked over my shoulder again. "Ask Hess what those rules are, and focus on bodies that were assigned to other mortuaries." I looked back at Elijah. "If he's hiding from us, it makes sense that he's hiding from you, too."

"But why?" asked Elijah. "He couldn't have known I'd end up working with you."

"But he never contacted you," I said. "Gidri was trying to recruit you, but Rack didn't bother—from what you've told us he didn't bother trying to recruit Gidri, either. He just let them wage their war and attract all our attention, and meanwhile he worked in the background planning this attack."

"So what is he planning?" asked Elijah. "He wouldn't go to all this trouble just to fool you for no reason."

"I assume he's planning to kill us," I said. "That's what I'd be doing in his place. But we think we've found him, through another connection, and we're taking the fight to him. That's why we need to know everything we can about how he works."

"He'll kill you," said Elijah.

I didn't flinch. "Tell us how."

"By being smarter than you," said Elijah. "His powers are one thing—don't get close, don't let him attack you in person, and definitely wear some kind of face mask to keep him out of your mouth. Ripping hearts out isn't the only thing his soulstuff can do, but it's a big one."

"What else can it do?"

"He can talk with it," said Elijah. "He leaves a bit of soulstuff behind when he goes for the heart—it's the conservation of mass, he can't absorb new flesh without expelling something else. Or I guess he could, but he'd be enormous. He leaves a bit of soulstuff behind in the corpse, and then he can animate it—not the whole body, but the mouth and lungs. The part his soul has touched. It's the only way he can speak out loud."

"I remember Brooke saying something about that, too," I said. "She gave us more than I realized." Had I been ignoring her, just like the rest of the team ignored me?

No wonder she'd started looking to the Withered for friends.

"Who is Brooke?" asked Elijah. "You've mentioned her three times now, but I've never heard of her before. She's the friend of a friend, I assume?"

"She has all of Nobody's memories," I said.

"That sounds like a story I need to hear sometime."

"Later," I said. "We don't know how long it will be before he kills again, or before he tries to contact her again and realizes we've discovered him. If you can tell us how to kill him, we can go in and do it now, in force, before he has a chance to reach whatever end game he's been building toward."

"That's what you tried with Gidri in the mortuary," said Elijah. "You lost two men, and at least two more are injured."

"Isn't that worth it to kill someone like Rack?"

He paused, saying nothing as he looked at me. I tried to read what he was thinking, and found him more humanlike in his facial expressions than I expected—certainly more human than Potash. His brow was furrowed, his eyes slightly squinted, his mouth grim and flat. He was concerned. He probably thought we were all going to die. How he would react to that concern, though, I couldn't guess.

"Let me come with you," he said.

"We still don't trust you."

"I've done nothing but help," he said. "I haven't attacked anyone, I haven't done anything alarming, I've answered all of your questions." He leaned forward. "I'm more human than any thousand other people you could ask—put together. I want this shadow war over, and I want your side to win. What will it take to prove that to you?"

"Tell us how to kill Rack."

"You can't," said Elijah. "He regenerates too quickly. He's faster, stronger, and smarter than any other Withered. I've known him for ten thousand years and he's never lost. Even if you overwhelm him, he'll just retreat and keep killing and come up with another plan. You're too close now to let that happen, so bring me on your raid. Get me close enough and I can drain his memory—even if he attacks me first, even if he knocks me down and breaks my bones and reaches in to steal my heart, I'll be touching him, and that's all it takes. I can empty his mind and stop him."

I stared at him. Was his description of Rack's abilities accurate? Would his plan to get around them work? It all seemed to make sense, but it was so hard to trust him. I wanted to trust him—I felt a . . . kinship to Elijah that I'd felt with barely a handful of people in my entire life. It had scared me before, because he was a Withered, and it still scared me, but . . .

But the rest of my team were humans, and they'd done worse things than Elijah had ever even tried. I couldn't define my morality the same way anymore. There was too much gray area. But how could I judge him without knowing him? I needed time to get inside his head, time I didn't have.

Or maybe I only needed one more question. "What about his thoughts?" I asked. "Drain his mind into yours and for all intents and purposes you'll be him. What's to stop him from continuing his plans in another body?"

"I'm easier to kill than he is," said Elijah simply. "If his mind takes over, kill me."

I looked at the mirror again. "I trust him," I said. "Let's move."

16

We moved silently through The Corners, under cover of darkness. Elijah had warned us that Rack would see us coming—that his senses were just as superhuman as his strength—but still we tried to be quiet, if for no other reason than to keep the neighbors asleep and unaware. They had no idea of the combat we were about to engage in: the final battle with the king of the demons. The less they knew the better.

The plan was simple: to trick Rack into a confrontation and get Elijah close enough to drain his mind. Seeing it through would be much harder. Potash was leading the way, a cannula in his nose and a portable oxygen tank strapped securely to his back; he wore his steel machete in a sheath beside it, a combat knife on his belt—a new one, since I still had his old one—and enough guns to arm half the police department. Diana was with him, armed more simply but looking no less imposing. I had, again, suggested that we leave her outside to guard an entrance, but Trujillo had insisted that she be in the first wave. If Rack tried to flee, we'd lose him, no matter how many police officers surrounded the building with automatic weapons. We had to force a showdown, and that meant bringing in the main team. We had to make him want to kill us.

I didn't *like* the plan, but I agreed with it. I hoped we lived long enough to see it through.

Ostler was outside, coordinating the attack, and Trujillo and Nathan were staying back in the office, as far out of harm's way as we could keep them. They weren't combatants. I wasn't either, but I was the only person willing to get close enough to Elijah to help him. I didn't want to like him, but I found myself trusting him in spite of myself. Maybe because we were both the outcasts on the team? I don't know, and I preferred not to think about it.

I kept my knife in my pocket, my fingers tight around the nylon-sheathed blade. Elijah had no weapons but his hands and whatever ancient power resided within them. He kept patting his pockets, then mumbling and shaking his head; after the fourth or fifth time I whispered softly.

"You missing something?"

"It's nothing," he said, "Just a nervous habit. I keep my keys on a lanyard, so I won't forget them during the times my memory's all patchy. Sometimes I can't even find my car, I'm so messed up, but I always have my keys. It's a comfort thing, I guess, and I'm nervous right now, so . . ." He shook his head. "I'm fine."

We were crouched in the shadow of a minivan parked on the street one door down from Rack's house. Potash was ahead, scouting, and when Ostler gave the word that it was time to move, we'd run up to join him in the first wave. I looked at the house: a blue two-story, made gray by the moonlight. Everything was dark. I looked back at Elijah. "You'll know him when you see him?"

"He's hard to miss."

"I guess that's true." I pulled out the knife, turning it slowly in my hands, thinking about the death of Mary Gardner. That's how I tried to think of it—not as my attack, but as her death. *I* had nothing to do with it, or at least I didn't want anything to do with it. I remembered the knife going in, coming out, going in. I remembered the feeling of it, a dizzying blend of horror and elation, of rage and unfettered joy. I had loved it, and that was the worst part: I was lost in a frenzy, far beyond my own control, and I loved every minute of it. I couldn't allow myself to do that again. To *feel* that again.

And yet there was a part of me that wanted to feel that more than anything in the world.

"Your knife's not going to help you," whispered Elijah.

"Not tonight," I said. I didn't say anything else.

The night was silent and dark.

"Go!" said Agent Ostler in my ear, and I rose to a run. Elijah stayed close behind me, and we reached the door just as Detective Scott broke it open with a heavy metal ram. Potash went in first, Diana right on his heels, assault rifles up and scanning the corners, hunting for monsters in the shadows. Elijah and I followed behind, hoping that Rack's attack, when it came, would involve something more targeted than a grenade or a spray of bullets. Everything about him suggested that he would want to finish this in person, face to face, and that was our only hope for success. I held my breath and stepped through the door. Detective Scott brought up the rear, with a half dozen armored cops behind him. Their whispers echoed in my earpiece:

"Clear."

"Moving up."

"On your six."

"Clear."

A stairway in the main entry led up to the second floor, and two cops watched it while the rest of us snaked through the main floor, making sure it was empty. The house seemed normal, almost disturbingly so, but here and there we saw a hint of something more: one of my Pancho's Pizza flyers, pinned to the wall with a thumbtack. News clippings about the three victims held with magnets to the fridge, like a proud display of a child's latest drawing. Stains on the living room couch and carpet, which might have been blood, or might just as well have been anything.

"Soy sauce," whispered one of the cops, as if he was trying to convince himself that the worst-case scenario wasn't true.

"He doesn't have a mouth," I reminded him. The cop gulped nervously.

We found a basement door near the back, and two more cops stayed to watch that, guarding against a surprise assault from below. Elijah and I stayed close to Potash and soon found ourselves back at the base of the stairs.

"It's now or never," said Diana. Potash grunted and started the climb.

"Go carefully," said Ostler, her voice crackling in our ears over the radio. "Don't try to kill him, just get Mr. Sexton close."

"Roger that," said Potash as he reached the top of the stairs. We paused to listen.

"Welcome to my home," said a soft, whispering voice. I gripped my knife, pulling it out of the sheath, knowing it was useless. Potash and Diana both turned to the left, identifying the source of the words, and we moved forward cautiously. A door at the head of the landing was open—the door leading in to the master bedroom, I guessed, based on what I'd seen of the house. Was he simply waiting inside for us? Had he known we were coming?

How was he talking?

Potash counted silently, locking eyes with Diana, and on three they burst into the room, all subtlety gone, shouting out commands to get down, to put his hands on his head, and the rest of us surged in behind them ready to run toward the killer, ready to sacrifice anything we could just to give Elijah the opening he needed, but nothing moved, and all we heard was a soft, wheezing laugh.

There was a body in the bed, lying on top of the covers: light hair and fair skin and most of the flesh on his torso missing, chewed to bits by human teeth. The head, as before, was untouched.

The lips were moving.

"Put my hands on my head," said the voice. The corpse's eyes were unfocused and glassy. "Of course you would say that. But which hands, and which head?"

Potash and Diana scouted the room quickly, checking corners and closets and any nooks or crannies that might conceal an attacker. The master bathroom was attached, and Diana opened the door only to stagger back, gagging. Potash looked at her in alarm, but she shook her head.

"Clear," she coughed, "and no need to double check. I can go my whole life not knowing what's in that tub."

"It's meat," said the body on the bed. There were flies on his wounds, buzzing in small circles before landing lightly and rubbing their forelegs together, licking the bloody flesh with tiny black probosces. The mouth moved by itself, as if it were completely independent from the rest of the body. "Puppets can bite," he said softly, "but they can't swallow."

I nodded. "If he'd left gobs of flesh behind anywhere we'd have found it," I said. "He had to hide it somewhere."

"He could have burned it," said Diana.

"I saved it for you," said the corpse. I walked closer, looking at the thing's pale skin, and its mouth twisted into a leer I could only assume was a smile. "Do you like it? I don't have guests often, you'll forgive me for not being here to receive you in person."

"Are you close?" I asked.

"Hello, John."

He could distinguish voices. Or was the room bugged? I didn't know what he was capable of supernaturally, and what he might need to augment with technology. I'd never known the Withered to have much range on their powers, though, so wherever he was he probably wasn't far. I frowned and thought of another mechanical question: how long could he use a corpse after he killed it? Elijah said he could only drain a corpse within about twenty-four hours—did Rack's power over the dead have a similar limit? Twenty-four hours ago we hadn't even known we were coming. I touched the body's arm and tried to lift it; it was stiff.

"That's evidence," said Diana.

"That's rigor mortis," I said. "This body died somewhere between ten and . . ." I tested it again. "Thirty hours ago."

"The mouth moves just fine," said Potash.

"I could—" said Elijah, but I cut him off with an urgent hand motion. If he was using the corpse's ears to identify our voices, he might not know Elijah was with us.

But then I realized with mounting horror that he might already know. He claimed to know everything. How could he have prepared this corpse to meet us unless he knew we were coming?

"We've got to get out of here," I said.

"We haven't even cleared the upper story," said Diana. "You're just going to trust him when he says he's not here?"

"I guarantee he's here," I said. "This is a trap and we need to get out now."

"Too late," the body whispered.

Someone downstairs fired a gun.

It started as shouts, shocked and desperate: "He's here!" "Look out!" "Behind you!" Urgent and angry, perforated by gunfire, and Potash ran for the door while Ostler screamed in our ears to know what was going on. All too soon, though, the shouting turned to shrieks of pain, howls and sobs and horrific death yells as whatever was attacking tore our armed escort to pieces. Potash roared in defiance, and we shouted for him to come back, to stay together and force the confrontation we needed, but he was gone. Diana swore and followed him back to the stairs, shouting at us to stay with her, and I ran after her with Elijah close on my heels. A spray of bullets tore the floor ahead of me, showering the stairway with splinters, and I fell back, covering my eyes. Elijah steadied me, and I counted to three before running again, steeling myself to face another barrage of friendly fire. As I ran I tried to visualize the house in my head, estimating that the errant bullets had come up through the floor from . . . the kitchen. The top of the basement stairs. We reached the main floor, jumping over the fallen bodies, slipping in the blood, and ran through the hall toward the battle. Another burst of gunfire tore through the wall, but it was ten feet to the side—a mile away in close combat—and we kept running.

"What's going on in there?" Ostler demanded on the radio. "Somebody talk to me!"

"We need—" said Diana, but she stopped abruptly. I reached the kitchen just in time to see her fall to the floor, her arm, still clutching her rifle, ripped from her body. Rack was no more than a shadow, seeming somehow unreal and enormous at the same time. He threw the arm at me and I ducked, and Potash roared again and attacked, muzzle fire lighting up the room in a staccato strobe. I caught only a glimpse of Rack's chest, a roiling mass of ash that seemed to burn his skin around the hole, the dirty yellow bones of his shattered rib cage protruding grotesquely from the edges. His face was a nightmare: wide eyes above, human and furious, a black, greasy hole beneath them. He had no nose, mouth, trachea, or chest. As he stalked through the center of that maelstrom, heedless of bullets, blood streaming from his fingers, I couldn't help but wonder: we got our concept of "king" from this creature?

Did we get "heartless" from him as well?

"We need backup," I said into my radio. "And every doctor you can find."

Elijah ran toward the Withered, screaming, but Rack turned suddenly and slipped through the door to the basement. Potash paused to reload his rifle, slapping in another magazine, but Elijah ran straight for the door, only to stagger back as a hail of bullets struck him in the chest. He fell, and Potash crouched just outside the doorway.

"He was ready for Elijah," I said. "He planned an escape and a ranged weapon to deal with him—he knew everything before we even got here."

Potash brandished his machete. "This ends tonight. One blow to the neck, remove the head before it can heal."

"You'll never get close enough."

"To hell with that," said Potash, and he fired his gun around the corner, clearing the stairs before charging in himself.

"Come back!" I shouted. "You can't kill him without Elijah!" Rack had known we were coming; he'd laid this entire thing as a trap—perhaps this was his end game, to lead us along with a false investigation, culminating in an obvious attempt to contact Brooke and lure us here, completely unprepared for what he really was. Even knowing what he was, we weren't ready.

I flicked on the light and crawled across the bloody floor to Diana. Her breath was coming in short, pained bursts. Her arm had been torn off at the shoulder, and I shuddered to think of the strength it must have taken to do such a thing.

Diana looked at me, her gasps arrhythmic, almost like hiccups, too weak to speak or even move her remaining arm. As I looked around for something to stanch the flow of blood, Elijah sat up with a grimace.

"That hurt," he said.

"You'll be fine," I said, grabbing a towel from the stove handle. "I've seen you heal from worse. Find me more towels."

"The only injury I've had that was worse was . . ." He grimaced. "Getting hit by that truck."

"And you were fine," I said. "Now find me some towels!"

He looked at me oddly, then stumbled across the blood-slick floor to rummage through the cupboards. I folded my lone towel into a tight wad and held it to Diana's bloody shoulder as tightly as I could, gritting my teeth against the pain I imagined when the touch made her wince. Her muscles convulsed, her chest curling forward as her body tightened, her breath coming in ragged, desperate gasps.

"Death is weak," I hissed at her, trying to think of anything I could to keep her fighting. "You will not die because you're not going to let him win, all right? We're going to stay alive and we're going to find that demon and we're going to kill him together. Are you with me Diana? Can you hear me?"

Her eyes started to roll back in her head.

"I found more towels," said Elijah, dropping down beside me, but we both started suddenly when Ostler shouted in our ears.

"Everybody fall back! He's outside! Fall back!"

I looked at Diana's stumpless shoulder. "I don't even know how to put a tourniquet on that."

"Here," said Elijah. He took off his belt and wrapped it around Diana's shoulders, covering my hand on the towel. He cinched it down and I pulled my hand free; he tightened it further and Diana groaned.

"Did you hit me with that truck on purpose?" asked Elijah. I didn't answer.

"You're going to be fine, Diana," I said, hoisting her onto my back. "We're going to kill that thing together, do you hear me?" I stepped carefully across the floor, staggering under the weight, headed for the front door. "You and me," I said, "up close and personal. We're going to tear off *his* arm and beat him to death with it." My radio was filled with screams. I clenched my teeth and walked to the front door. "Elijah, can you see anything? What's going on out there?"

There was no answer. I turned, slowly, and saw no movement in the house behind me. Orange light spilled out of the kitchen, glinting off the pools of blood and shining on the dark black helmets of the fallen police.

"Elijah!"

He was gone. I struggled to the door, murmuring "fight back, fight back," to Diana, and when I looked outside, the screams were finished, the gunfire was gone. Even Diana had grown silent and motionless on my shoulder. I turned, trying to see her, but her one arm hung limp and lifeless.

My radio crackled with static, empty white noise seeming to fill the entire world. Everyone we'd brought was dead. I let Diana's body slump softly to the ground.

A tiny whisper came over the radio: Ostler's voice, thin and reedy, like all the strength had been pulled out of it, and nothing was left but the words.

"Isn't this what you wanted, John? Calm, peaceful silence, and all the dead bodies in the world."

17

I ran through the darkness, dodging pools of lamplight, slipping on ice and snow. All around me the world came slowly to life, waking up from one nightmare to another—lights came on in bedroom windows, terrified faces peeked out through windows splashed with blood. The street was a scene of gruesome devastation, and somewhere in the middle was the creature who had done it, the Withered king, smiling with another man's lips and speaking with a dead woman's voice. I had to get away—I didn't know where, I just knew I had to go, to run, to get as far from that place as I could.

"You can't run forever, John."

I tore my radio from my vest and threw it down, leaving Ostler's dead voice to whisper alone in the shadows.

Had Elijah betrayed us? I didn't think so—he didn't feel like a traitor—but how could I possibly trust my feelings? I didn't even know how to use them. Elijah was nice to me, he was similar to me, and I felt that we shared some kind of . . . what? A bond? Because we lived on the fringes of the world, avoiding other people? That didn't make us instant friends, it made us two people with all the more reason to avoid each other. He worked in a mortuary—for all I knew that was part of the trap, to win my confidence through association with the one thing left that I loved.

I'd built my life around this: getting to know people, making them think I was their friend, all so I could find their weak spot and hit it as hard I could. Now someone had done it to me.

But Elijah had been helping us. Even after the trap was sprung, he'd stayed with me, he'd tried to save Diana, he'd even tried to attack Rack. If he was part of Rack's plan, wouldn't he have turned on us? He could have drained my mind a dozen times tonight, leaving me in a blank, mindless coma. Instead he'd run away. Was he too much of a coward to fight us directly? Or had he felt the same link to me that I'd felt with him, and when the moment came he couldn't go through with it?

Or was the traitor someone else?

I stopped running, leaning on a fence to catch my breath. I was blocks away from the scene of the attack, and once again the world was quiet—I couldn't even hear screaming in the distance. Was Rack killing more people? The neighbors, or the EMTs who showed up to help? It seemed like the kind of thing he would do, but not tonight. He was on a vendetta and he wouldn't stop until our team was dead—all of us. He hadn't chased me, and I wondered if maybe he was saving me for last; the ones in danger now would be Nathan and Dr. Trujillo.

And Brooke.

I started running again, pulling my phone from my pocket. Was Brooke more Withered than human? I didn't know, and as I ran I realized I didn't care. She was my friend—maybe not a good friend, but I wasn't exactly a role model either. Maybe my only friend left in the world. I didn't know if Rack was planning to kill her or recruit her or something even worse, but either way I had to save her. I dialed Trujillo's number.

Ring.

Snow was starting to fall, and my breath came in ragged gasps, visible like smoke in the streetlights.

Ring.

"John?" It was Nathan's voice.

"Nathan," I said, clenching my teeth and trying to breathe. "Where's Trujillo?"

"I can't find him; I didn't even know his phone was here until it started ringing. What's going on?"

"Were you monitoring the radio?" I asked.

"It was a closed channel," he said. "It didn't reach this far. Did something go wrong? You sound terrible."

"I'm running," I said, and paused again to catch my breath. "It was a trap, and everyone's dead. I'm the only one left—"

"Dead?"

"Rack killed them all," I said. "Not just us but the police. Ostler, Potash, Diana, Detective Scott—"

"That—" he stuttered. "That's impossible. How did you get away?"

"I think he's leaving me for last, which means he's coming for you."

"Dammit, John—"

"Listen, Nathan, you have to find Trujillo and get Brooke and get away from there. Check her out, break her out, do whatever you have to do. I'll call you when I get closer."

"You brought this on us," he said angrily. "This is your fault, everything you've—"

"You can yell at me when Brooke's safe," I said. "Are you already moving? I don't know how much time you have."

"Somebody had to be on the inside," said Nathan. "If this was a trap, someone tipped him off."

"It wasn't me," I said.

"It was Elijah," said Nathan, "which makes you just as guilty—you're the one who brought him into the team."

"It wasn't Elijah," I said fiercely. "He was . . . he was helping us. He didn't leave until we'd already lost—the same as I did, he just ran away first."

"If he was trustworthy he would have stayed to help you," said Nathan.

"Why?" I asked. "So we could lock him up again? So we could run him over with another truck? He gave us everything he had, and we tried our plan and failed. He's probably running right now, and we need to do the same. Get Brooke—"

"If it wasn't Elijah then it was obviously Brooke," said Nathan. "We know she was communicating with Rack, she must have warned him we were coming."

"We didn't plan this attack until after the letters were cut off," I said. "Brooke didn't even know about it at all—Trujillo wouldn't let us tell her, just in case—"

"Do you think it was Trujillo?" asked Nathan.

I stopped, shaking my head. "I don't . . ." I tried to control my breathing. "Why would he betray us?"

"He knew everything we were doing," said Nathan, "and he had the time and the means to tip Rack off. Dammit, John, he had hours alone with Brooke, for weeks on end, to be seduced by whatever promises the Withered were making."

"Seduced?"

"Trujillo practically lived over there, and you honestly think he didn't know about the letters she was sending? I'm the one who found them, not him—if I hadn't been there to force the search, we might never have found out about them. And now we've been betrayed and he's disappeared, and there's no way that's a coincidence."

"Trujillo wouldn't just turn like that," I said, though I knew as I said it that I couldn't be sure. "He worked as a profiler for years—he put dozens of serial killers in jail."

"Because he trained himself to think like them," Nathan countered. "Obviously some of it rubbed off, and now a few talks with Nobody, maybe a talk or two with Rack directly, was all he needed to tip over the edge."

I stopped on a corner, looking at the street signs: Leonard and Morgan. Whiteflower was still miles away. "I'm going to try to grab a bus, but I'm still at least a half an hour out. If Trujillo is the traitor and you're not dead, he'll be going after Brooke next."

"He won't kill her, he'll just take her to join them."

"You think that's better?" I asked. I turned and started jogging toward the nearest major street. I was covered with Diana's blood; I'd have to find some way to clean up, or at least hide it. "Do you still have a gun?"

"Are you kidding? With all the crap we've been through I don't let that thing out of my reach even to shower."

"Get Brooke and get out. Take her somewhere we've never been before—a Denny's or something, something that's open all night—and make sure you walk. Your car is traceable, especially to someone with Trujillo's police contacts. Call me when you have her, and I'll call you when I'm close. And Nathan?"

"Yeah?"

"Brooke is literally, without exaggeration, the only thing I have left in my life. If you let anything happen to her, you'll wish Rack had gotten to you before I do."

I met up with Nathan and Brooke in an old movie theater, where they huddled in the back row while a late night horror movie flickered on the screen. There were only a handful of other people in the theater, most of them either high or making out in the corners. I sat down next to Brooke; she was dressed in her plain cotton pajamas, with big rubber boots and Trujillo's long trench coat over them. Trujillo was a wide man, and it dwarfed her like a circus tent.

Brooke grabbed my hand. "I missed you." She stopped, frowning, and held my hand up to the faint light from the screen. "Your hands are sticky, here between the fingers." She peered closely. "You have blood on you."

I nodded. "I don't know if the guy at the ticket counter noticed, or if the police even have time to respond if he calls it in. Either way, we shouldn't hang around here much longer."

"Where are we going?" asked Nathan.

"Did you find Trujillo?" I asked.

"I don't like him," said Brooke.

Nathan shook his head. "No sign of him at Whiteflower or the office." He held up a cell phone. "I've got his phone."

"Too bad," I said, "I wouldn't mind calling him if he ever came back to get it."

"You want to talk to him?"

"You don't?" I asked. "The least he could do is tell us why he turned."

Nathan swore. "I don't even care anymore. What's our plan to get out of town?"

"I've been thinking about that," I said. "We can't trust any of our own homes, any of our own cars; we can't go anywhere Rack might be expecting us to go. Even the bus station out of town is too risky."

"That leaves stealing a car," said Nathan, "do you even know how to do that?"

"I do," said Brooke.

"If we steal a car then Rack *and* the police will be looking for us," I said. "We need to go to the one place no one's going to expect us."

Nathan frowned. "Back to the crime scene?"

"To the mortuary," I said. "Elijah's car is still there from the night he was captured, so he'll go straight—"

"Absolutely not," said Nathan.

"He's not a traitor," I insisted, "but Rack knows we think he is, and that makes him the only person we can trust right now. His entire cover in Fort Bruce is blown, so he's probably just as desperate to leave town as we are. If we get to him soon, we can leave with him."

"Are we talking about Meshara?" asked Brooke. "He's so sad."

"I don't like it," said Nathan. "He's a Withered—Brooke is *half* Withered, for crying out loud."

"Keep your voice down," I urged.

"Trusting the Withered is what got us into this mess in the first place," Nathan hissed.

"Do you have any better ideas?"

"Call the FBI and wait for backup?"

"If you want to," I said. "But let's at least wait outside of town somewhere."

He growled, but finally nodded. "Let's get out of here, then. I hate this movie."

The bus service in Fort Bruce cut off at ten, with a late service on a few lines that ran until two in the morning. It was nearly midnight. We walked a few blocks to the nearest late-line station, keeping our heads down, listening to the whispers of drunks and hookers and other late-night denizens as we passed them:

"Did you hear what happened in The Corners?"

"Dozens are dead."

"I heard it was hundreds."

"It's like the end of the world."

Brooke walked close to me, shivering, and after a moment of hesitation, I put my arm around her.

"I love you, John," she said.

"I'm only doing this to keep you warm."

"That's why I love you."

I thought about Boy Dog, back in my apartment. If we left without him he'd starve, or at least dehydrate, alone in there maybe for days. I had rules to keep me from hurting an animal, even by neglect . . .

Who was I kidding? I'd broken all my rules. I couldn't trust them, I couldn't fall back on them, I couldn't even blame them anymore. What did I have, if I didn't have those? No family, no home, no life. A mad girl in my arms, and a dead one in my dreams. I didn't even have myself.

I wasn't even sure who I was.

I used to know. I used to be the weird kid, the one who sat in the corners, who didn't talk to anyone, who hung around with the other weird kid because he never expected me to say anything back. I kept my rules and I kept to myself, and then the Clayton Killer came to town and everything changed. I had to hurt one person to save a bunch of others, but it didn't stop at one. Now Marci was dead, and my mom, and so many more. Could I justify it with math? How many people haven't died because I killed the Withered that would have killed them? How many people *have* died because I kicked the hornet's nest and woke the hounds of hell? If I stop will it get better? If I kill them all, will it stop?

"Where do you want to go?" whispered Brooke.

"We're going to Elijah's mortuary."

"I mean after," she said. "When we're free."

"Free from trouble?" I asked. "I don't think we can go far enough for that."

"There's the bus," said Nathan. "Run." We sprinted the last block and made it to the bus just in time, climbing on breathlessly as it pulled out from the stop. Nathan paid, and we sat on an empty bench. He flopped down across from us and pulled out his phone.

"Ordering a pizza?" I asked.

"An air strike," said Nathan. "I want Langley to wipe this hellhole off the map."

I glanced at the driver, but he seemed to be ignoring us. I pulled out my own phone and connected to the e-mail server.

You shouldn't have run, said the message from Rack. *We have things to discuss.* I disconnected without sending a response.

Was I really ready to just walk away from this? To let a monster that dangerous keep killing? I didn't know how to stop him—except I did. Elijah was still our greatest weapon, and now we were going to find him. Yes, he might help us get out of town, but there were other ways. Was I going to him because I wanted to escape, or because some part of me still wanted to fight? Was I lying to Brooke and Nathan about leaving? Was I lying to myself? Brooke asked me where I wanted to go, and I didn't know. I wanted everything to end.

I wanted to end it.

We rode for fifteen minutes, and then walked for seven more through back streets to the mortuary. The light was on in the garage, and we reached the big bay doors just as one of them started to open. I pulled Brooke to the side, and Nathan ducked behind me, and when the door was fully raised we peeked around the corner. The garage held four vehicles: two of them were hearses, behind the second bay door that was still closed; the third was Elijah's car, and the fourth was a heavy pickup truck, with a snowplow on the front and some kind of plastic tank in the trunk. The garage had its own private gas pump, and Elijah was using it to fill up his car.

Nathan had his gun out, but I frowned and waved him

back, mouthing "put that away." We didn't want to scare our only ally.

Elijah must have heard us, because he looked up, his eyes wide with fear, and then swallowed nervously when he recognized my face. His body shook with a tremor of agitation and he went back to his work.

"Wasn't expecting to see you," he said.

"Hello, Meshara," said Brooke softly. "It's been a long time."

He looked at her more closely. "You're Brooke?"

"Sometimes."

"You're leaving town," I told him. "We want to come with you."

"So he can find us all at once?" Elijah shook his head. "No, thank you."

"Just far enough that we can lie low," I said, walking in. Brooke and Nathan followed. "Just the next town over, that's all we ask." I was about to tell him that we trusted him, that I wasn't like the others in the police station who'd been to afraid even to talk to him, but Elijah's next words shocked me.

"I don't trust you," he said.

"You don't trust *us*?" asked Nathan.

"Why should I?" asked Elijah, looking up again from his work. "You hit me with a truck."

"I'm sorry," said Brooke.

"Look," I said, but Elijah shook his head and stormed toward me; Nathan cringed and stepped back a few steps.

"No," said Elijah, "you look. I left the Withered years ago—millennia ago. I don't like them, I don't like their methods, I don't like the way they think they can do anything they want to anybody just because they're stronger. They used to be gods and they think they still are. Humans are their playthings. And then when I finally got back in the fight and I picked a side because you—you, of all people—convinced me that it was worth it, it turns out you think exactly the same way. We're your playthings, and you can play god with our lives. I thought you were different."

"I told you we were right," I said. "I never told you we were different."

"Maybe you should have," said Elijah. He glared at me a moment longer, and the age behind his eyes seemed suddenly overwhelming, ten thousand years of weariness. I didn't have an answer, and he turned back to his work. "I'm leaving," he said again. "You can find your own way out."

He pulled the gas-pump nozzle out of the car and turned to put it back on its hook, when suddenly a loud crack split the air and Elijah dropped to the floor. I stumbled back, my ears ringing from the sound, and looked at Nathan. He didn't even have his gun out—his empty hands were clamped tightly over his ears, his face locked in a grimace. Brooke looked like she was screaming, but I couldn't hear anything. I looked back at Elijah, struggling to get up, but he was hit by two more shots. I could barely even think from the shock—could barely process what was happening—but Brooke grabbed my arm and pulled me past Elijah to the end of the car, yanking me down into cover. I peeked around the edge of the hood in time to see a dark shape hurtling in through the garage door, a man streaked with dirt and blood. Elijah groaned, regenerating too slowly; the intruder raised his arm and a long, sharp machete flashed brightly in the light. He swung once and took off Elijah's head.

It was Potash.

I staggered to my feet. "You killed him!"

"That was the point," growled Potash.

"He was on our side!" I shouted. "He wasn't even that—he was on a better side. We're the ones who betrayed *him*!"

"He was a Withered," said Potash. "We've danced around too long, trying to understand them, to ally with them, and what has it gotten us? The whole team's dead, and I'm done dancing. It's time we kill who needs to be killed, and finish this once and for all."

"He didn't need to be killed," I said, dropping to my knees beside the body. Elijah was good—he was better than we were. It wasn't supposed to go like this.

Elijah's body collapsed, turning to ash and grease before my eyes. Soulstuff, he called it. Too corrupt to do anything but rot. In seconds his body was a bubbling pool of gritty black tar.

I felt the knife in my pocket.

"You were right," I said, climbing slowly to my feet. I looked at Potash, covered with cuts and scrapes, his chest heaving from exertion, his ruptured cannula held to his nose with one hand. He had killed one of the only good people I knew. I said it again. "You were right." I pulled out my knife. "It's time to kill whoever needs to be killed."

18

"Everybody calm down," said Nathan.

Potash looked at me, leaning slightly back, as if reconsidering me. "What do you think you're going to do?"

I looked at him closely, my hand tight around the knife. "Why are you doing this, Potash?"

"I think I just explained myself pretty well."

"Why are you on this team?" I demanded. "What brought you here? Who are you? No one knows anything about you: not your background, not your motives, not your outlook on life. Why are you doing *this*? What are you doing that you don't have to do?"

"I'm not just a killer you can analyze, John."

"But you could be," I said. "In another situation, in another place, if you'd gone down a less official path and I'd gone down a better one, I might be tracking you right now as the worst serial killer in history. You kill people—why? You live apart from the world, even more than I do—why?"

"Because someone needs to do it."

"So it may as well be you?"

"Better me than someone who doesn't know how," said Potash. "I fought that bastard Rack to a standstill—I almost had him—where anyone else would have died. Everyone else did die. I followed him through a cellar so messed up I can't even describe it to you, and I'll have to live with what I saw down there for the rest of my life—and anyone else would go mad even trying to."

"And you haven't?" I asked, glancing down at the ashy remains.

"Elijah needed to die," Potash insisted. "They all do."

"Why?"

"Do you think he's the traitor?" asked Nathan.

I shook my head. "No."

"Then why are you asking him all these questions?" asked Brooke.

"Because I want to know!" I yelled. "I want to know what he's doing here—I want to know what I'm doing here! Is any of this wrong or right? Have I been wasting my time trying to be the good guy, when good and bad don't even make sense anymore? Elijah was one of the best men I ever met, and this guy just cut his head off, and he'll probably win a medal for it and I want to know why! Why do our choices even matter if someone can just decide what right and wrong mean? Why did he have to die if this is all just arbitrary?"

"You're asking why a Withered had to die?" Potash asked. "Do you even hear yourself?"

"What if he wasn't called a 'Withered'?" I asked. "What if he was 'Cursed'?"

"The word doesn't change what he was," said Potash.

"What he was was a man," I said. "He was a driver, and a mechanic, and a regular visitor in a rest home, and yes he made a mistake and yes he was dangerous, but he spent more time trying to be good than any of us have ever spent trying to be anything."

Potash looked at me, the seconds ticking by, until at last he shook his head. "Making these decisions is the hardest part of our job, but we still have to do it. Killing isn't just pulling a trigger or swinging a blade—it's making a choice about who deserves to live and who deserves to die."

"Elijah deserved to live."

"That decision will hurt me for the rest of my life," said Potash, "but now I'm the only one it will ever hurt. He won't drain another mind, and he won't make another Merrill Evans, and he won't endanger another Rose Chapman. The FBI won't spend any more time or money hunting him down and confining him, which gives them more time and money for the bigger threats, which gives the rest of the world fewer threats to worry about. The world is better off without Elijah Sexton in it."

"And you?" I asked. "Would it be better off without you in it?"

"Everybody take it easy," said Nathan, stepping closer to Potash. "Nobody's going to start anything crazy, or do anything stupid, or—" His hand came up behind Potash's back, and he shot him through the head.

My ears rang again.

"No!" screamed Brooke.

I jumped back, my eyes wide, my mind reeling. Nathan looked at me and rolled his eyes.

"What, like you weren't planning to do the same thing?"

"He was . . ." I didn't even have the words. I was used to violence, to death and pain and terror, but this was too much, and too random. Ostler and Diana, and now Elijah and Potash—it was all so senseless. "Why?" I demanded again. I tried to follow it up with another question, something biting and insightful, but all I could manage was another "Why?"

"Because he was dangerous," said Nathan. "He was a wild card we couldn't predict or control, and he could have outfought all of us put together."

"But we didn't need to fight him at all."

He gestured at me with his pistol. "Then what were you planning to do with that knife?"

I looked down at it, clasped so tight in my hand my fingers were as white as bone. "I don't know," I said, closing my eyes. "I don't know what I was going to do, or what I wanted to do, or anything else. But I didn't want to kill him."

"Yes, you did."

"But I knew it was wrong!" I shouted.

"No, you didn't." Nathan shook his head. "You can't have it both ways: you just spent five minutes telling the guy he was a dangerous psychopath and the world would be better off without him, and now you're freaking out because you weren't the one to do it? Like you're the world's sole arbiter of justice?"

"That's not what I mean," I said.

"You don't know what you mean," said Nathan, and I had no response because he was right. I'd wanted Potash dead—when he killed Elijah I wanted him dead more than anything in the world—but now that I'd seen it happen I couldn't bear it. I knew that sometimes people had to die; I'd had that realization before. But I knew now that I had no idea how to make all the other decisions that come with it: who had to die, and when, and how. Humans and demons were categories that made sense to me, or at least they used to. Now nothing did.

Nathan nodded, prodding the corpse with his foot. "I was lucky you were distracting him—there's no way I could have taken him if he was paying attention to me. A quick shot in the back of the head was my only chance and I had to take it."

"No you didn't," I said. "He was . . . on our side."

"Don't be naive," said Nathan. "He was on our *team* but he was never on our side. Maybe Ostler's or Diana's side, but not yours, and definitely not mine. We've gone our own way, and whether we abandoned them or they abandoned us, it's all the same in the end."

"They didn't abandon us," I said, "they died."

"You left them long before that," said Nathan. "Or are we pretending you weren't sending e-mails to Rack?"

I looked up suddenly, focusing on his face. How did he know that? Nobody knew that but me and Rack. And since I didn't tell him . . .

"You were talking to him, too," I said.

"Of course."

I nodded. "You're the one who told Rack all those secrets, aren't you? Who better to dig up our buried pasts than the doctor of library science? All of it was public information, except yours, and we couldn't figure out who had told him because no one knew it. No one but you."

"I didn't really want any of you to know, either," said Nathan, "but I figured you'd be dead soon anyway."

"So you just turned on us," I said, "just like that."

"Just like that," said Nathan.

"Why?"

"You aren't smart enough to figure that out on your own?" asked Nathan. "John Wayne Cleaver, the great psychological mastermind?"

I nodded, trying to think—not just about his motives, but about our situation. What was Nathan planning? How could we get out of it? Was he keeping us alive just to gloat, or did he have something else in mind? He didn't want to kill us, or he could have done that an hour ago. That meant he was waiting for something—for Rack? Was he handing us over to Rack?

"All Rack's letters were addressed to me," I said. "He wants to talk to me."

"He'll be here soon," said Nathan. "I sent him a text on the bus."

Then we didn't have much time. "He wants to talk to me, but he offered something different to you."

"We don't want to be here if Rack's coming," said Brooke. She'd come up behind me and gripped my arm tightly. I couldn't help but have a quick flashback to Potash and what had happened when Nathan came up behind him, but I pushed it from my mind. Brooke wasn't there to kill me.

I looked around the room, trying to see what we had to work with. The white plastic tank in the back of the truck just held water, now that I saw the label up close. That wouldn't help us. The garage door was still open—should we run? Would that solve anything, or just postpone it? Our only real weapon against

Rack was Elijah, and he was dead now; Nathan had tried so hard to keep us away from here because he knew Elijah was Rack's only weakness.

But no. He had other weaknesses, too. He needed hearts, for one thing. His body was strong and fast and regenerated at a ridiculous rate, but it was still a human body, and it still functioned the way a normal human body functioned. It couldn't function without a heart. He had other weaknesses too: he didn't have a mouth or a nose, so he couldn't taste or smell. I could use that. More than that, though, maybe more than anything, was Rack's biggest weakness of all—his one glaring blind spot.

He'd never lost. So he didn't think he could.

I studied the garage carefully: the fuel pump, the tool bench, the water pump on the white plastic tank. The knife in my hand. I could do this, but I didn't have much time. And I needed one more piece of information.

"You joined Rack because he offered you something big," I said, not looking at Nathan but circling away from him, looking at the water pump. How long was the hose? How big was the nozzle? "You'd done the research on us, so you already knew we were a pack of degenerates: killers, gangsters, psychos. A former rapist. I assume Trujillo is dead, by the way?"

"I killed him right before you called," said Nathan. "We timed it to coincide with the attack on your strike team."

I nodded. "And you were fine with that attack because we had no moral high ground. Compared to people like Cody French and Mary Gardner, our team was equivalent at best, and compared to Elijah Sexton we were monsters." I read the label on the water pump: sixty psi at the lowest setting. It was high, but it could work. I circled past Nathan, stooping down to study the floor.

"You think you offended my tender sensibilities?" asked Nathan. "I sold drugs for five years, kid. I've seen people do some of the darkest stuff you can imagine."

"Exactly," I said, studying the subtle slope of the floor. "You've already proven that you're willing to get your hands dirty if you get something out of it, but with us you weren't getting anything out of it. You spent your days in a rented office and your nights in the cowboy bars of scenic Fort Bruce." The floor was relatively clean, with two good drainage holes. I nodded and stood up, circling back toward Nathan. "You figured you deserved better," I said, "and since you were working for a bunch of killers anyway, why not switch teams to a killer who could actually offer you something? What did he promise you, money? A big house somewhere, maybe a prestigious post at a university?"

"Money's all it took," said Nathan. "That'll buy me all the other stuff. And you'd better believe that a man who's been alive for ten thousand years has a lot of money to offer."

"I bet he does," I said, stopping beside him. He looked at me uncertainly, his eyes flicking over my face and body and arms as if he wasn't sure what to expect from me; whether he should pat me on the shoulder or shoot me in the gut. I assume Rack had ordered him not to shoot me, but if I made any sudden moves he'd react without thinking. Unless I made him think about something else. I looked him in the eyes. I still needed to know one more thing. "Did you tell Rack how much I hate you?"

He made a sort of half frown, half smile. "Why . . . is that relevant?"

"Did you?"

"Why do you care?"

"Because I need to know what to expect when he gets here," I said. "I want to be ready."

"You think he's going to hurt you any more than otherwise just because I told him what a little prick you are?"

"So you did tell him?"

"That you're insubordinate and mouthy and stubborn as hell?" asked Nathan. "Yeah, I told him. I told him no matter what he wants you for, you'll never do it, and you'll be completely useless, and anything he needs I can do a better job of."

"Thank you," I said. Our eyes were locked, each sizing the other up, each waiting for the other to blink. Would he make a move? Would I? How long did we have until Rack arrived? Time to move. I tried to smile, to unnerve him with my confidence at the last second, but I couldn't do it. Nothing I was about to do made me happy. "If you think Rack's going to share his power with you, maybe you should remember what we learned about Gidri."

Nathan frowned. "Gidri? What's he got to do with this?"

"He's gorgeous," said Brooke. She slammed her hand on the hood of Elijah's car. "I hate him!"

"Oh, come on," said Nathan, rolling his eyes. "Now you've done it, she's going to freak the hell out again—" He turned toward her, and I stabbed him. Up under his ribs, as deep as the knife would go. I put my other hand on his back to hold him place, shoving the knife in further, clenching my teeth and twisting the blade. He tried to turn but I had him in a lock, wrapping my arms around him, practically hugging him, turning as he turned, so he could never get a shot. His body twitched against mine, convulsing with pain, doubling over and then curling back, and I pulled out the knife and slammed it in again, hearing him grunt and grunting in time with him. He dropped his gun, and his body went slack, and I lowered him gently to the floor. He twitched again, and his eyes rolled back in his head, and he was gone.

19

Brooke was screaming in a rage, beating the wall with a heavy metal wrench. "I hate him!" she shouted, "I hate him I hate him I hate him I hate him!"

I collapsed on the floor, exhausted, between the bodies: Potash and Nathan, and Elijah's smear of ash. I looked at the garage door, but no one was there yet. I took a deep breath, dropping the knife, pausing only a moment before clambering back to my feet. We didn't have much time.

"I hate him!" screamed Brooke. "I hate him!"

"Be quiet," I said, "you're going to wake the neighbors."

I looked at Potash's body; his forehead was mangled by the bullet, but his face was intact. Nathan's face was untouched. I only had time to prepare one body, so I had to choose the right one. Whose voice would Rack try to use? What did he want to say to me, and how would he choose to say it?

That's why I'd asked Nathan that question. Rack was arrogant; everything about his letters told me that he'd want to gloat. The gloating would hurt more coming from someone I hated. Did Rack know how much I hated Potash? Maybe. He definitely knew how much I hated Nathan, though, and after this betrayal he'd know I'd hate him even more. Nathan it was.

I dragged Nathan's body closer to one of the drains, setting his head almost exactly on top of it, then ran for the water pump. They must have used it for washing something, or maybe for watering the plants around the grounds; it had a long rubber hose, ending in a smooth metal nozzle. I screwed the nozzle off, leaving a slim metal tube about a half centimeter in diameter, and then opened the tank's dump valve, letting all the water splash out onto the floor.

I looked at the garage door again. He wasn't there yet.

While the tank drained I ran to the tool bench, ignoring Brooke's rant, and searched for a roll of wire or duct tape—anything I could use to clamp down on an artery to create a seal. Brooke seemed to calm slightly, distracted by my actions. I combed through the bench and found nothing but a vise grip and decided it would have to do. The water tank was nearly empty now, so I closed the valve and pulled the gas hose as far as it would go, sticking it into the top of the water tank and setting it to fill as fast as it could. It would be easier if I could use the gas pump directly, but the pressure would be wrong. I let it fill and sat down next to Nathan, with the water pump in one hand and the vise grip in the other. My knife lay beside me.

"What are you doing?" asked Brooke.

"I'm embalming him," I said. I took a deep breath. *Let's do this.*

I set down the tools and picked up my knife, wiping away the grime from the floor and then carefully slitting open his neck. The skin split open like a piece of raw chicken, blood welling up at the wound. I'd never worked on such a fresh body before. I lengthened the hole, pulling it wide, and reached inside with my finger to find the jugular artery. It felt like a thick hose, not much different from the water-pump hose by my feet. I pulled out a loop of it, and looked around for something to anchor it.

"What do you need?" asked Brooke. Her eyes were wide, watching the process with morbid fascination. I didn't know if it was Brooke or Nobody or some other personality I hadn't even met yet.

"A screwdriver," I said.

"Phillips or flathead?"

"It doesn't matter."

She brought me a screwdriver from the workbench, and I placed it under the loop of the artery to keep it from sliding back inside the neck. I looked up at the door. Empty. I took my knife and slit the artery carefully, making a hole big enough for the slim metal water pump. I slid it in about two inches, pinched the artery closed around it, and clamped it in place with the vise grips.

I stood up gently, trying not to disturb the body. The water tank had several inches of gas now, and I turned the pressure dial as low as it would go. Sixty psi was the upper limit for most embalming pumps; anything higher might tear the blood vessels apart. I put my hand on the switch, ready to turn it on, then stopped suddenly and looked wildly around the room.

"What do you need this time?" asked Brooke.

"A ventilator, a fan, something like that."

"The door's open," she said, "we're not going to choke."

"Call it a superstition." I spotted a vent in the ceiling and took a deep breath, nodding. These things had to be done right. "Let's hope that fan doesn't give out on us," I said, and flipped the switch on the pump.

The hose jumped, and Nathans's body lurched at the sudden influx of pressure. I ran to him, holding the bloody artery in my fingers, trying to add more pressure to the seal. Gas leaked out onto my hands, but only a little; most of it seemed to be going inside. If I'd done it right the gasoline would run through his system, filling the blood vessels and pushing out the blood. Filling the heart with poison. I held my breath, staring at the neck, never taking my eyes away from the hole I'd cut in the artery. Gas was flowing in one end . . .

. . . and very slowly, in bigger and bigger drops, blood was coming out the other.

Soon the blood was flowing freely from the artery, and I did my best to angle it so it flowed down the drain. I looked at the open door, but still saw nothing.

"I'll go watch," said Brooke, wrapping Trujillo's old coat tightly around her as she walked to the edge of the garage.

How much longer did we have? A minute? An hour? All this work would be for nothing if Rack appeared while the hoses were still attached. I let go of the pump-to-artery seal, hoping it would keep working on its own, and when it didn't immediately explode I dug through Nathan's pockets for his phone, hoping to find Rack's text conversation. The phone was locked, and I didn't know the code. I tried a few random patterns, then gave up and threw the phone in frustration. I instead used my time cleaning up, putting away the extra tools while the hose steadily pumped gas into Nathan's body.

A chemical embalming could take several minutes, but I didn't need the whole body filled, just the heart. How long was that? I thought again about leaving—just hopping into Elijah's car and driving away—but I couldn't do it. Killing was a choice, like Potash said, and I had made a choice to kill Rack. He couldn't be allowed to continue. Ten thousand years of terror would end tonight, and if I had to die to make it happen . . . I looked up at Brooke, blond hair limp and stringy against her skull, her frail body lost in the folds of that giant coat. She watched the darkness intently, and I watched her. Should I tell her to leave? Was her life in any less danger out there than in here? I might have to die to kill Rack, but she could get away. I owed her that much.

It was the least I could do.

"You should go," I said.

"Go where?"

"Anywhere," I said. "Away."

"But I love you."

"No, you don't—"

"I know you don't love me," she said, and though I couldn't see her face I could hear the emotion in her voice, choked and cracking. She was crying. "That doesn't mean I don't love you."

I watched her a moment longer, but said nothing.

A full embalming used about a gallon of fluid for every fifty pounds of body. Nathan was what, two hundred pounds? Two twenty? I tried to calculate the flow of volume at sixty psi, wondering if I could even do it in my head, when Brooke stiffened suddenly.

"John . . . ."

Rack was coming. I unlocked the vise grips and yanked the pump free of the artery, trailing gas across the floor as I ran to the tank and shut it all down. I threw the hose up into the bed of the truck, hiding it, and ran back to Nathan, spreading his blood around the neck wound, pulling out the screwdriver, doing everything I could to make it look like his throat had been slashed in a fight. It looked too clinical, and I slashed at it again with my knife, feeling only an echo of the fury that had made me want to stab him before. Really, all that was left now was fear. Brooke backed up slowly, taking my hand when she reached me, and we backed up together to the end of the garage. I held up my knife like a cross, as if I was trying to ward off a vampire. It made me feel stupid, but lowering it made me feel vulnerable, so I kept it up. Better stupid than terrified.

Rack walked slowly around the corner of the garage door, a monstrous giant nearly seven feet tall. He wore a long black coat, stained past his knees with blood, and a thick black scarf around his neck and face. Only his eyes were visible over the top, gleaming in the light of our lone yellow bulb. He stopped before the corpses and watched us.

This is what it all came down to. Had I read him right? Did I understand the way he worked and thought and acted? He'd never lost, not in ten thousand years—he was so confident in his own strength that he'd never suspect a trap of mine could work. He'd told Nathan to hold me here because he wanted to talk, and that meant he'd use one of the bodies to speak to me. *Come on*, I thought, *do it. Take Nathan's heart.*

The room reeked of gasoline. Would he really be done in by something as simple as the lack of a nose?

He unwrapped his scarf and opened his coat, and I saw again the black pit in the place of his heart. He watched me in hideous silence as thick tendrils of his charred black soul reached out and down—

—toward Potash.

The sludge clutched at Potash's face, surging into his mouth, shredding his insides. I stepped back, too shocked to think clearly. What could I do? I only had one plan. I'd considered every variable and I was wrong. Potash's body flopped and wriggled, and then his throat bulged out, and then his mouth was forced open impossibly wide and his slick red heart emerged from between the teeth, wrapped in black tentacles of ash. Rack raised the heart up, pulling it into the mass of sludge in his chest, and with a ghostly gasp Potash began to speak.

"You have given me more enjoyment than I expected," said the dead voice. "I haven't felt this thrill from a hunt in a thousand years or more."

I had to summon all my courage to speak. "That's it?" I asked. "You keep me alive this long, and tease at some big final climax, and all you're going to do is hunt me down and kill me?" Why hadn't he taken Nathan's heart? Had I read him that wrong? Was he trying to send some other message than I expected, or did he simply not care which voice he used?

The Withered stood still as dark stone, watching me, while the soft, dead words whispered out of Potash's throat: "I don't want to kill you, John. I want you to join me."

He wasn't here to gloat. He was here to recruit me.

That's what all of this had been about, all the letters and the messages and the hints and temptations. He didn't just want me to kill, he wanted me to kill for *him*. I embalmed the wrong body because I completely misread his intentions: he wouldn't use the voice I hated for a recruitment speech. I gestured at Nathan's body, my careful trap completely untouched. "You want another Nathan Gentry?" I asked. "Another human thrall?"

"I've had my fill of human thralls," said Potash's head. "These puppets are of limited use in the coming war."

"What else is there?" I asked. "You want a . . . partner? I told you before, I'm not like you."

"But you could be," he said. The ghostly whisper filled the room. "We can perform another ritual."

"No . . . ," said Brooke.

"The time is coming," said Rack. "The conditions are right. What would you give up to become Gifted?"

20

I stared at him in shock. "You're going to make more Withered?"

"Gifted," said Potash's voice. The ashy soulstuff in Rack's chest shifted and bubbled as he watched me. "The ones you call Withered were weak. They allowed themselves to grow soft, or tired, or sloppy. I can teach you how to stay strong."

"So I can kill homeless people in a Midwest backwater?" I asked. "Is that the glory you're offering me?"

Brooke's grip tightened on my arm. "Don't make him mad."

Potash's voice laughed: a dry, empty chuckle. "You think you could do better?"

I realized with a start that I did think so. I'd seen so many Withered wasting their lives in dead-end towns, hiding or coping or merely surviving, pointless and lost and alone. All that power, and this was all they could think of to do with it. I had nothing—all weakness and no strength—and I'd still managed to kill four of them. I'd maneuvered myself onto a government strike force. Give me some actual power and I wouldn't let it rot in a one-bedroom apartment. I ignored the talking head and looked at Rack, looked right into his eyes. "You used to be gods, and now look at you. You're damn right I could do more with your 'gifts' than you have."

The head laughed again. "This is why I chose you. You can see the possibilities in a way most others can't."

"But I'm not like you," I said again, though it felt different this time. Was my life really any different from theirs? I had the same kind of apartment Cody French had lived in. I even had the same dog. I mocked them for their empty lives, moving from one kill to the next with no higher ambition, but how was my life any better? At least they were acting. I was only reacting: traveling where they traveled, living where they lived. I was letting them dictate the course of my life, as much a puppet as Nathan, or Potash's lifeless head. That most of them didn't even know they were controlling me only made it worse.

"You say you aren't like us," said the voice. "You aren't like them, either. You never have been. The freak in the shadows, the killer in a little boy's body. Do you really want to spend your life like that? Never peaceful, never happy—"

"I've been happy," I said fiercely.

"Once," said the voice. Rack stared down like a monolith. "Once, for a few weeks, long ago. But she's dead now, isn't she?"

"Don't you dare talk about—"

"Marci Jensen was everything you'd ever wanted," said Potash's voice. Rack's head nodded. "Yes, I know all about her. I've done my research—I've e-mailed at length with your aunt and your sister. Lovely people. I have been following you almost as long as Nobody, watching your methods, waiting to see how you'd react to each new thing. You have a cold-blooded calmness no Gifted could ever match; a precision, a gift for making death. The war is coming now, relentless and inevitable, and you will be its greatest soldier. I want you on our side."

"So you talk about Marci?"

"Marci was the personal connection you'd never thought you could make," he said, "filling your life with a joy you'd never experienced from any other person. But she's gone now. You're emptier than you ever were before. She gave you a heart, but all it does is break."

"And this is your sales pitch?" I asked. My voice was louder than I intended, harried and desperate. These were the feelings I tried to keep hidden, because I didn't know what else to do with them. They were too raw, too loaded with guilt and anger and bottomless despair.

"It's okay," said Brooke, but I yanked my arm harshly from her grip.

"No, it's not! You're just a crazy, stupid—" I stopped myself before I said any more, knowing I was only making it worse. I screwed my eyes shut, trying to think of something, of anything that wasn't Marci, and when Potash's dead voice started to speak again I roared back in a rage. "Is this your big plan, Rack? To tell me how much my life sucks so I may as well become a monster? I am already a monster, and nothing you say can change that: your threats won't work because I have nothing left to lose. Your stupid little hints about my aunt and my sister mean nothing to me, because I am already so profoundly alone that there is nothing you can do to make it worse. You want to threaten them? You can drink their hearts and cry all night in their voices and it won't mean a thing to me because the only thing that ever mattered is already gone. I let her die because I wasn't smart enough to save her. I watched my mom burn to death because I wasn't good enough to keep her alive. So if my broken heart was your big trump card, and now I'm supposed to realize my life is hell and throw in my lot with yours, you can forget it. My life's been hell for as long as I can remember, and there is nothing left that you can take away from me."

Potash's voice rattled through his throat like dry leaves across a grave. "I can take away your pain."

"Don't listen to him," said Brooke.

"We became the Gifted by giving something up," said Rack's dead puppet. "The worthless human weaknesses that held us back. Your heart is broken? I got rid of mine ten thousand years ago. You don't want to be sad anymore? I can cut your sadness out like a tumor."

"It doesn't work," said Brooke. "Nobody gave away her body because she hated it, and Rack gave her the power to take any body she wanted. She hated them all, John, because her body was never the problem. Your heart was never the problem. You can't just get rid of pain: you have to deal with it."

"You just have to give up the right thing," said the voice.

I'd seen so many Withered, all of them trying to run from their problems, all of them trapped in the same unbreakable cycle. Mary Gardner could cure herself of any disease, but only if she stayed in the hospital, constantly getting sick. Elijah Sexton could forget every bad experience he ever had, every loss, every pain, every death, but that only made him repeat them, over and over. His only choices were to dwell on his mistakes, like a wound he could never let heal, or to make those same mistakes again.

I pointed at the smear of ash that was all that remained of Elijah. "You want me to give up my memory of Marci? Of everyone I've ever lost? I've seen how that works and I don't want anything to do with it."

"Your memories only hurt because you care about them," he said. "What if you didn't have to care?"

And there it was.

If anything could make me turn my back on the world, it was that. For years I'd used sociopathy as a shield, as an excuse not to care about anything, not to be hurt by anything, not to love something so much that it destroyed me when it was gone. I needed it because my father was gone, and now my mother and the rest of my family. My friends. The rest of the team. Marci. If I said yes and he made me a monster, gave me some kind of devastating power that ruined the world around me, it would still be worth it because I wouldn't care. The pain would roll off. The unwinnable bargain would corrupt me, destroy me, turn me into a Withered even worse than the ones I'd faced, but I wouldn't care. An unholy anesthetic to hide the pain of a heart I didn't know how to use.

I would be dead and alive at the same time. A walking corpse in an endless, unbreakable peace.

I felt myself crying.

"Don't do it," Brooke whispered.

"You don't know," I said. "You don't know what it's like."

"Yes, I do."

I opened my eyes and looked at her, thin and pale as death, lost in the folds of her coat and the thick black pillars of her oversize boots. I could snap her like a twig. How much pain was in that tiny body? How much loss? My heart had been broken once; how many heartbreaks were buried in her mind?

"Bring her with you," said Potash's voice. Rack stepped closer. "A link between the past and the future we'll create."

I looked down at Potash's body, a bloody, crumpled heap on the floor. His mouth moved faintly, but his eyes were open and dead as glass. What had those eyes seen in that basement? He'd followed Rack down into the darkness, and said the things he'd seen would haunt him until he died. That hadn't turned out to be very long.

What had he seen? What was so terrible that the most vicious killer I knew could be haunted by it?

A broken mirror and a bathroom covered with blood. The most horrific thing I'd ever seen. If I said yes, those horrors would never haunt me again.

What choice would Potash make, if Rack had offered this to him? "Choosing was the hardest part," he'd told me. Killing was easy, choosing was hard. The power to kill meant nothing if you didn't know where to apply it. Sometimes Potash made the wrong choices and good men like Elijah died. But Potash chose anyway, because somebody had to, and all the guilt and the pain and the darkness stayed on him, and no one else would ever have to face it. Elijah had made the same decision, living with the pain he'd caused Merrill Evans to make sure it never happened to anyone else.

I couldn't make that choice if I didn't care. I couldn't make any choices at all. And if the right choices hurt the most, then fine. I'd hurt the most. But it would be me.

I closed my eyes and said goodbye to peace.

"Are you ready?" asked the corpse. "We have people to meet."

"I need something first," I said, and stooped down to search Potash's pockets. The weapon I needed was on his shin: a small leg holster, holding a slim, two-shot handgun. I pulled it out and stood up.

"You won't need that puny human weapon," said the voice, but I shook my head.

"We're not actually going with you. Sorry if I gave you the wrong idea."

The dead voice laughed again. "You can't possibly hope to use that gun against me—"

I shot Potash in the face, shattering his mouth and jaw with both bullets, *boom boom!* The voice disappeared. "Not really," I said. "I'm just sick of your evil-villain monologue." I looked Rack straight in the eyes. "If you're going to kill us, shut up and kill us."

Brooke grabbed my arm again, trying to put herself in front of me, as if her frail body could shield me from the demon king's wrath. I pushed her gently, stepping up next to her, and we faced the Withered side by side. He stepped toward us, looming like the shadow of death.

"What's the matter?" I asked. "Were you not done talking?"

Rack flew into a rage, smashing the cars and the tools and the entire garage in a frenzy of destruction—hands and feet and charred black tendrils lashing out in a primal fury. He paused to look at me, then smashed another window and threw Potash's body at the wall in a burst of terrifying strength. He paused, his chest heaving, the soulstuff swirling like a hurricane of tar, and I gripped Brooke's hand tightly as he stalked back toward us.

"It'll be okay," said Brooke. "I'm ready to die with you."

I shook my head, trying to sound braver than I felt. "Not yet."

Rack stopped, his eyes seeming to burn with an inner fire, and then he stooped and swallowed Nathan's heart.

I locked eyes with him, and never looked away.

"You fool," said Nathan's body. "You insignificant, asinine fool! I've offered you power! I've offered you a seat on my own right hand! And you throw that all a—" He stopped suddenly, his brow creasing sharply in an expression of concern. His chest was roiling, the poisoned heart already absorbed into his body. Spreading the poison as fast as he could heal it. "What have you done?"

"Kind of fitting that Nathan should be the one to kill you," I said. "He's the one who helped me to figure out how you work." He fell to one knee, clutching at his chest. "And that means I know how to make you stop working."

He dropped his other leg, sagging on both knees. "I . . ." Nathan's voice was thin and desperate. "I am invincible!"

"Obviously not," I said. I took a step toward him. "You need hearts to sustain you, just like Elijah needed memories. You can't live without them. And your regeneration won't work right if you're drawing your power from a poisoned heart."

"I have lived ten thousand years," said the voice, and there was almost a whine in it now, a petulant scream of a spoiled child. "I will not die here, like this, like nothing! I will have the death of a god!"

He was practically lying down now. I walked closer, stooping to pick up Potash's machete, testing the weight, feeling the handle firm in my hand. "This is the other big difference between you and me," I said. "If I want something dead, I kill it. No pointless monologuing."

He started to speak, and I cut off his head.

"Ssssssssssssss," said Nathan's mouth, dead in midsound, and then it went slack. Rack's skin spit and popped like a pot of hot tar, and his body dissolved into ash.

We took Elijah's car to my apartment, where I peeled off my bloody clothes and piled them in the sink. I took a hot shower, scrubbing the rest of the blood away, and when I came out Brooke had changed into some of my clothes. She was sitting on the floor scratching Boy Dog behind the ears, whispering to him in a language I'd never heard before. I got dressed, too, and filled my backpack with all the food and water I could carry.

I didn't have much to leave behind. I packed another few sets of clothes and all my cash, and then looked through Potash's duffel for any cash he might have been hiding. True to his word, there were no weapons, but I found a stash of small bills and documents and addresses—his "go bag," I assumed, for if he ever had to disappear. He'd lived in the darkness his whole life, and being on our team hadn't changed that. The passports with his name and face were useless to us, but I took the rest.

It was nearly 5:00 A.M. and the city would be waking up soon. Most of the night's horrors would be new to them—the slaughter in The Corners, the devastation of the police force, even the inexplicable double homicide at the mortuary—but the worst horrors were gone now. Rack was dead, and the man who'd helped him. The killers who'd stalked this town for months were done forever. And now the Demon Girl and the Murder Boy were leaving as well.

What did I do that I didn't have to do? That was always the question. Figure out what we choose when we're free to choose anything, and you'll know who we really are. I saved Brooke when I could have run. I chose to be hurt when I could have chosen to never be hurt again. I was a killer, cold-blooded and ruthless, but I was a hero, too. Or at least I was trying to be.

Elijah's car was damaged from Rack's rage, so we took mine instead. Brooke climbed in the passenger seat, and Boy Dog in the back, and we drove for three hours before the winter sun finally peeked up behind the horizon.

"I love you, John," said Brooke. Or maybe it was Nobody. I kept my eyes on the road.

"Rack said he had people to meet," I told her. "Let's see if we can find them."